"Just let me go," she pleaded.

"Nay." He crossed his arms against his chest. "You betrayed us, and now you've been caught thieving on our land. You will answer for your crimes."

He'd also not allow her to venture alone to the MacNabs, especially not with his son.

She frowned at him. "You jest. Becoming laird has addled you."

"Perhaps." He frowned and led her by her bound hands to his stallion, which grazed on a tuft of grass along the hillside. "Now mount."

"I will be no one's prisoner, least of all yours," she answered, struggling in his hold.

He stopped and released her, his fingers tingling for a brief moment with memories of the past, which he batted away. "You are no prisoner. If you do not wish to answer for your crimes, you may leave, but not with my son."

Author Note

One might say that my obsession with the Highlands began during my study-abroad experience in college when we visited Edinburgh and then took a snowy train ride up to Inverness, but I believe it may have begun much earlier. Either way, the origin story of the Campbells and MacDonalds first forged its way into my heart in 2013, and the story of Brandon and Fiona breathed itself to life soon after. Their romance is anchored in the struggle for self-acceptance and redemption that fuels my stories. I hope you will come to love them for all of their beautiful strengths and flaws as much as I do.

Happy reading, and I hope you enjoy this trip into Georgian Scotland!

JEANINE ENGLERT

The Highlander's Secret Son

HARLEQUIN®
HISTORICAL™

Recycling programs
for this product may
not exist in your area.

ISBN-13: 978-1-335-50628-3

The Highlander's Secret Son

For questions and comments about the quality of this book,
please contact us at CustomerService@Harlequin.com.

Harlequin Enterprises ULC
22 Adelaide St. West, 40th Floor
Toronto, Ontario M5H 4E3, Canada
www.Harlequin.com

Printed in U.S.A.

Jeanine Englert's love affair with mysteries and romances began with Nancy Drew and her grandmother's bookshelves of romance novels. When she isn't wrangling with her characters, she can be found trying to convince her husband to watch her latest *Masterpiece* or BBC show obsession. She loves to talk about writing, her beloved rescue pups, and mystery and romance novels with readers. Visit her website at www.jeaninewrites.com.

The Highlander's Secret Son
is Jeanine Englert's debut for Harlequin Historical.

Look out for more books from Jeanine Englert coming soon.

Visit the Author Profile page
at Harlequin.com.

To my husband, Brian, who helped me
learn how to become the heroine of my own life.
Thank you for always believing in me...
I love you beyond measure.

Chapter One

Glencoe, Scotland, May 1743

'Put your hands up, you thief,' Brandon Campbell bellowed, staring at the young lad.

The bastard stood waist-deep in the dark waters of Loch Leven. The boy stilled. Brandon edged his stallion closer to the bank. He almost felt sorry for the wee bastard. No doubt he was daft as a rock. Why stop to bathe after thieving hens' eggs and dried beef? He was but a half-day's walk from disappearing into the shadowy depths of Glencoe Pass.

A shiver of warning lit up Brandon's spine as he squinted into the glare of the sunrise. *Why, indeed?*

He raised his hand in the air, to signal for the two men behind him to yield. Dismounting, Brandon pulled his dagger from its sheath along his waist belt. If this was a lure, the boy would take out him alone. He'd not risk further casualty. Clan Campbell had suffered enough loss over the last year or so. The MacDonalds had seen to that.

With each step closer to the loch Brandon's chest

tightened. Scars puckered and threaded the lad's back. The braids of raised pink skin were a testament to the fact that his flesh had been broken and healed over, only to be broken again.

Brandon paused and watched. The lad hadn't moved. The water about his waist remained tranquil and still. His form was lean, his muscles sinewy and under-developed. His dark wet hair barely touched the base of his neck. Could he even be over one and twenty? Brandon doubted it.

Lord above. He didn't want to cut down a wee boy with barely enough hair to coat his upper lip. He'd killed enough men to haunt his dreams. No need to add to that count this morn. But thieves couldn't be allowed to go free either.

A plain grey blanket rested in the grass. The brown shells of hens' eggs and the dark hunks of dried beef beckoned him on.

There had to be order. Consequences. Punishment if needed. As the new Laird, he now had to be the one to provide it, even if he didn't wish to.

'Turn,' he ordered.

The lad didn't move.

'Turn, you thief. Or I shall wade in after you.'

The boy shifted and pulled his arms towards his body.

'Ack. Not likely, lad. Put your hands to your sides, palms open, and turn. I'll see the face of the thief stealing from me.'

Brandon thought he heard a curse from the boy, but it failed to carry across the water. The lad relaxed his arms, placed them to his sides, opened his palms, and turned.

The sight of a pair of perfectly formed breasts knocked the breath right out of Brandon.

'Turn away!' he growled to his men.

They obeyed his command. And as he stared at the lass a surge of loss and anger rose from his belly like bad ale. He sheathed his dagger. Of all the breasts he would have liked to see this morn, hers weren't included.

Fiona bloody MacDonald.

'If I believed in ghosts, I'd say you were a ghastly spirit, Fiona MacDonald.'

Brandon rolled his shoulders and shifted on his feet. Seeing her again after all this time unsettled and angered him all in the same moment. Just as it always did. He swallowed hard.

Bollocks.

Instead of covering herself, she ran her hands through her wet hair, causing her breasts to rise and fall in a very becoming way. Fiona's green eyes shone with mischief, just as they had when she was a wee girl. Then they darkened with anger as her smile fell into a flat line.

'I could say the same of you, my laird.' She popped her hands on her hips.

Brandon's body twitched at the sight of her. *Ack.* Her beauty was a distraction. It always had been. One he didn't need. Not today. And now that she'd been found on Campbell land—stealing, no less, and after all the chaos and destruction she'd already caused—she'd have to be dealt with. No Campbell had any softness in his heart for any MacDonald right now—especially not this long-lost ewe.

'Come out of the blasted water before I come in after you. I've more pressing things to do this day.'

'If you insist,' she answered, and began to stride out of the loch, taking no heed to cover...*anything.*

'Stop,' he commanded.

She paused with the water lapping just below her navel. A navel that still haunted his dreams.

Fate was a wicked temptress.

He hated this woman. She'd betrayed him, his clan, and broken his heart, but he couldn't suppress his base need to protect her. She was still a woman, and she deserved some semblance of decency even if she was a traitor to her core.

He scanned the ground around her. *Where were her clothes?* Rolling his eyes, he headed over to his mount and pulled an extra Campbell plaid from its strap. She wasn't worthy of wearing its stripes. He threw it at her anyway.

She caught it and gifted him a smile full of daggers. Brandon responded in kind.

He studied her as she exited the loch and climbed the bank. She secured a knot of plaid at the shoulder to hold it in place. The light green twinkle of mischief returned to her eyes, and Brandon fisted his hands by his side. Unease skittered along his limbs. The lass was up to something.

'Malcolm, bind her hands,' Brandon ordered, and the soldier turned to face him.

Sensing his man's hesitation, Brandon stopped cold. Malcolm was new to the clan and didn't know what she was capable of.

'She may seem a soft woman, but you don't know her. She could drop you where you stand, wipe the blood from her hands, and then enjoy an apple under the shade of a bough tree. Do not be fooled by her beauty. She is a warrior and a traitor. Bind her. Now.'

Fiona smirked at him.

Oh, no.

Brandon made a move towards Malcolm, but it was too late. Fiona snatched the man's blade from its sheath, twisted around him, and slammed her foot into the back of his knee while elbowing him in the neck.

One of Brandon's best men crumpled to the ground like a rag doll. This was the last thing he needed today. He sighed.

'Fi!' he shouted, irritation coating the name. 'Do *not* make me wrestle you to the ground.'

'What makes you think you can?' She moved loosely back and forth on her bare feet, like a wolf assessing her prey. She scanned his form and frowned. 'You seem a bit softer than I remember.'

'My laird, would you like me—?'

'Nay, Hugh,' Brandon growled. 'I'll deal with her. It's time we settled what has come to pass between us.'

And he meant it. Rage flooded his body and he heated with the need to punish her for what she had done to his clan, his family...to him.

But he'd not pull a blade on her.

He removed his waist belt and set it off to the side. He rolled his neck and shoulders and settled into his sparring stance.

'Do you really refuse to use a blade?' she asked, shaking her head.

'Aye.'

'Fine.' She tossed her own blade into the grass.

'Then I shall best you without it.' She smiled and gazed up at him.

'Or you could allow me to bind your hands and bring you in without this skirmish,' he said. 'I shall best you in a fight, as I always do.'

'Ah. This new role as Laird has made you far more arrogant than I remember.'

'A role *you* thrust me into…if you remember.'

Her steps faltered for a mere second, and he seized the advantage. Lunging at her core, he tackled her, and they tumbled to the ground in a tangle of limbs. She landed several kicks to his thighs and one blow to his nose before he had her pinned to the ground.

Panting for breath, he whispered in her ear. 'Give up, Fi. I do not wish to hurt you.'

'You already have,' she answered softly, and stilled under his hold.

Gooseflesh rose along his skin, and the feel of her beneath him flooded his mind with memories of a far different kind. Of a time when he would have given anything to spar with her, in the field or otherwise.

'And so have you hurt me,' he bit back. He cursed under his breath, stood, and pulled her to her feet. 'The rope,' he commanded.

Malcolm, who stood sheepish and red-faced a few lengths away, tossed it to him.

Brandon caught it with one hand and bound her wrists in front of her. He wiped the blood streaming out of his nose on his tunic sleeve and stalked over to the wool blanket that held the thieved hens' eggs and dried beef. Another bundle lay next to it. When he kneeled to pick it up, it squealed. He froze.

Lord above.

As he pulled back the material his footing almost gave way, but he caught himself. Running a hand down his face, he leaned back and stared into the bright blue eyes of a beautiful baby with a head of chestnut-coloured hair.

This morn was full of surprises.

Giving a delighted squeal, the wee thing smiled at him and clapped its hands together. Brandon couldn't help but smile back.

Then he turned to face Fiona.

She lowered her eyes. 'Brandon, meet your son. William.'

Chapter Two

His son?

Brandon blinked at the beautiful little creature gurgling at him. The boy smiled with joy, glee. *Hope.* The kind of smile he hadn't encountered in some time. He swallowed hard and stared. He and Fiona had shared more than one clandestine night together and he'd planned on making her his bride, despite the objection he knew her father would have had against the union. The night of the MacDonald attack on Argyll Castle had severed any such plans.

It was more than possible that the boy was his, but was it a trick? She'd deceived him before, and people he'd loved had died.

'Why should I believe you?' he asked.

'Because I give you my word.'

He released an ugly laugh. 'Your word? It will take far more than that for me to believe you. Not after all you've done.' He stood and crossed his arms against his chest.

'Curses! Look for yourself, then. He bears the mark

of the Campbell upon his arm.' She glared at him and nodded towards the boy.

Brandon squatted and gently tugged back the grey wool blanket that surrounded the boy. The sight of the pink egg-shaped birthmark along the wee babe's forearm sent a ripple of recognition scampering down his body. His heart beat feverishly in his chest. The mark was identical to his own, and that of his older brother Rowan.

Glancing up, Brandon met Fiona's gaze. The mask of indifference, anger and mischief was gone. The softness of her features and the longing in her eyes confirmed the truth. His stomach dropped.

The boy was his.

And he knew she needed his acceptance of her and their son as she needed air to breathe, but he'd not give it. Not now. Perhaps not ever.

The choices he could have made a year ago were his to make no longer. He was Laird of Clan Campbell now. The MacDonalds had seen to that, and Fiona had led them to it. When her family and clan had attacked Argyll Castle without cause, by a hidden tunnel entrance, Brandon had known instantly that she had betrayed him. She was the only person outside of his clan who knew of it, as they'd used that tunnel to keep their clandestine meetings a secret.

So many of those he cherished had perished, including his brother's wife and son, because of his folly in trusting her. After the attack his clan had survived but spiralled into chaos after such heavy losses. His brother the Laird had been crushed by grief and thrust to the brink of rational thought, his decisions becoming more unsound and erratic as time had passed. Desperate to save the clan from ruin, Brandon had finally agreed with the elders' demand to remove his older brother as Laird and take on the role himself.

A role I never wanted.

What had begun as a temporary solution months ago now seemed more resolute with each passing week, as Rowan's demeanour and behaviour continued to decline, and Brandon had to accept his new responsibilities. All he did impacted his family, his clan, and the future of over a thousand people. His wants, his desires and his hopes mattered little.

And now it seemed he was a father. Yet another yoke of responsibility he wasn't ready for, but one he couldn't deny. He had a son, a beautiful boy, and the shaky ground Brandon stood upon as Laird shifted once more beneath his feet.

My son.

Drawing a deep breath, he cradled his son to his chest and stood. He'd have to keep his distance from Fiona until he could find a real solution. Even though they shared a child, he couldn't marry her. Not now. But he also couldn't banish his son, and nor did he wish to. He had to gain some time to think and unearth a plan. What he did now would impact his son for ever, and there would be no second chances. Emotion would only blunt his reason, and the longer he held his son, the more he felt emotion stir in his gut. As the new Laird, and as a new father, he couldn't afford mistakes.

'Take the boy back to the castle, Hugh.' He walked over to the burly soldier and handed the babe to him.

He received the boy gently, as Brandon had known he would, and tucked the babe within the folds of his plaid. Until Brandon could gain his footing his son would be safer with Hugh, his most trusted soldier.

'You bastard. He's *my* son. You will not take him from me!' Fiona yelled and started towards them.

Malcolm grasped her shoulders and held her as she struggled against him. Hugh rode off, and Fiona watched as he disappeared around the bend.

'I've got her, Malcolm.' Brandon grabbed Fiona's elbow and pulled her against his side, hard. 'You ride ahead and share word of our…*guests*. Have my sister tend to the babe until we return. And send word to Miss Emma. Lord knows what the child has been through after being out of doors for such a time. Have her check him over. Thoroughly.'

'Aye,' Malcolm replied, sending a cutting glance to Fiona before he rode off.

When his man was out of sight, Brandon turned to Fiona, gripping her harder. 'Stop. Struggling.'

'I will not. You fool! That is your son. He bears the mark of the Campbell upon his arm. You cannot deny this,' she hissed, and stamped on his foot.

He groaned, clutching his toes through the thin hide of the boots he wore. He was grateful she was barefoot.

'Fi…' He grimaced. Irritation coiled through him. 'I know that. I saw it with my own eyes. I did not deny him to be mine.'

'Then why did you not say as much?' she asked.

'Because the babe does not change the past. Your actions…' he paused, trying to keep his voice below a shout '…killed many people. My sister-in-law…my nephew…both died that night because you shared the secret about the tunnel into our castle—one that was meant for no one else to know of. I trusted you, and you betrayed me. You betrayed all of us.'

She trembled and began to speak.

'Don't,' he said, and held up his hand. 'Don't utter a word. I don't want to hear any explanation.'

'You've always been so bull-headed,' she complained. 'If you would just listen—'

'Nay. I cannot trust you again. Not after all that's happened. Whatever kindness had finally come to pass between us and our clans when we were children, since the Glencoe Massacre of decades ago, has been severed once more since the attack. Coming here onto my land was a mistake.'

'I wasn't coming here. I was trying to go south to the MacNabs. I've a cousin who married within the clan. I hoped they might take me in, as they despise my family and yours just as I do. I paused here for a bit of respite, a wash, and to...to gather some food.'

'You meant to travel there alone with a wee babe— with my son? What were you thinking? British government soldiers are scattered amongst our borders even now, planning their next attack. And you—you are a woman, Fi. You know what could happen.'

Her head whipped up. 'Aye, I do. You need not remind me.'

Warning lit her gaze and Brandon pressed his lips together. Her sister had been lost to such savagery years ago, when rogue soldiers had woven in and out of the borderlands, plundering the clans—mostly its women, but their stores and cattle as well. It was a loss they had borne together as friends. One of the many sorrows of the past decade.

He didn't need another one.

'Just let me go,' she pleaded.

'Nay.' He crossed his arms against his chest. 'You betrayed us and now you've been caught thieving on our land. You will answer for your crimes.'

He'd also not allow her to venture alone to the MacNabs—especially not with his son.

She frowned at him. 'You jest. Becoming Laird has addled you.'

'Perhaps.' He frowned and led her by her bound hands to his stallion, which grazed on a tuft of grass along the hillside. 'Now, mount.'

'I will be no one's prisoner—least of all yours,' she answered, struggling in his hold.

He stopped and released her, his fingers tingling for a brief moment with memories of the past, which he batted away. 'You are no prisoner. If you do not wish to answer for your crimes you may leave. But not with my son.'

Chapter Three

She balked. 'I'll not leave without *my* son.'

'Then mount and answer for your crimes. 'tis your choice.'

'Stop being so stubborn, and let me and William go,' she answered, glaring at him.

His shoulder-length brown hair fluttered against his flushed cheeks in the budding breeze and his deep brown gaze held her own. No deception edged his handsome aquiline features. He was the same boy she had known all her life—the same man she had loved all those days until the night of the battle.

She'd hoped to be bound to this man by handfasting, not treated as a common thief. Yet now he was Laird and her enemy. Hardness rested in his dark eyes in place of what had once been carefree joy. Had she caused that?

She looked away, unwilling to discover the answer.

Her well-hatched plan to escape to her cousin seeking asylum was evaporating like the morning dew. If she'd only had ten more minutes she would have been on her way.

Ten bloody minutes.

When she didn't move, Brandon frowned. 'Shall I throw you atop myself?'

What choice did she have but to go? She'd never abandon her son. He was all she had now—all she had left in the world to care for and believe in. She'd not sacrifice him to this brute.

Glaring at Brandon, she struggled to mount and eventually leaned into his offered hand to let him hoist her up. He pulled himself up smoothly behind her and cinched his arm about her waist—a familiar action she'd felt a thousand times.

Her body shuddered in betrayal. She'd missed him, and she hated herself for it. His solid strength eased through her like a warm sunny afternoon and for a moment she allowed herself to be soothed by it. After months of battling for the life and the safety of herself and her son, feeling at ease was a blessing. One she had taken for granted. One she never expected to have again.

She could depend on no one but herself now.

The last year had taught her that.

Her future had changed in the blink of an eye. After her father and the MacDonalds had attacked Argyll Castle, using the secret entrance, Brandon had abandoned her as her own mother had a decade earlier. Fiona had sent letter upon letter, pleading for his forgiveness and help to escape her father's brutality and to protect their babe, but he'd never come. Then her own clan had banished her, and a woman unprotected in the Highlands was destined for certain death.

And now it was time to plan yet another escape—

an escape from a man she'd once loved. She almost laughed aloud at the irony.

He'd reminded her of a horrible truth: that sometimes love wasn't enough. Just as her love for her mother hadn't been enough for her to stay.

Fiona scanned the familiar horizon of grassy meadows and gentle grey sloping mountains, inhaling the sweetness of new growth that only springtime could muster. Glencoe Pass wasn't far in the distance, and would serve as the very route for her future escape to the MacNabs. If she could endure whatever punishment the Campbells sought to place upon her for her 'crimes', and find time to be alone with her son, she could hatch another way out of this mess.

All her past secret meetings with Brandon in the dark of night would aid her in such a plan, and her skills with the blade would help her to down any soldier bent on halting her escape.

Doubt sliced through her as she studied the dark shadowy coves and outcroppings surrounding the pass. Could she truly survive alone along the road with her son in the dark of night? It was two days at least to the MacNabs, and long, desperate and dangerous hours such travel would be.

It had been difficult enough to remain alive in her own clan, despite the sparse protection her aunt and brother had been able to provide. How would she fare alone amidst British soldiers or rogue rebel clansmen bent on robbing any stranger they encountered along their journey?

The hills provided shelter for men who'd lost their way and lacked any code of decency. She still trembled at the memory of finding her sister having succumbed to such an attack so many years ago.

The wool plaid itched along her scars—a reminder of all she had already survived. Lashing after lashing she'd endured from her father for being with child—especially with a Campbell bairn. Rage had fuelled every slap of her father's whip against her flesh. Even now she could hear her aunt and her brother Devlin pleading for him to stop. Telling him that the punishment was enough. But her father the Laird hadn't paused until she'd passed out, so determined had he been for her to lose her babe.

But the boy had a strong will to survive—as did she. And they would survive this challenge as well.

Stiffening her back, she resolved that she and her son would be no one's casualty. Not the Campbells', the MacDonalds', or the Highlands'. They would leave here and begin a new life on their own.

But she'd have to have coin, a fool-proof plan, and an accomplice. Right now she had none of those, but she knew Argyll Castle held all three. She didn't know exactly where each would be hidden, but she'd uncover them one by one until she had all she needed to make an escape with her son.

She frowned as she scanned the hillside. 'Why are we going this way? Is it not shorter to cut across the field?' She needed to see her son and know he was safe.

'You dare question the path I take to my own castle?' said Brandon.

She rolled her eyes. 'I wish to see my son.'

'You will take the time to see what you have done.'

'What *I* have done?' she replied. 'What are you talking about?'

'Cease,' he commanded, tightening his hold around her waist.

She bit back a retort as impatience brewed. *Insufferable man.*

They rode on in silence. Only a rogue birdcall or a snuffle from the stallion as it began to climb a steep incline interrupted the quiet. Finally they crested the first hill on Campbell lands, and Fiona sucked in a breath at the sight of the outskirts of the village.

Shock roiled through her and she shifted on the mount to lean closer. The thriving, tidy row of thatched cottages she remembered sat in a row of charred ruins and burned-out mounds full of memories. Where were the families, the livestock and the children?

'Your warriors burned them out and burned every last home to the ground,' Brandon stated, as if reading her thoughts.

Ice laced his words and Fiona could only stare. The place she had loved as much as her own lands was in ruins, and her misplaced trust in her family had caused it.

Shame budded anew in her chest…followed by anger. 'I did not do this,' she stated.

'Aye, you did. I'll hear no more of it,' he commanded.

But he would listen one day. He would hear what *he* had done. Hear of all the pain *his* abandonment had caused her and her son. But he'd not listen now—she knew that. Nor would she listen to his ramblings of blame.

She bit her lip and counted to a hundred to keep her temper in check. She'd accomplish nothing by getting herself killed before they even reached the castle walls. Her focus had to be on reuniting with William and planning their future far from here. What Brandon thought of her didn't matter—not any more.

Chapter Four

Staring out at the horizon, Brandon watched the misty fog hovering along the base of the Glencoe Mountains that surrounded the village ruins before him. He settled into a slow, rhythmic canter as they made their way to the castle. Birds called along the hillside and water trickled along the gentle slope as it made its way to the loch.

He missed the simplicity of the past...the feel of Fiona pressed against him and his unburdened duty as second son. But such a time belonged to another man. It belonged to him no longer, and it was high time he accepted it.

A hint of the rising sun's rays warmed his face, beckoning him to move on, move forward. He was a father now—a heady and jarring development on what had begun as a regular morning. At one time he'd longed to be a father and to share a life with Fiona as his wife, but this... This was not the future he'd envisaged and the timing could not be worse.

His people were still teetering on the edge of ruin and he had only gained a foothold as the new Laird over the last several months. He also had little idea how to be a father. All he knew was that he'd not be like *his* father. He'd not place clan duty before family.

He swallowed hard. Being a good uncle to little Rosa was a far different beast from being a father, and he was uncertain how to begin. Then there was Fiona to contend with. She had to answer for her crimes to the clan and to him. He didn't know which would be more poorly received.

A wisp of her hair skimmed his neck, and the faint tickle was a memory of their rides along the glen when they had been in love and had had few cares in the world. Now his burdens were many.

He clenched his jaw. Her presence was a complication he didn't need—especially with Rowan to contend with upon his return to the castle. Despite not being Laird any more, Rowan still exerted his power when he could. Seeing Fiona and wee William would bring out the worst in him after losing his own wife and son. It didn't matter how much time had passed. His grief was as fresh and new as if the loss were but yesterday.

Gripping the reins too tightly, Brandon felt his stallion pull and heard him neigh. 'Sorry, boy,' he murmured, relaxing his hold.

Rowan would be enraged at the sight of Fiona—perhaps even to a breaking point. Which was exactly what Brandon didn't want. Since his wife's death, Rowan had teetered back and forth between the past and the present, as well as between sanity and blinding grief.

Fiona settled back against him and a whisper of the scent of greenery, the budding fresh, clean hint of new growth, tickled his nose. His stomach hitched and squeezed. She'd always smelled this way to him—as if she contained a hint of hope for the future...*his* future.

Acid filled his throat and he moved back to create a hint of space between them. Now such 'sweetness' reminded him of the bitter seed of betrayal.

They passed another string of burnt-out cottages as they neared the grain keep and the drying sheds for herbs. They'd be upon the beginnings of the cottages being rebuilt soon. Once the first clansmen spotted her word would spread through the clan like wildfire, and there would be little he could do to stop it.

Thankfully Hugh would have William safely to the castle by now—which was another reason Brandon had taken the long route back with Fiona. His son's safety was the most important thing to him. It was an unexpected and unsettling feeling, but he'd not have his son become a casualty of the chaos his parents had created. The boy deserved better than that.

Brandon guided his mount around the corner. Men were beginning to gather their tools and new logs for their day's work. At first the men cast only a casual glance his way, nodding in respect in his passing in deference to his position as Laird. But as they came closer one man paused, and then another, and soon all set aside their work.

'That be her!' One man pointed her out, aghast at the sight of her.

'Traitor!' another yelled. 'Curses to ye, Fiona Mac-Donald, and to all of yer family!'

Brandon said nothing. It was not the time for him to intercede. He would let them vent their hatred upon her; she deserved no less. He would keep her alive and nothing else. He wouldn't protect her from her past.

She tensed against him as the men and women lobbed their diatribes at her one after another, but she said nothing in response and met their gazes. It surprised him. The Fiona of old would have shouted back a challenge, or something far worse.

Pulling back his shoulders, he brought his stallion to a gallop, eager to return to the castle before a riot ensued at the main gates.

Soon Argyll Castle's tall limestone walls glowed before him in the sunshine, sitting like a beacon on the hill. The sight of it always stole his senses. Blue and green Campbell flags rippled in the breeze, filling his chest with pride. This was his clan, and he would bring it back from the brink of ruin. They would be stronger than they had ever been before.

His limbs tingled at the knowledge that one day he would leave all this in the hands of his boy.

His son.

They crossed the small bridge that led over a shallow murky moat. In twenty lengths he'd see his son once more, and to his surprise a bit of eagerness threaded through him.

He pulled his stallion to a slow stop and dismounted, handing the reins to Joseph, a small lad with a large grin and floppy brown hair. The boy had quickly become a favourite of Brandon's when he'd become Laird. He was quick to learn and eager to please, spending all his days in the stable since his mother had died—a loss Brandon understood keenly.

'My laird.'

Joseph nodded in greeting, and Brandon patted the lad on his shoulder. He hoped his son would grow to be as sharp and keen to learn as Joseph.

He turned from the boy and faced Fiona. He extended his hand to assist her, but she ignored it. She scowled at him and slid off the mount awkwardly, a hint away from falling face-first into the grass. He shook his head. Evidently the stubborn, headstrong Fiona of old was not entirely lost to him.

A small crowd of clansmen had already clustered outside the gate, easily filling the space between it and the castle doors. His stomach knotted and he gritted his teeth. If he'd been much longer the throng would have been twice as deep.

He nodded to Fiona to walk ahead of him. When she hesitated, he grasped her bound hands and tugged her forward, eliciting more calls and shouts from the Campbells.

Why the woman thought now was the time to test his patience further, he didn't know. Perhaps she didn't fully grasp the severity of her situation. He alone stood between her and death at the hands of an angry mob of Campbells. Perhaps he should just leave her here and let them decide her fate…

Then he thought of his son.

Brandon swallowed hard and dragged Fiona forward. He knew what losing a mother did to a boy, and he wished to prevent such pain for William if he could.

Two soldiers carved a path through the throng of clansmen that still shouted, raising their fists in the air, threatening Fiona with every step.

'Your days are numbered, wench!' one man called, and spat upon her as she climbed the stairs to the castle doors.

Others shouted in support. A couple of them followed suit and spat at her as she passed.

Brandon smothered the flare of protection welling up in him. A year ago he would have brought a sword to the neck of anyone daring to disrespect her. Now he was torn between his own anger and that of his people.

She had betrayed them.

She had betrayed *him*.

He kept silent. He didn't trust himself.

Only the briefest of hesitations hinted that Fiona had heard or felt the insults. Then she squared her shoulders and continued on, staring straight ahead.

Brandon found her restraint admirable and quite unlike her.

He closed the gap between them and nudged her forward as she reached the top of the stairs. He turned to the crowd and raised a hand to silence them. He couldn't come to her defence. Not after what she'd done. It didn't matter that she was the mother of his child, or that he would have given his life to protect her once before. That was the past. The present was all that mattered now.

'Fiona MacDonald will answer for her crimes against us. You must trust in that. Go home. Work your fields, rebuild what we have lost, and care for your livestock. When there is a decision reached as to her punishment, the news will be shared with you. You've my word.'

'What is there to discuss, my laird?' asked Old Man Purdy, the clan's master blacksmith. 'If she were a man, we would be measuring the rope for her noose.'

'Aye,' Brandon answered. 'But she is not a man, is she? Her punishment must be befitting. Give me time to reach a just decision.'

'How much longer shall we have to wait?' a man shouted from the back of the group.

'As long as is needed to decide her fate,' Brandon answered. 'Now, go,' he ordered.

The men began a slow shuffle away from the castle, conversing amongst themselves, no doubt disgruntled by Brandon's command. He was disappointed that he could not offer them a speedy and just response as well. But dealing with Fiona was complicated—as it always had been.

Hugh opened the castle doors and stepped aside to allow them entry, a deep scowl on his brow.

As Brandon followed Fiona into the castle he could guess why his friend and most trusted warrior was in such an ill humour.

The disorder in the Great Hall screamed of Rowan's knowledge of Fiona's arrival. He'd had another episode, it seemed, which was why the men were waiting outside, rather than within, as they might have on any other given day. Broken pottery lay scattered about, a ripped tapestry hung haphazardly by a metal hook above the hearth, and a pair of large wall sconces appeared to have been ripped from their holders and now lay splintered on the stone floor.

'Seems you've done a bit of redecorating since I've been here,' Fiona mumbled.

On another day and in another life Brandon might have laughed, but not today.

'You will only speak when spoken to—unless you wish to lose your tongue,' Brandon bit back.

The sight of the chaos sent weariness through his bones. Would his brother ever be the man he'd once been? Would his melancholy and rage over losing his wife and son ever subside enough for him to be Laird once more, or even a helpful source of strength for

Brandon and the clan? For months Rowan had been little more than an added strain and worry upon all of them, and poor Rosa, his daughter, had borne the worst of it. To all intents and purposes, it seemed she had lost both parents the night of the attack.

Another crash sounded from an alcove off the Great Hall, and Brandon's elder sister Beatrice came rushing from the room. At the sight of Brandon, relief spread through her features and her shoulders relaxed. Then she spied Fiona and stopped, frozen, halfway across the hall from him.

Brandon turned to Hugh. 'Watch her,' he commanded, sending a warning glance to Fiona before he approached his sister.

When he reached her, he grasped her hands, which were ice-cold and trembling.

'So it is…it is true?' Beatrice stuttered, glancing over Brandon's shoulder to Fiona.

'Aye, but we will speak of her later. What of Rowan?'

Brandon squeezed his sister's hands and spoke softly to her. She was the only person he could depend upon these days besides Hugh, and he knew the toll all this had taken on her—especially in providing the care of their brother and young niece as she'd had to. His strong, spirited sister was becoming worn, timid and harried. It was a sight that pained him deeply.

'Garrick heard word of Fiona's capture.' As one of Rowan's most trusted friends and supporters, Garrick's actions did not surprise Brandon. 'He rushed back to the castle before you and told Rowan. He…' She looked around the room at the damage. 'He did not take it well. I have tried to console him. I even made him one of Miss Emma's tonics, to try to soothe him, but he smashed it to the ground.'

'And now?'

'He is outside the study. I locked it, so he would not go within and destroy Father's things, but he is enraged at me for it.'

'And the babe?' Brandon whispered. His heart thundered in his chest. He needed to know his son was safe.

Beatrice's face lit with colour and warmth, as he had known it would. 'He is a fine healthy boy. Miss Emma tends to him now, above stairs in the old nursery.'

'Good.' He smiled at her. 'Go to him now and I will get Rowan in hand. Once he is settled we will talk.'

Beatrice's eyes slid back to Fiona. 'And Fi?'

'Aye, we will speak of what to do with her as well.'

'Do not let her weave her spell over you brother, while I am away.' She winked at him.

Brandon chuckled, enjoying this small reminder of the teasing older sister of long ago. 'Not likely, lass. Now, go on.'

Before he could go to find Rowan, his older brother rounded the corner and walked into the Great Hall.

Chapter Five

Fiona wiggled her toes as her bare feet gripped the cold stone floors of the Great Hall at Argyll Castle. She studied the room, startled by the change since her last visit. What on earth had happened here after the attack?

A bedraggled bearded man entered the Great Hall from an alcove and advanced towards them quickly. Fiona squinted, but couldn't recognise him.

'Brother!' the stranger called angrily. 'How dare you bring her within these walls?'

Sucking in a breath, Fiona froze. *Rowan?*

'That is close enough, brother,' Brandon commanded, pressing a palm to Rowan's chest to keep him an arm's length from her.

She gasped aloud and stared. The once strong, tall, dark and forbidding man she'd known as a wolf among men stood before her in a stained, torn tunic, with greasy long hair and a beard that seemed to be holding the remnants of his last meal. His eyes were wild and unfocused, his breathing a bit uneven.

Feeling the heat of Brandon's gaze upon her, she

commanded herself to close her mouth and pressed her lips together in silence.

Although she'd always respected Rowan, they'd never truly liked one another. Ever. He had a streak of cruelty like her father, and a wicked temper. Being the oldest, and having become Laird before he was even twenty, he'd been naturally arrogant, which had only added to his predisposition to demanding his needs be met quickly.

It seemed most lairds had such characteristics, and Rowan had continued the tradition. It was the very reason she'd been drawn to Brandon's innate kindness like a moth to a flame.

But this man... He was not that Rowan—not the man she had known all those years.

'You dare tell me what I can and cannot do as your laird?' Rowan seethed, a bit of spittle coating his beard.

Laird? Fiona watched Brandon's shoulders sag forward, and his hand fell away from Rowan's chest.

'Rowan, we have discussed this before,' he began, speaking patiently and quietly, as one might address a child. 'You are no longer Laird. I am. The elders commanded it. Do you remember? To give you time to overcome your grief.'

Rowan paused, considering his brother's words. He looked around the room with wide eyes, as if seeing it for the first time. Then he clenched his fists by his sides and seemed to awaken from whatever place he'd been in. He began to sob.

Discomfort roiled through Fiona, and she almost wished to excuse herself and return out of doors to face that angry mob of clansmen. She glanced back to Hugh, who met her gaze with accusation and then looked away from the scene before him, apparently discovering a spot above her on the far wall to hold his attention.

Confusion swam through her as she turned and watched Brandon pull his brother into an embrace.

'My Anna is dead,' Rowan mumbled against his brother's shoulder, followed by another sob.

'Aye,' Brandon replied in a low, soothing tone.

'And my son…' Rowan swallowed a sob and sniffled.

'Shh, brother. I know. And I am sorry beyond words. Let Hugh take you to your chamber. Perhaps a bath and a shave will set you to rights. The servants will be sent to help you. We shall talk later, when you are ready.'

Brandon squeezed his brother's arm and pulled out of their embrace. Nodding to Hugh, he guided Rowan to him, and Hugh took Rowan by the arm and led him from the hall.

Fiona couldn't move. Shock roiled through her once more. She had a thousand questions, but her mouth didn't seem able to work and ask even one of them.

Once Hugh and Rowan had exited the hall, Brandon whipped around to face her. Hate burned bright and hot in his gaze, and she instinctively took a step away from him.

'You see what you have done to my family, my clan? *This* is what you have done. My brother is consumed with grief, my sister is in tatters, and my people are thrust into the chaos of anger once more at the sight of you.'

She blinked back at him and said the only words she seemed able to muster. 'I'm sorry. I never meant for any of—'

'Do not attempt apologies. I'm in no mood for them. Follow me now, before I change my mind.'

Falling into a quick step behind him, she wove around the shards of broken bowls and tankards and hurried to keep up with his long strides.

'William?' she dared say.

He didn't answer, but continued on up a set a stairs to the first floor, where guests stayed. Relief coiled through her. At least that ruled out the possibility of her being forced to stay in the hold for prisoners beneath the main level, or within the damp walls of the root cellar.

Malcolm, whom she'd met earlier in the day, stood at the top of the first floor, as if awaiting their arrival. He frowned at the sight of her. She frowned back.

'Have Jenny bring fresh clothes and have the kitchen prepare hot water for a bath for our guest. Then gather two more men to stand guard outside her door.'

'Aye, my laird,' Malcolm answered, and left.

Brandon continued on, passing several open doors before stopping at the one closed door on the floor. She worried her hands. She knew this room, and the fact that he'd chosen to put her here made her uneasy. It held far too many memories for them both.

He unlocked the door and gestured for her to enter.

She hesitated. 'So I am to be a prisoner here after all?'

'Nay.' He sighed, gesturing to the key resting in the lock of the door. 'As I said before, you are welcome to leave and take your chances on being torn to bits by the fine men and women of Clan Campbell. In the end, it would make my life far easier.'

'Then I shall gather my son and be off.'

He stepped closer—so close that the edges of his

boots touched the tips of her bare toes. Awareness fluttered in her stomach.

'You may leave, but not with my son. Understand? I'll not be repeating myself again.'

'Aye,' she answered.

'Then go.' He gestured into the room. 'I've far more pressing matters to tend to besides your comfort.'

'And to think I was beginning to feel sorry for you.'

'Save your pity for yourself, Fi. The more days you spend here, the more you'll need it. If you survive that long, that is.'

She walked past him, wishing to cut him from nose to navel. Her blood heated her veins and she swallowed the pride that beckoned her to spit in his face. She'd be leaving sooner than he thought, with her son in her arms, and Brandon would be the last dim-witted Campbell to realise it.

Chapter Six

It was hardly mid-morn and exhaustion pressed in on Brandon. A dull, throbbing ache was beginning at the base of his skull. He'd get a tonic from Miss Emma after he'd checked on his son.

His son.

He hadn't tired of the sound of the words in his head, and it was eagerness to see that his boy was unharmed that beckoned him onwards, away from the chaos of Fiona and the damaged crockery strewn about the Great Hall below.

As he reached a room on the second floor, a sense of calm began to spool through him. The room had served as a nursery for him and his siblings, and it was where Rowan and Anna's children had spent many an hour.

The irony of going there now to see his son, when Rowan had lost his own but a year ago, soured Brandon's stomach. It was time he told Beatrice the truth and enlisted her help to tell Rowan of the boy's lineage. He'd not keep secrets from them. They were all the family he had left in the world, and he'd not betray them with omissions that would affect them deeply.

Even if such truths would bring pain to both of them, as he knew it would.

The sight of Miss Emma holding his son and Beatrice cooing to him soothed Brandon's worry. He stood and watched the women fuss over his boy until they realised he was there.

'Come, come, my laird,' Miss Emma beckoned him. 'We are fussing over this handsome babe. I've checked him over thoroughly, and he appears healthy and thriving. A strong lad, I'd say.'

The wistful look in her gaze told him she had discovered the birthmark, but no such awareness rested in his sister's eyes. He almost wished she already knew.

'Thank you, Miss Emma. I'm grateful for the care you've provided him. May I trouble you for a tonic? My head aches.'

'Ah, I've just the thing for ye.' She smiled and handed the babe over to his sister. 'I'll run along and bring it to ye shortly,' she whispered in his ear as she headed out through the door, closing it quietly behind her. 'She already adores him. The truth will not endanger that.'

'He is lovely, brother.'

Beatrice smiled at him. She longed to be a mother, but time had not gifted her a babe yet, despite her married state. She would be pained to know that nature had skipped over her once more, despite her many prayers, and granted him a gift he'd never even asked for.

He held her gaze and said the truth of it. 'Aye, I'm glad you think so. He is my son and your nephew.'

Her eyes softened and her shoulders drooped. 'What?'

'You heard me. This is my son, William. Fiona car-

ried my child, but I did not know of it until this morn.'
Brandon walked over and sat beside her on the settee
near the window. 'He even bears the mark.' He nudged
back the plaid covering the boy and showed the birthmark to her.

'This beautiful creature is your son?' Tears welled
in her eyes and spilled down her cheeks. 'What a blessing!'

'Aye, an unexpected one.' His sister's joy brought
him some much-needed relief, and he chuckled aloud.

'Let me see you now,' she added, placing William
in his arms. She watched them and clapped her hands
together. 'I wish Mother could have seen you two. It
would have filled her with such joy. He has her eyes,
you know.'

'Does he?' Brandon asked, staring into the depths
of his son's clear blue gaze. 'Aye, you're right. Beautiful eyes they are.'

Beatrice wrapped her arm around his shoulder and
hugged him. They sat in silence for a while, just like
that, staring down at their tiny gift, the only one they'd
had over the last year. Gratitude settled deep in his
gut, and contentment followed close behind. He ran his
thumb over William's soft wee cheek, and then down
his arm. His son clutched greedily at Brandon's thumb
as he touched his tiny hand, and the boy's grip surprised him.

He laughed. 'He's a strong boy.'

'Aye, like both his parents.'

Both his parents.

Too bad the boy would never know his parents in
the traditional sense—not in the way Brandon would
have imagined for him. He didn't know how to man-

age this untenable situation. He was Laird. William's mother was an enemy and a traitor. Everyone in the clan wished her harm.

Especially Rowan.

'I do not know how to tell him, Trice,' Brandon murmured.

'You will find the words and we will tell him together. We are family, and so is William. Rowan will not cast such bonds aside.'

'I hope you are right. Bring Rowan and meet me in the study in half an hour, if he has recovered enough to join us. I asked Hugh to see if the servants could entice him to a bath and a shave. Perhaps even a haircut. My hope is that it will help give him some calm and bring him back to the present. Ask Daniel to join us too. Having your husband there will help Rowan feel less…outnumbered.'

She nodded and stood to leave. 'I'll go and check on our brother now and meet you later. It will work out…it *will*.'

Rowan, Daniel and Beatrice were already waiting for him inside the study when Brandon arrived. The quiet tones of their voices drifted out into the corridor. The calm, even cadence of his brother's voice put a bit of ease in Brandon's steps. Rowan sounded aware and present—a plus for the conversation they were about to have.

'After all we have been through…after the destruction, betrayal, and pain she has caused all of us—especially him—why would he bring her here, sister? Why?' Rowan asked as he sat down on one of the large benches that flanked the table in the centre of the room.

'I did not *bring* her to the castle,' Brandon answered, entering the room and closing the door. 'I discovered her stealing by the loch. It is our duty to punish her for her crimes.'

Rowan crossed his arms against his chest. His dark gaze challenged Brandon. Rowan had bathed, shaved, and wore clean clothes. He almost looked like the Rowan of old. It was the best he had looked in ages, which gave Brandon renewed confidence that their conversation might go better than he expected.

'Why was she even stealing anything from us in the first place? She is a MacDonald. She doesn't want for anything.'

'She was hungry and had stopped to bathe. I offered her escape, but she would not take it,' Brandon answered, holding his brother's gaze.

His brother shook his head. 'That is nonsensical.'

Beatrice nodded to Brandon, urging him to continue. But suddenly Brandon's mouth felt full of sheep's wool. 'She would not leave without her son.'

'So why did you not allow her to take him? Why would it matter at all to you if—?'

Rowan froze, and the way he watched Brandon told him he had finally stitched it all together. Daniel was not far behind, and he scrubbed his hand through his hair and sighed.

'She says he is *your* son?' Rowan asked. His words were sharp and brittle.

'Aye.'

'And you believe her?' He laughed aloud.

'He bears the mark, brother, and our mother's eyes,' Beatrice added. 'I have seen it. He is a Campbell. He is your nephew—our nephew.'

Rowan stood and laughed aloud—a long, eerie laugh. 'He may be *your* nephew, sister, but he will never be mine.'

Anger brewed in Brandon's gut. 'You will not reject my son. He will be respected. I demand it as your laird.'

'You *demand* it?' Rowan bit back. 'As Laird, your duty is to this clan first…but you have always had a softness…a weakness for her. That cannot change overnight. You will be back in her bed doing her bidding before the week is out. She has come back to destroy this clan once and for all…through *you*!'

He paced the study like a trapped animal.

'It has not been overnight, brother. The past between us lies buried in the graves of our clansmen, your wife… your son. There is no going back.'

'Nay,' Rowan growled. 'There is not. Which is my point.'

'Brothers…' Beatrice began, no doubt noting the heavy edge in Rowan's words. She made a move closer to them, but Daniel stilled her with a hand to her shoulder.

'We shall leave this for your brothers to discuss,' he said.

She nibbled the corner of her lip but nodded to her husband. Daniel clearly knew that what would come to pass between his brother and himself would be ugly and far beyond what even their sweet older sister could manage. Ever since their mother had died, over ten years ago, the wedge between the brothers had been edging into a chasm. Anna's death had made it even wider, and only duty kept them together.

Brandon sent his sister as reassuring a look as he could muster, and then watched her and his brother-in-law leave the room. Rowan stood silently staring into the fire, and Brandon waited. Waited for whatever it was Rowan needed to say to settle this new rage that Fiona's arrival had stirred up within him. Brandon would listen. He owed him that.

When Rowan turned from the fire that crackled in the large hearth to face him, raw grief greeted him. Pain shone in his brother's glassy eyes, and Brandon felt all the heat and colour drain from his own face. He swallowed hard and held his brother's gaze. Knowing that he had played a part in his brother's sorrow cut him. Again and again and again.

Rowan held a silver brooch in his hand and his thumb rubbed over it in a rhythmic fashion. Brandon recognised it immediately and his breath hitched.

'Do you remember when I gifted this to her?' Rowan's words were low, raspy, and coated with emotion.

'Aye,' Brandon answered. 'I do. Weeks you had spent, working the silver time and again to make it just right.'

Rowan chuckled. 'And still it was an ugly, dreadful piece of work.'

Brandon risked a small laugh in kind. 'Aye, it was.'

'But she loved it. Adored it. Because I had made it with my own hands. She wore it every day.'

Until she died.

Words would not come. Apologies fell unspoken in the air. The din of regret chimed in his ears.

Brandon had said all the words he could think of in the past to release the guilt and change the outcome, but nothing ever could.

His sister-in-law was still dead.

His brother was still a widower.

His beautiful sweet niece was still motherless.

His nephew had died.

Because of him.

The pit of shame he'd felt time and time again in the years since it had happened returned and threatened to pull him under once more like a bog.

Rowan shook his head. 'And yet when I saw her this morn... Fiona MacDonald, standing there pale and thin... I did not slay her as I thought I would. I can only think. Only imagine it was *her*...' He met Brandon's gaze and a faraway look was reflected in his eyes. He swallowed hard and struggled to speak. 'Anna...'

Her name had not been spoken out loud in so long it sounded foreign in the air.

'*She* must have guided me. Because I have dreamed of killing her. Of killing all the MacDonalds in revenge.'

Brandon couldn't move. He'd never truly believed Rowan would kill Fiona for what had happened. *She* had not killed Anna. *She* had not killed his son. But her family had—her clan had. Shock and awe flooded Brandon. He'd known his brother was angry. He knew he grieved. But he had not known the depth of his brother's rage until now. Nor had he realised how much he had risked in bringing Fiona and his son into this castle.

'I see surprise in your eyes, brother...'

Rowan walked closer, his boots echoing against the stone floor. He stopped an arm's length away.

Brandon held his ground. 'I am surprised.'

'You should not be. I have always had the blacker heart of the two of us—which will serve me well as Laird.'

His dark eyes narrowed in on Brandon. At last the truth was out in the open between them. Rowan wished to regain his role as Laird, even if it would bring the clan to its final demise.

'Do you also wish *me* dead, brother?' Brandon shifted on his feet and held his breath. Did he even wish to know the answer?

His brother's silence struck Brandon with a violence he hadn't expected.

Rowan *did* wish him dead, and the painful, brutal truth of it made Brandon's toes tingle.

'And if I killed Fiona what would you do, *my laird*?' Darkness had settled deep in Rowan's glare.

'I do not believe you would ever do as such. 'tis not within the brother I know.'

'Then you know me little.'

'Perhaps I do not know this new brother, but my brother of before was not so dark and unforgiving as our father. He would make decisions of the mind, not out of anger.'

'That was before.'

'Why tell me all this now? I could imprison you for such treason, and for disloyalty to me and our clan.'

'I tell you this because every day it will be a struggle to keep the rage at bay…' A lock of Rowan's dark hair vibrated against his temple. 'You best not hold any illusion of Fiona remaining alive for long. It matters not to me that you favoured her, bedded her, even loved her once. I imagine there will be a moment when even Anna cannot keep me from killing her. Nor will you.'

Brandon squared his shoulders and fisted his hands by his sides. Rowan baited him even now. His brother wanted and needed a reason to let his rage free, but Brandon would not give it. He would hold his own anger in check. And he would protect Fi and his son with his life if he had to.

It was *his* decision as to how she would answer for her crimes, not Rowan's right to dispense justice as he saw fit. Even if he had to go against his brother. With word. Or deed. Or sword.

'Is that all, *my laird*?' Rowan's words were tight and low.

Brandon studied him a moment longer. 'Aye. For now.'

Chapter Seven

Fiona paced about the small room, burning off her fear and energy as her mind twined through the possibilities. She'd not be able to rest until William was here with her. But how did she demand her child be brought to her when everyone hated her?

She could just storm every room until she found him, fighting off one soldier after another. She was a bit tired and underfed, but she was strong. If only she had a blade…or two.

She stood staring out through the small arrow slit window. Could she lower herself from this window down to another? She was thin enough now to do so. Or perhaps jump and hope that cart filled with wheat below would break her fall?

She nibbled her lip and chided herself. *Ridiculous.* She couldn't think clearly without her boy. They'd never been separated for this long.

'Miss, I've yer bath for ye.'

A voice called from outside the open door to her room, startling her. Fiona turned. It was Jenny, a young lass she had befriended during her affair with Brandon.

The girl had often helped her sneak in and out of Brandon's chambers without being seen. Seeing such a familiar face brought a smile to Fiona's lips.

'Greetings, Jenny. I'm pleased to see you,' Fiona offered, walking towards the door.

Jenny took a step back and allowed two soldiers to enter. They carried a large tub full of steaming water. They glared at her and left. Jenny thanked them and entered silently, closing the door behind her. She clutched a bar of lavender soap and towels for drying tightly against her chest, as if they served as protection, and hesitated to move closer.

Fiona's smile faded away. 'I cannot imagine what you think of me,' she offered, trying to put the girl at ease.

'I think nothing,' Jenny said quickly, rushing forward. 'I have brought soap and towels for yer bath. Do ye need assistance?'

Poor Jenny. She lied as badly as Brandon. Her unease reflected off her like sunlight. But Fiona was desperate for some female company—so desperate she would take advantage of Jenny's former kindness and try to befriend her once more.

A whisper of guilt made its way into her thoughts, but she slammed it back. This was for her son…for William's life. She would use whoever she had to, to fashion an escape?

'Aye, if you could help me I would be grateful. It has been some time since I've had a bath.' Fiona chuckled, trying to add a touch of levity to the situation and put Jenny at ease. 'Well, other than in a loch.'

Questions registered in Jenny's furrowed brow, but

the lass held them in check and nodded to Fiona. 'Let me help ye then.'

She set aside the soap and towels on the bed and began to untie the sloppy knot in the plaid Fiona had fastened along her shoulder. The material slid easily to the ground.

Jenny sucked in a breath. 'Oh, miss...' she offered, unable to hide her shock.

Fiona tensed. She had forgotten about the scars. She met the girl's wide, pained gaze and squeezed her hand. 'They pain me no longer, but they look a fright.'

Nodding, Jenny walked away to retrieve the soap, and Fiona took her first step into the hot, steaming water. She sank down and sat in the tub, sighing as the water lapped about her shoulders. Bliss filled her and she closed her eyes.

It was heaven.

'Miss, may I pour some water to wet yer hair before I scrub it?' Jenny asked.

'Aye,' Fiona answered with her eyes still closed.

Soon after, water streamed slowly over her head and down her neck, soaking her hair. She sighed once more.

Jenny rubbed the bar of soap along her head and ran her fingers within it to bring the suds to a frothy lather. Such kindness of touch and care Fiona had not felt in a long time, and hot tears gathered in her eyes.

She blinked them back and shoved aside her sentiment. Had she learned nothing? Now wasn't the time to be soft. She needed to befriend Jenny and use her as a means of escape, nothing more. A friend, some coin, and a way to get William away from here—they were the only things that mattered now. She could trust no one but herself.

'Shall I rinse?' Jenny asked quietly.

'Aye, thank you.' A waterfall of water cascaded over Fiona's head again, and once more until all the suds were gone.

Jenny handed the warm, soft bar of soap to Fiona. 'I'm off to fetch ye a new dress and underclothes, miss.'

'Would you mind bringing me something not too fussy, so I may get in and out of it myself? It makes it far easier to nurse my son.'

'Aye.' At last the corner of a smile emerged from Jenny. 'He is a fine boy. Congratulations on yer bairn.'

'Thank you… Do you know when I may see him?' She couldn't stop herself from asking, a thread of urgency heightening the pitch of her voice.

Jenny's smile disappeared. 'He will be brought to you shortly. Do not fret. He is being well tended to by Miss Emma and Lady Beatrice.'

'Good. Thank you.'

Jenny left and Fiona leaned back into the tub, allowing the tension and aches to ease away slowly in the hot water as she washed herself with the lovely scented bar. Soon she would have fresh clothes on and her boy in her arms, and all the fragments of the day would come together to make her feel whole once more.

Shortly Jenny returned, and Fiona rose from the tub, allowing the maid to help her dry and dress. It was only after glancing in the looking glass once she was fully clothed that she recognised the gown. Her heart squeezed at the sight of the familiar grey frock with its bell sleeves. It was one of Anna's gowns. Fiona could remember her wearing it, and teasing Anna for its ridiculous wide sleeves, and Anna telling her she loved it, for the extra fabric kept her and her son warm as she nursed him.

'Does it not suit?'

Fiona glanced up and met Jenny's gaze in the reflection of the mirror. A line of worry etched in the lass's young brow.

'Nay, it is perfect for me. I was just thinking of Anna and the last time I saw her wearing it. It pains me to think of it.'

Jenny dropped her gaze. 'As it does all of us.'

'Does everyone wish me dead here?' Fiona asked, venturing into dangerous waters she could not keep herself out of. If she was to craft a suitable and reasonable plan of escape for her and William, she needed to know the truth of how difficult such an escape would be.

Jenny stepped away and busied herself with folding the damp towels and the Campbell plaid Fiona had worn into the castle.

'You may speak plainly to me. We were friends once, were we not?'

She faced Jenny, whose busy hands came to a stop. When the girl looked up to meet Fiona's gaze, pain showed in her wide glassy eyes.

'Aye. We were once friends—but now...? My brother and my betrothed died that night. I shall not forget it, and nor shall I forgive ye for yer betrayal. I will serve ye as the Laird commands it, but that is all. We are not friends, miss,' she answered, and anger vibrated off her now, in place of the meekness Fiona had seen earlier.

'I appreciate your honesty. Thank you. That will be all.'

'Aye,' Jenny answered, neglecting to add any nod or salutation of respect before she left the room.

Fiona sat down on the bed with a thud and cradled her still damp head in her hands. Finding an ally would be harder than she'd thought, and facing the daily wrath of a castle full of people who hated her and her son would be difficult. Some other opportunity would have to present itself—or perhaps she'd have to create one. Either way, she'd have to be creative and careful...far more careful than she'd ever imagined.

Chapter Eight

Brandon closed the door to his bedchamber. Exhaustion, confusion, and worry battled within him under the pressing weight of duty, and yet he could not sleep. Not yet. Too much swirled about in his head.

Moonlight shone through the series of arrow slit windows facing east. The torches had already been lit in his room, along with a slow rolling fire in the hearth, casting flickering shadows along the stone walls.

What a day it had been. When he'd left this morn, he'd been a laird off on an exploration along the borderlands, in search of new ways to enhance his defences and strengthen farming, trenches, and stores in hopes of making his people as self-sufficient as possible.

He'd returned with Fiona and his son.

He'd returned as a father—a *father*, of all things.

He scrubbed a hand through his hair. It was a role that filled him with hope as well as dread.

And the woman he'd once loved, lost and mourned, and now loathed, sat in a room two floors below.

Hell.

His sweet son's face swam before his mind. What a

life they could have had together as a family. He and Fiona could have united their sparring clans and laid to rest a long-held grudge, as they had once dreamt upon, with William as a reflection of a strong, united future. Now he had little idea how to unravel the tangled net he found himself in.

How could he protect his son and have Fiona answer for her crimes while still trying to become the strong, powerful laird that his clan needed? His own brother wished him dead—it was a sombre reminder of the chaos of the day and difficulties his clan had had to overcome.

Brandon stared down at his thumb. It still tingled with the memory of his son's wee hand wrapped around it. How could such a beautiful creature have been born of that dreadful last night together with Fiona?

But if he was honest with himself, their last clandestine meeting had been anything but dreadful, and his body heated at the memory of the passion and love they had shared. It was in the hours after her departure that the horrors of her betrayal had been brought to light, and the death and destruction that had followed had changed their lives for ever.

How could he bear the sight of her, knowing what she'd done? Perhaps the men were right. He should just hang her for her crimes and be done with it. But then how would he ever be able to look into the eyes of his son, knowing he had ordered the death of his mother?

Hell. There was no way through.

He stared out of the window along the hillside and felt a cool breeze ruffle his hair. Breathing in some of the night air helped to slow the uneven cadence of his heart. The smooth cast of moonlight against the rolling fields of darkness acted like the cool, crisp lines of charcoal against parchment, and he smiled.

He gathered the bound ledger he used for his sketches from under his bed, and the charcoal from where he'd left it on the windowsill. He settled onto the ledge and shifted against the cool stone beneath the window until the light shone on his page just right.

Sketching would settle his mind, just as it always did.

Perhaps the parchment would yield answers, as it had in the past. Answers his mind could find in no other way except through the work of his hands.

He flipped past pages of sketches. Many of them were of Fiona, and his heart squeezed at the sight of her looking back at him with her clear unflinching gaze. So many secrets they had shared, and so many dreams they had forged together. Ever since that fateful day when they had met along the border almost a decade ago, when they'd both been in their teens.

Her heart had been full of mourning over her mother leaving and he had been enraged by the crushing disapproval of his father the Laird.

Their emotion had bound them instantly, just as it always would.

He smiled at the memory of that first meeting. She had been throwing daggers at a tree target even then, her red hair long, loose, and falling wildly about her shoulders, her freckled, tear-stained cheeks flushed with exertion.

'Who are you?' she'd demanded as he'd emerged from the rowan trees that edged the border wall between their two clans.

'I might ask you the same,' he'd replied, clutching

the dagger he'd held in his hand. He'd been cutting a branch from a nearby tree to fashion into a gift for his ailing mother.

'I am Fiona MacDonald, daughter of the Laird Audric. And you?' she'd asked, levelling her gaze at him as she'd shaded her eyes from the sun that burned high and bright at his back.

'Brandon. Brandon Campbell—son of the Laird Malcolm.'

Her eyes had scanned his features. 'And...?' she'd enquired, lifting her eyebrows at him.

He had frowned and crossed his arms. 'And nothing.'

'Why do you interrupt me?' Impatience had threaded through her voice.

He'd chuckled. 'I didn't plan to. I was here gathering a branch when I heard...crying.'

Her cheeks had flushed and her eyes had filled with more unshed tears. 'I was not crying.'

He'd shrugged. 'Makes no difference to me if you were or you weren't, but it does look as if you have run out of daggers.'

He had extended his blade to her, his heart softening at the battle he'd seen raging in her even then. The desperation not to care or feel when her heart felt and cared about everything.

It was a desperation he understood keenly.

One that stirred within him even now.

They'd met in secret for some years before their friendship had been discovered. Then their parents had forbade their meetings. They'd ignored them, finding ways to meet, which had intensified their feelings and their determination to continue to see one another.

Brandon let his fingertips trail upon her features in

the sketch before flipping on. Longing for a different past would not change it. Just as his desire to be a valued second son would not be realised.

Sketches of his designs for the Campbell lands followed. He allowed himself to linger upon them for a few moments before continuing. For years he'd laboured over his ideas for crop rotation and a new water trench, but his new duty as Laird had thrust such work to the side. Each page reflected details that had taken him painstaking hours to calculate. But would anyone else ever see the value in them? Especially now, when they had so many other worries pressing so closely upon them?

Like how to refortify their borders and train new warriors to replace the many lost in battle. Where to find the funds to pay their taxes. Or whom he might eventually have to marry to help them gain a better standing within the Highlands.

Ack.

He tapped the pad of his finger on a sketch.

They were things he cared little about. Things Rowan and their father had cared deeply about. They had been born with the hovering expectation of duty. He had been born with the idea of never having any of those burdens. He'd been an invisible and independent presence most of the time, and he had preferred it that way.

He shifted in irritation and saw his father's old sword, hung on the back of his chamber door, reflected in the moonlight.

Brandon glared upon it.

He had felt the pang of loss for his mother and had grieved over her, but would he ever shed a tear for his father, the man he'd despised for half of his life? It was what a good son would have done. It was what he'd done for his mother. What he still did for her each year on her birthday and each anniversary of her death. Sometimes he wandered to her gravestone and just sat, merely to be near her bones and dust.

The memory of his father only stirred rock-hard anger in his gut. But it reminded him that he would not be his father and put his duty before his family. He would be a better man. He would listen and show his son how to possess bravery, courage, and power without crushing his inferiors beneath his feet.

Reality pressed in upon him and he sucked in a breath. And he would respect and protect William's mother, even if he could never marry her. Even if he couldn't trust her. He wouldn't squeeze the very life from her with his hatred, as his father had done to his mother.

His body and his heart had ached at the mere sight of Fiona this morn. Despite all the chaos and pain she had caused him, he could not deny how much he had missed her—still missed her—and how just seeing her had cut him to the bone.

They had made such lofty plans together, of uniting their clans and ending the feud that had put them at odds for generations.

How many nights had they met in secret and basked under the moon along the cliff's edge, or nestled on the bank near Loch Leven, dreaming with one another? She had been tucked smoothly against his side, her hair pressed against his cheek, counting stars. She had listened to his ideas for improving the clan with interest and intellect, and he had talked strategy with her on fortifying their borders with the English.

There had been a time when he'd known every part of Fiona as he knew the lines on his own palms. They had shared a closeness which had made the loss of her feel as deep today, when he'd set eyes upon her in the loch, as it had during the night of the attack when he'd realised her betrayal. There had been a time when the only person he'd felt he'd needed in the world to survive was her.

But he'd found a way to survive without her, and now he'd find a way to survive *with* her until he could come up with a better plan.

Staring out at the sky, he focused on the single bright star his mother had taught him to find if he ever got lost and needed to find his way home.

'I will protect them with all I am, Mother. I have no idea how, but I will. I wish you could see your grandson. He is handsome and strong. And he shall be the best of all of us. I promise.'

He stared back at the blank page before him and then began to sketch. After a few minutes, the charcoal stilled in his hand. Warmth spread through him as he gazed upon his first sketch of his boy—*his son*. After less than a day he knew the dimple of the boy's cheek, the lift of his brow, and the slight curl to his chestnut hair around his ears.

A beautiful boy had resulted from his fateful last night with Fi, and Brandon wouldn't forget that.

Beauty could come when one least expected it, and he knew that all too well.

He set the drawing in the windowsill. 'Take a look at your grandson, Mother. I miss you.'

Glancing outside, Brandon noted a few torches heading to the castle. It was late, and the sight of an organised cluster of village men sent a warning along his spine. The small group of men approached the door, spoke with the guard, and then waited. Not long after, heavy steps could be heard echoing up the stairs towards his chamber.

He frowned, jumped from the windowsill, and swung his door open to find Hugh frowning back at him.

'May I enter, my laird?'

'Aye.' Brandon allowed him inside and closed the door behind him.

'Seems the news of Fiona MacDonald's arrival has made its way all through the village, as we expected. A group of concerned men have come to express their displeasure at her not being hung already for her crimes. I believe you should speak to them before your brother does.'

'I will speak with them when I am ready, and not before. Tell them all their questions will be put to rest in due course.'

Brandon crossed his arms against his chest. The men of the village would demand nothing of him; *he* was Laird, not them.

Hugh widened his stance and clutched his hands together behind his back—a sign he disapproved of Brandon's words.

'And...?' Brandon asked, knowing his long-time friend had something else he needed to say.

'I know not why you brought her here. She will be the ruin of you and of this clan.'

'I could not abandon her.'

'Why not? After all she has done to our people and to you, does she not deserve hanging?'

''Tis not so simple a thing, Hugh.'

'Oh?'

Brandon released a breath and stared Hugh dead in the eyes. 'The boy is my son.'

Chapter Nine

Lavender permeated the air of the chamber. The hot bath had been bliss, and now that Fiona had William in her arms she wanted for little. They had a roof over their heads, and soon she would have food in her belly.

William began to mouth along the bodice of the grey dress Jenny had given her to wear. She settled on the edge of the bed, cradling him in her arms.

'You must be hungry, my sweet boy. We have had quite a day, have we not?' She cooed at him, unlaced the front of her bodice, and guided her nipple into his mouth.

He suckled greedily and snuggled in closer. His soft warm skin against her own comforted her. She wrapped the plaid around them tightly and rocked back and forth on the edge of the bed.

Soon a tune her Aunt Seana had used to sing to her twirled from her lips, and she sang to William as he ate. Despite how the day had begun, they were safe. *For now.* Tomorrow was a question mark, but now was a certainty. She would savour this moment while she could.

Approaching footfalls along the corridor outside her room shattered her sense of calm. She slowed her rocking and took a deep breath. She had nothing to fear. Not yet. Brandon had sworn to protect their son, and she had no choice but to believe him.

She recommenced the slow rhythmic movement and stared into William's eyes. He smiled and wrapped his hand about her finger.

A knock sounded. 'I must speak with you.'

Relief feathered through her. It was only Brandon.

'Aye,' Fiona called.

Brandon entered the room and closed the door, dropping the latch to bar it. A bit of unease replaced her relief. Was he barring others out or her within? She released a breath and met his gaze, only to find him staring dumbfounded at her. Disbelief registered along his slackened jaw and wide eyes.

'Perhaps you thought him not my child? You seem addled at the sight of him at my breast.'

Fiona almost smiled. His surprise and confusion amused her, which was a welcome feeling after the strains of the day.

He sat next to her on the edge of the small bed and nodded. 'I had not imagined to see you so…content. And knowing he is mine…it brings me to my knees.'

She sucked in a breath. His kindness, his honesty, his willingness to be vulnerable was a heady reminder of why she had once loved him. Of what might have been. She wished they could have shared such a moment in another way and in another time. One when they were husband and wife, revelling in the beauty and magic of their child, rather than Laird and enemy.

'Does this mean the talk with your family went well?

Do they now know William to be your son?' she asked, readjusting the Campbell tartan wrapped about him, casting aside her memories of happier times and of what might have been.

Brandon averted his gaze. 'I wished to speak with you and see William. They know not that I am here.'

Nerves bubbled up under her skin. What wasn't he telling her?

'You are Laird,' she scoffed. 'They are bound to serve *you* and follow *your* command. You need not ask their permission or keep any secrets from them.'

'I underestimated Rowan's anger. Best you always keep the door latched when you are inside, for your own safety. Daniel and Hugh shall be the only men allowed into this room other than myself until your fate has been decided. They will knock and reveal themselves to you. No other man may enter.'

A flicker of uncertainty flashed in his eyes before he could veil it, and Fiona's stomach dropped.

'What are you not telling me?'

Again, he would not meet her gaze.

She pressed closer to him. 'It shall be hard enough to muddle our way through this situation and keep our son alive. We can have no secrets between us. You must trust me even if you do not wish to, and I you. For William's sake.'

'Rowan wishes you dead, Fi. He wishes me dead as well.'

'While I'm not surprised to hear he wishes to end me, I do not understand his blame of you. Are you certain his wrath is for us both?'

'Aye. And while I can protect you and William when I am with you... I fear the moments when I am not.'

He met her gaze. 'There is a darkness, a wildness in his eyes that even I have not seen before. You must take heed.'

'All the more reason for you to set me free, to let me escape from here.'

'Nay. I...' He paused and his gaze drifted once more to her exposed shoulder and back, where her bodice drooped now that she'd loosened it to feed William.

She looked away and attempted to cover herself with the plaid, but he stilled her hand.

'I cannot pretend I do not see it.'

Brandon's thumb caressed one of the long, braided scars along her shoulder blade, sending a quiver through her body. Gooseflesh rose on her skin.

'Who has done this?' he asked.

She didn't need to meet his gaze to see his scowl. It echoed in the dark-edged timbre of his words.

'My father.'

His body tightened, and the pressure of his hand upon her own increased. 'Because of the babe?'

'Aye,' she whispered, clutching the wool of the tartan in her hand. Her heart pounded in her chest.

'While you were with child?'

She hesitated. He knew the answer. She'd just clearly stated it. Why did he wish more to be said?

'Fi...' he began. 'You will tell me.' Anger had dropped the pitch of his voice lower.

'Aye.' Shame budded in her, hot and full. Her father had lashed her. Not once, not twice, but multiple times, trying to cause her to lose her bairn. Trying to make an example of her to the clan.

Her own brother had been unable to stop the lashings. Only her aunt's actions had saved her life. After the lashings, she'd nursed Fiona back to health each time. Her aunt's love and the love of her unborn child had given her the strength and the will to live.

Brandon cursed and pounded a fist against his thigh, which sent a jolt along her body.

'Why did you not send word?' His voice cracked. 'A note? A plea for help? If I'd known I would have come for you. Stormed the walls if—'

What?

She balked, met his gaze, and scooted away from him, clutching William tighter in her arms. 'How dare you utter those words to me? I sent you letter upon letter…risked sending messages through my servants to your door to plead for your help…but you never answered. You never came.'

Never.

His mouth gaped open and a muscle worked in his jaw. The colour drained from his face.

'So I fled with my Aunt Seana to the borderlands under cover of night, to hide for as long as I could until after the babe was born. Anything to survive. But when she died I could not manage alone. I felt my only option was to continue on and to seek asylum with my cousin. The MacNabs seem a more forgiving lot.'

Her hands shook as she studied Brandon. The rage, anger and desperation at her abandonment pressed upon her fresh and new. She could scarcely breathe.

'I thought you had cast us aside…' Her voice betrayed her and her breath hitched in her chest. 'Abandoned us.'

He said nothing.

His gaze roved over every feature of her face as if he were seeing her for the first time. Heat crept into her cheeks at this intimate assessment of her, and then he clutched her hand in his.

'Nay...' he began, his voice scratchy and rough. 'I never received even one of them. On my life—on the life of our son, Fi—I swear to you, if I had known I would have come. I would not have abandoned you and our child, no matter what had happened between us.'

He stood abruptly and walked away from her towards the hearth. He stared for long minutes into the fire as she let what he'd said soak in.

All she could do was stare after him and take in his tall, familiar form as he stood silently with his back to her. Could it be that all the rage, anger and abandonment she'd felt and relived day after day over the past year had been for nothing? That the truth she had held so close to her heart had been a falsehood?

She covered her mouth to smother a sob. *He'd never known... He hadn't abandoned her in anger...*

All this time she'd believed the worst of him. That he had abandoned her as her own mother had. That she was not worth loving or protecting.

She took deep, greedy breaths, trying to regain her composure.

'When you told me of William at the loch this morning,' he began quietly, staring into the fire that danced before them, 'I believed you had intentionally kept him from me. That you had done it in order to affix some further pain and betrayal to me. That you hated me enough to keep him from me. Even when I saw the scars I did not think... I didn't wish to believe anything else.'

He leaned a hand against the mantel and faced her, pain etched in his tight features. She met his gaze, realising that his pain had been her own. He had grieved the loss of her as she had of him. Such a waste...of everything.

'It seems we believed the worst in one another.'

What else could she say to such a revelation?

Nothing, it seemed, for no more words formed in her mind or on her lips.

Her heart thundered in her chest. What could come of this? They were wedged tightly in between the past and the present, all because of one mistake: her uttering a secret out of turn. One stupid lapse of reason that had shattered the connection between them.

Time could not be unwound. They could not pretend that they did not hate one another now, even if it had been a misunderstanding. Too much had passed between them. Too many walls of protection had been built.

Could they ever begin to tear them down? Could she dare to do it?

Her sorrow, her guilt, and her shame over what her family had done to Brandon and his clan, and her part in it, threatened to swallow her whole. She couldn't undo the past, but she could attempt to free herself from the guilt of it—especially now that she knew he had not abandoned her in anger and punishment.

She could not stop the words from finally spilling unbidden from her lips. 'I am sorry...so sorry, Brandon. For all that has happened. For the attack, for the deaths of those you loved, and...and for my horrid part in all of it.'

'Fi—' he began.

'Nay,' she interrupted. 'You will let me say this. I wish with all that I am that I could undo that one ridiculous moment when I blurted out the location of the secret passage. I was foolish to trust Eloise. I believed she would never betray me…that she was a sister to me.'

He lifted his brow at her.

'I know… I know. You had warned me more than once about her loose lips, and reminded me that she was my maid, not my friend or my sister.' She fiddled with the edge of the plaid. 'But you know how lonely I was. After my mother left…'

Her breath hitched and she began again.

'After she abandoned us I needed someone to share my life with, my joy with. I was so happy. I loved you. I believed we would have the happy life I had always imagined. I did not think of the possibility that my joy at meeting you in secret and the place where we met would be shared beyond the walls of my bedchamber. Nor did I believe she had been sharing my secrets with Father all the years she served me.'

Heat flushed her face and she shifted the plaid off her shoulders.

'She was the one who told Father of the babe. It was she who brought the first blow of ruin upon us all.'

Brandon frowned. 'It doesn't surprise me. Nor do the actions of your father.'

Fiona nodded. 'Aye… I wish my father and my brother were better men and had not resorted to deceit and trickery to try to destroy your clan. I trusted them. I did not wish to believe them capable of such cruelty and devilry.'

Brandon sat down next to her and clasped her hand. His fingertips skimmed along the smooth inside of her wrist, sending chills down to her toes.

'I understand the cruelty and the weight of family and the choices they make.' He let go of her hand and

studied his open palms. 'I wish I could miss him—
my father. But nothing comes. Not even after all these
years. No grief. No sorrow. Seems he was hollowed
out of me long ago, after my mother died. He did that
to her. His lies, his meanness, his other women…they
squeezed the very life from her heart.'

She knew of the stories of the Old Laird of Campbell,
but Brandon had never confirmed their truth before.
Nor had she ever asked him to. That he had told her
now, after all that had passed between them, plagued
her further—as if she did not deserve his truth.

'I'm sorry. I didn't know. But you must believe I did
not plan such a deceit. I wish I could prove it to you,
yet I know not how. It was Father. He has lost all reason. He is consumed by a lust for absolute power. It is
one of the reasons I fled.'

''Tis why I never longed to be Laird. Why I was
happy as a second son, left to my own interests in agriculture and mining. Being Laird makes one cruel.
Hard. Immovable. I fear I will become so, as it is what
is required. I'm sorry I did not know all you had endured. That I wasn't there to protect you and William
before. But I shall do so now, no matter what it takes.'

He smiled down at their son, who now lay nestled
between them.

'I don't understand. What do you mean?' she asked,
but he ignored her questions.

'I must go. I've much to consider.'

He studied her face, as if searching for something.
Finally he bent over and pulled a small dirk from his
boot and pressed it into her hands.

'Keep this hidden for your protection. I know not yet
who to trust. Someone has gone to great pains to keep

me from my son and from knowing what was happening to you. It may be someone within these very walls, and I do not want you left without a weapon to defend yourself, if need be. Do not make me regret such an act of trust, Fi.'

His gaze was hard, unflinching.

'I won't,' she answered, knowing full well that she might be pushed to break that promise. It all depended on how the next few days unfolded. No doubt he felt as conflicted and confused as she. Could they trust one another? Did they dare? Did they dare not to with William's life at stake?

She turned the dirk in her hand and felt an ache grow in her chest. It had been his mother's, and Fiona knew how he treasured the small blade with its single ruby set in the carved wooden handle. He'd never used it in battle, but he always carried it. It was a way for his mother to be with him in all the years since her passing, he'd often said.

'I will take great care with it.'

'Just take great care of our son. I shall do the rest.'

'Rest of what?' she called, but he was already gone.

Chapter Ten

The wooden latch lifted within Fiona's chamber, and Brandon opened the door. He stilled at the sight of her holding his son on her hip, and reminded himself that this was the best of the poor options he had to choose from.

It had been two days since her arrival. The clan demanded an answer for her presence, and he would give it. Then he would handle whatever consequences he had to as Laird—but he would do what was best for his son first.

He nodded to her. 'Come.'

Her gaze narrowed on him. 'Where?'

He didn't answer, knowing full well she would refuse if she knew the details of his plan.

'You wish me to come with you?' she asked. 'Why? Where? I'll not go anywhere without knowing why.'

He steeled himself and sucked in a level breath. 'Come with me so we may speak with the clan. You will answer for your crimes against us this day.'

'To those who hate me and wish me harm?' She shook her head. 'Nay, I will not. Not with William.'

'Then my sister can care for him.'

He reached for her arm, but she stepped out of his grasp. What was wrong with her?

'Nay.' She took a step back into the room, shaking her head. Her words fell to a low whisper. 'I…' She faltered. 'I do not trust you.'

Her words silenced him. And then, 'Nor I you,' he whispered.

She cut her gaze away from him and stared down at their son. 'Then where does that leave us?' she asked.

'Uncharted waters. But we've no time to worry about what lies beneath. Unrest bubbles in the clan. I must address it at once.'

He stepped towards her and she retreated further. Frustration threatened to overtake his calm. He had no time for this. Neither did William.

'You will explain yourself,' she said. 'Otherwise you will have to drag me from this very room.'

'We've no time for this. Come with me, answer for your crimes, and then let us try to build some sort of new foundation for our son.'

White-hot urgency flooded his body. She *had* to agree; he could see no other way through.

She wrapped the edge of William's blanket around her finger silently for a few moments, before nodding to him. He released a breath and briefly squeezed her hand in his own. The warm, familiar feel of it eased some of the tension from his shoulders. They could only protect William together.

He opened the door, and she fell into step behind Hugh, who stood waiting at the ready. Brandon followed her down the corridor and onto the landing, above the throng of villagers gathered in the Great Hall below.

The room threatened to overflow with noise and the mass of people filling the space. But as he, Fiona and William appeared at the railing a hush fell over the room and all eyes were upon them.

There was no going back. There was only going forward, as his mother used to say.

Forward it was, then.

'Clansmen,' Brandon began, in a loud, clear and steady voice. 'You have heard talk of Fiona MacDonald being on our soil, and as you can see the talk is true. She is here.'

Grumblings began and disapproval travelled through the crowd in waves.

'We know that!' Old Man Purdy called from the back of the room. The crowd parted to let the respected elderly blacksmith come forward. 'What we want to know is why she's still alive. She's a traitor—just like all the MacDonalds be.' He spat on the floor. 'She should be hanged for what she's done. What shall be the punishment for her crimes? We have waited two days for yer decision. We can wait no more.'

Roars of agreement rose and the rafters reverberated with the noise. Brandon scanned the room. Peace would be slow and hard-won, but he knew this was the only course.

Steeling himself, he lifted a hand to silence them, and after a few moments the crowd fell into quiet once more.

'What you do not know…' he paused, letting his gaze settle on Rowan '…is that she has brought my son William with her.'

Not only could he see the awe and surprise in many faces, he could also hear the sharp intakes of breath, the subtle murmurs of unrest along with the fierce resentment in his brother's scowl.

Garrick shook his head and smirked. 'And how do you even know the bastard is yours?' He crossed his arms across his chest and shot Rowan a triumphant look.

The crowd shifted and unease rippled through the soldiers at this direct challenge to the Laird. All would note Brandon's response. If he balked, then he might as well return the title of Laird to Rowan now.

'Take heed on how you refer to my son, Garrick.' Brandon stepped forward and leaned upon the railing, sending a glare in his brother's direction. 'I have no doubt he is mine, so none of you may have any doubt…' He nodded to Fiona. 'Show them his marking. My son will be protected by everyone in this clan from this day forward.'

Fiona hesitated for only a breath. Meeting her gaze, he nodded to her. In that moment she revealed the birthmark on the boy's arm to the crowd. The mark that mirrored Brandon's own. The one that everyone in this clan knew.

No one would dare deny William's heritage now. No one who wished to continue to draw breath, anyway.

Rowan crossed his arms against his chest and said nothing. It was a sign that Brandon had made his point.

Now it was time to settle any additional questions that remained. Brandon swallowed hard, squared his shoulders, and made his stand. He set his hands on his waist belt and met the gaze of every man who dared meet his own.

'But what of *her*, my laird?' Old Man Purdy called out before Brandon could utter another word. 'What is to be done?'

Brandon hoped against all hope that his gut was right this time. That what he was about to say would not get them all killed and thrust the clan into greater chaos.

'She will answer for what she has done by providing us with all the information we desire in regard to her clan. Their resources, their battle strategy, where they are mining, and what secrets and treasures their own castle holds.' He faced her. 'She will tell us all or be cast from here without a care.'

Fire blazed in Fiona's gaze, and he watched as she brought William closer to her chest.

Grumblings of protest began.

'That is no punishment!' Rowan cried out, moving through the crowd, closer to the front. 'Not after what that wench has done. I will not stand for such softness. No laird would ever pass such a ridiculous judgment! You know she should hang!'

Two soldiers held Rowan by his arms. Another episode of his anger seemed about to unfold, and Brandon could do nothing to stop it. However, he *could* try to prevent an uprising.

'Aye,' he responded, 'she should.'

Rowan stopped struggling and waited to hear more.

'But I will not murder the mother of my son…even if she does deserve it.'

Silence settled among them. Perhaps revealing the painful truth of his own struggle with such a decision would help calm the dissent—for now. However, he was under no illusion that it would last for ever.

'No harm shall befall either of them,' he continued.

'If you pledge allegiance to me and this clan, you also pledge allegiance to their safety. Anyone unwilling to do so should leave this clan. *Now.*'

He didn't need to turn fully in order to see and feel the weight of Fi's surprise. He heard her small gasp, and out of the corner of his eye he saw Hugh move to steady her by resting a hand on her elbow.

Perhaps she had thought Brandon unwilling to claim them, or too weak to bear the brunt of the consequences that would come from his actions. He wasn't. He might have been years ago, but not now. She would know by his actions and not just his words of his loyalty in protecting his son.

It didn't matter whether or not she deserved such kindness after her treachery. She was the mother of his child. She would be protected. His son would not be denied the love and care of his mother. Brandon was not his father, and nor was he his brother. He would not sacrifice his family for his duty as Laird. He would try to mesh the two worlds into one.

Rowan seethed with rage. He didn't even bother to hide it. 'She has bewitched you as I said she would!' he shouted, and spat at the ground. 'Fiona MacDonald will be the end of you, my brother…or perhaps *I* shall end you!'

'Remove him!' Brandon commanded the soldiers below. He'd not entertain any more of his brother's threats, nor allow him to inspire any sort of uprising against him.

A few men called out their displeasure and disapproval. Had Brandon expected anything else? Nay, he hadn't. He knew his words had planted a seed of outrage underground, where it would grow quietly, fester, and then rot into something far more dangerous: treason.

'Those who wish to discuss the matter further will come to me and me alone. That will be all,' Brandon added in a final dismissal.

The crowd shifted and the talk grew louder as the men and women headed to the large castle doors leading outside. He watched them as they mingled, wanting to see if he could determine who the early dissenters might be. A group of young soldiers stood along with his brother-in-law in a small circle around Rowan. His brother spoke in animated short bursts, shaking his head at times as he listened to the men. Then he glanced up and caught Brandon's gaze, falling silent for a moment before he was ushered out by the guards.

Brandon frowned. 'I see that didn't take long. He rallies against me even now.'

'It began long before, my laird—you know that. Now he has even more reason to focus his anger fixedly upon you,' Hugh answered. 'Best you hurry along with whatever plan you have now that you have shaken this clan to the ground.'

Brandon sighed. 'Aye... I'll be sure to let you know what it is once I have it.'

Hugh chuckled. 'I look forward to that day.'

'As do I.' He clapped a hand on his trusted warrior's shoulder and turned to Fi. 'Come,' he ordered. 'We've much to discuss.'

She nibbled her lip, but said nothing.

They walked in silence to her chamber. After entering the room, Brandon nodded to Hugh. The warrior closed them into it for privacy. Fiona strode to the crib and nestled William in his blankets and furs. Brandon smiled at the sound of her cooing to him as she tucked him in.

He grabbed an iron poker from its holder near the stone hearth and jabbed the small winking fire back to life. Tossing in a new log, he watched the embers pop and dance in the air as it caught flame. Despite what she believed, he would not fail to protect her or their son, and his gesture tonight had proved such.

He rolled his shoulders and faced her, eager to bring the discomfort he felt at her doubting him to an end.

'So this is it, then?' Fiona demanded, facing him. Ire laced her words and her eyes burned a wild emerald. 'We are to stay here. For ever? I as some sort of prisoner to be bled of information and William as your bastard son?'

'Did you have any better options available?' he answered, frowning at her. She'd found her tongue and seemed bent on using it. 'You are no prisoner—as I've told you time and again. But you will not take my son from me. I've taken the risk of losing my title by daring to keep you alive and by claiming William outright, and now you don't wish to be here?'

Frustration flooded through his veins and he scrubbed a hand through his hair.

'You are the fool who did that, not I. I told you we have never wished to be here.' Anger laced her words and she propped her hands to her waist. 'You captured me, remember? I begged you to let us continue on. Everyone here hates me—and my son. What life will there be for us here? I have no wish to be controlled once more by a man who does not...'

She faltered and turned to walk away.

He clutched her forearm to halt her retreat. They'd finish this. There'd be no more running.

'Who does not what?'

She hesitated and faced him. Sadness and anger glistened in her gaze. 'Who does not love me. Who does not want us. I have endured enough from men like my father, who wish to control me and who value me as little more than property. All I want is to be free to make my own choices, but you have trapped me once more.'

A tear spilled down her cheek and she wiped it hastily away with the back of her hand. She struggled to free herself from his hold, but he could not, *would* not, let go.

He had to make her understand. He was trying to protect her and William the only way he knew how. *Why* didn't she understand? He'd risked everything. His heart pounded in his chest, but he'd forgotten to breathe and no words would form on his lips to respond.

'I will not allow my son to see this as an example of how to be a good man. I will not allow him to see me as some whore to be used at your whim.'

'What?' He spouted the word in shock, releasing her arm. 'You speak drivel. You will be no such thing to me. I would not debase you in such a manner. I am to marry another. We are in the process now of selecting my bride. You will be free to make your own choices as long as William stays within the walls of Argyll Castle. All you need do is prove your value by telling us about your clan, so we can protect ourselves from them in the future.'

'Oh, is that all?'

'Would you prefer to be hanged at first light? I'm

sure my men would be eager to measure your rope at my word.'

'And do you think any of those soldiers shall see me as anything but property, kept here for your pleasure? No other man will dare touch me now that you have claimed William and ordered me protected. And how do you believe they will treat our son? He is the Laird's bastard in their eyes.' She stared at him coldly. 'And do you believe your future wife will want me here underfoot, with a boy who would make her son second? You are daft! She will order her men to end us in our sleep. We will not last a year. It would have been an act far kinder if you had just cast me out.'

'Cast you out?' Brandon echoed. 'You've gone mad. You speak in circles. I've risked all to protect you and William. The clan may fall into greater chaos because of it.'

'But I did not *ask* you to.'

'What should I have done?'

'What I begged you to do. Let. Me. Go. *With* our son. Now we will always live in fear, in hatred, and never be free.'

'They will come to accept you,' he said.

'In how long? Years? A decade? Our son will not live like that. I will not allow it.'

'You have no choice in the matter,' he answered flatly.

'Drivel. I have *every* choice in it.'

'You may leave if you wish, but he will not.'

'So I truly am a prisoner?'

'Only if you see it as such,' he answered, and left, slamming the door behind him.

Chapter Eleven

Did Brandon truly believe that she was safe here at Argyll Castle? The man had clearly lost his mind in his quest to protect her and William. Not only was he making himself a target, by forcing a clan of men who hated her and her son to vow to protect her, he had made them prisoners within these stone walls in the process.

Fool of a man.

If he'd told her of his feeble plan before announcing it to all the clan she would have told him what a ridiculous notion it was and been done with it.

She paced the room. And what kind of information did he and his elders think she possessed? Her father had never trusted her within his study, where all the real battle planning and strategy had taken place, and the few attempts she'd made to eavesdrop had been thwarted.

Only her brother and her trusted guardsman Oric had ever treated her as an equal within the walls of Glenhaven Castle, her childhood home. And Brandon.

He had treated her with respect, valued her mind and her strategy when they'd loved one another and thought they would build a life together by joining their clans in something other than dispute and warfare. Even when her father had ordered her to stay away from him she'd risked all to see him, and he her, but now...? Now they seemed unable to grasp the past hope and the sense of possibility that had once bound them together. Now she could hardly think straight.

A knock sounded on the door. She frowned. 'Leave me be!' she shouted.

'''Tis only me, miss.' Jenny's soft voice carried through the door. 'I just wished to see if I could get anything for you.'

'Could you bring me a cup of willow bark tea before I undress? It will help to calm my nerves.'

'Of course, miss,' Jenny answered, and padded away down the corridor.

Fiona sat with a thump on the bed. How would she possibly be able to escape the castle grounds with her son? All the men would be on guard, watching her, waiting for her to prove her devilry. They would capture her so she could be hanged as they wished.

Thankfully William slept soundly in his crib, oblivious to her fears.

And even if she could somehow sneak past the guards, she'd be taking a risk travelling at night alone, without anyone to protect her and her son. While travelling during the daylight would still be dangerous, travelling at night along Glencoe Pass could be downright deadly.

The tea would help. It might just clear her head, so she could have one lucid thought.

Maybe.

Rolling her eyes, she flopped back on the furs and

covered her eyes with her forearm. Such hastiness had caused her to be in this mess to begin with. If she planned to flee, she had to plan her escape carefully, and she needed help. And right now help was in short supply. Unless Jenny…

She heard the door open. It closed again softly and the slight tinkling of a cup sounded as a tray was placed on a table. Perhaps now would be a good time to attempt to befriend Jenny once more.

'Jenny, thank you for the tea, my sweet…'

'I do not think you will be thanking me for my visit.'

Rowan's deep voice sent tendrils of alarm down her body and she scrambled upright to her knees on the bed and watched him. He leaned his arm against the hearth, where a small fire flickered, and smirked at her.

'What have you done with the guards?' she asked, wondering if they had been killed so Rowan could reach her.

'They are responding to Brandon's urgent need of them. I offered to stand watch until they returned.'

He offered her a wicked toothy smile. *Blast*.

'They still follow my word,' he said. 'It matters not that I am not Laird in name.'

'Get out of my chamber,' she seethed.

'I think not. It is you who should leave *my* castle.'

'Perhaps you have lost your wits this day. It is not *your* castle. 'tis Brandon's. And I know no matter what tricks you play, it will remain as such.'

'You accuse *me* of tricks?'

Rowan's hand rested on the dagger at his waistband and she shifted away from him, knowing her own blade was far across the room, hidden from view.

'I know not what spell you have cast once more upon

my brother, but I will not stand for it. He will marry another, and you will be thrown from here like dung from a stable. And your boy—'

'You will not speak of my son!' she shouted.

He stepped forward and grabbed her forearm, yanking her from the bed. She struggled to gain her footing and wriggled to free herself as his fingers bit into her flesh, but she made no progress. He drew his blade.

Footfalls sounded in the corridor. A loud, masculine pair, followed by the light, scurrying steps of a woman.

'I tried to stop him, but he insisted,' Jenny chattered in a high, eager pitch. 'Took my tray and ordered me from here. But the Laird bade me tell ye if anything unusual happened, so I…'

Relief poured through Fiona. *Thank you, Jenny.*

'Let go of me!' Fiona shouted, in the hope of being heard outside the door.

The footsteps picked up speed, and soon the door burst open. Hugh crossed the threshold, with Jenny but a step behind.

'Go to the first soldier you see and tell him to get the Laird and bring him here at once,' he ordered her.

Jenny hesitated and cut her gaze to Fiona.

''Tis in hand, Jenny,' Fiona called. 'Do as Hugh commands.'

The maid nibbled her lip and ran from the doorway.

'Release her,' Hugh commanded, drawing a dagger from its sheath along his waist.

'Why?' Rowan answered, pulling her into a tighter hold, so close she could feel the heat of his breath upon her cheek and see the glimmer of metal from his blade in her sights. 'She is but a whore and her son a bastard.

She has no place in this castle among us. Not after what she has done.'

Fiona held still, unsure of what Rowan might do. Before having her boy she would have fought back, grappled him to the ground to show him he held no power over her and drawn a dagger to his throat to free herself. But now…

She watched William awaken and stretch his tiny arms in the air. She would not fight back, nor provide Rowan the moment he needed to end her. His wrath would not cause her to leave her boy an orphan. She would trust Brandon's pledge that she and her son would be protected.

'You will release her and stand down or I will use my blade against you,' Hugh commanded. 'She is to be protected—even from you, Rowan. You can make no decision against the Laird.'

Rowan laughed. 'This woman has bewitched him. I do this to protect him and our clan.'

'Nay, you do not. You act in grief.' Hugh's tone softened and empathy registered in his eyes.

Rowan shifted on his feet and his hold faltered. 'You know not what I—'

'I *do* know. And you act from grief, not logic.' Hugh took a step forward.

'Stay there!' Rowan shouted.

Hugh paused.

'He has *what*?' Fiona heard Brandon demand as his booming steps echoed down the corridor towards her room.

She could hear him clearly, since the door was still open, and relief poured through her. For a moment she felt light as a feather from head to toe.

Brandon stopped at the door and scanned the room, taking in the scene. His shoulders tightened and the glare he set upon Rowan would have withered the heartiest of warriors.

'Release her,' he commanded.

'Shall I? Why? So she can further cast her spell over you, brother?'

An eerie laugh escaped Rowan's lips and he tightened his grip on her. She felt the cool press of metal to the flesh of her neck.

Brandon met her gaze, and the calm certainty in his eyes surprised her. She remained as still as she could.

'I will say it only once more. Release. Her.'

Brandon's tone sent a chill down her skin.

'All right, then,' Rowan growled, shoving her away from him.

Fiona skidded to the floor.

'We shall settle this between us.'

Fiona faltered before she regained her footing and hurried to pick up William. She stood far away from the three large men who filled the small chamber. Her son cooed in her arms and watched them all, unaware of the threat still looming. Fiona's hand shook as she traced a finger along William's cheek.

'Hugh, take Fiona and William from here. They are to be moved upstairs into the chamber next to my own. Permanently.'

The anger in Brandon's voice was something she did not recognise. Alarm buzzed through her. She hoped he would not do anything he might regret. He was Laird now, but even a laird could not slaughter his own brother. Not even when he threatened the mother of his child.

Hugh stepped aside and nodded to her. She fell in step behind him, stuffing the worry tightening her chest deep down in her gut. How she wished to say something to set Brandon's mind steady, but no helpful words formed on her lips.

Instead she said a prayer.

Please don't let them slaughter one another. William needs Brandon for a little while longer at least. As do I.

Chapter Twelve

'I did not expect this even from you. Fool!'

Brandon slammed the chamber door closed and it rattled on its hinges. He wanted to do the same to his brother. Rowan's dark eyes were wild, and he still held the dagger from his belt. The grief he had held in check so well these last few days shone bright in his eyes.

'You are the bloody fool. Do you believe for one moment that she will not bring the demise of this clan?'

Brandon edged closer to him, like a predator closing in on its prey. He'd not pull his weapon unless he absolutely had to. Rowan was still his brother—his only brother—and he didn't wish to lose him...especially when he knew he was broken by grief.

'I do not believe it. If I did, she would not be under this roof. What I do is best for the clan.'

He edged closer and Rowan jabbed at him with his blade. Brandon avoided it easily and settled back into his stance. 'You will give me the blade, brother. Now.'

Rowan cackled. 'Or what? You shall take it from me? Not likely!'

Brandon surged forward at the challenge and tackled his brother, taking him to the floor with a thud. He pinned him down, and used his extra weight to keep him down. He slammed his brother's hand to the floor and the blade slid towards the door.

'Aye. I will take it from you…every time. So I'd think twice about drawing a blade against me, Fiona, or my son. The next time I might just kill you.'

Rowan panted for breath. 'Not likely!' he said again, and he spat in Brandon's face.

Brandon wiped the spit from his cheek with his tunic sleeve and sat up, his legs still pinning his brother to the ground. 'I am glad beyond measure that Anna isn't here to see what you have become. She would not recognise you. I certainly do not.'

He got up and walked to the door, leaving his brother sprawled on the floor. A crowd of soldiers stood at the doorway.

'Deal with him,' Brandon ordered, and left the room.

He still had Fiona to tend to, and his heart would not be at ease until he had set eyes upon his son.

Brandon sucked in a fortifying breath outside the new chamber Fiona and William had been moved to. She would have much to say about what had happened, and his patience was as thin as the cotton on the dress tunic he had donned to make his announcement this eve.

'No one shall enter this room but her maid,' Brandon growled at Hugh, who stood watch outside the chamber door.

Brandon would talk with his most trusted soldier and friend later—when his mind wasn't spinning with images of what might have happened if he had been moments later in arriving. And when he didn't wish to draw a sword upon the men who had abandoned Fiona's door. Many of the soldiers still held a loyalty to Rowan…it was a truth Brandon would have to address.

'Aye, my laird.' Hugh nodded.

Once more Brandon thought how he hated being laird. The decisions he *wanted* to make were never quite aligned with those he *should* make.

He knocked softly and opened the door.

Fiona turned where she stood and stopped the soft tune she had been singing to William. He was wrapped in a fur, snuggled against her chest. She sat down on the edge of the bed and settled him in her arms before putting him in the crib next to the bed.

Brandon sat down beside her without a word. For moments he merely studied his son's peaceful face and let his heart settle into a more regular rhythm. They were alive and they were safe—for now.

The scene of Rowan threatening them was still fresh in his mind. If he had arrived minutes later, would they have both been dead?

'Did he harm you?' Brandon asked, noting the bruise forming on the inside of Fiona's pale wrist. He wished to touch her to be sure, but he clenched his hand into a fist instead. He didn't trust the emotion thrumming through his veins.

''Tis nothing. We are fine…for now.'

He frowned, facing her. 'What does that mean? You are protected. No harm shall come to you. Do you doubt the honour of my men?'

'Aye, I do.' Her bright green eyes glared at him. Hard, unflinching. 'And if you trusted them all, you would not have moved me up here to be next to your own chambers. Isn't that right?'

'This is the thanks I receive after all I have given up and suffered for you?'

Anger budded in his gut. His men would honour his command, and so would she. He was Laird, after all.

'And you think I...*we*...have not suffered because of you? Yet you keep me here by claiming me and William, placing us in unfettered danger by surrounding us with men such as your brother, who want nothing more than for us to both be dead. We are targets. We will be caught in the fray, and you know that. Set us free so we may be safe. Let us unburden one another. Nothing can be built from the ruins between us. It is far too late. You know this.'

Did he? When he'd seen her in danger, threatened by Rowan, all he'd wanted was to save her and hold her once more. But he couldn't say the words. Even though as he stared at her now, full of anger and sadness, he still cared for her.

Part of her was a seed in him that would always remain ready to bloom, full of love, if she would just say the word or if they could but erase the past. Perhaps it was time he squashed it—for his sake as well as her own. But his son...? He couldn't take the boy from his mother or her from him. He was trapped in misery, and nothing seemed a solution for it.

'You and William will stay here as long as I command it.'

He stood and headed for the door. He'd not let her go, but he'd not let her close to his heart.

'You have become what you promised you never would,' she spat.

He turned to her. 'And what is that?'

'Your father.'

His fingers tingled. He said nothing and left the room while he still could. Anger pumped wildly through his limbs. He clenched his fists. He was *not* his father, nor would he ever be.

Hugh greeted him outside the door. 'Your brother has been sedated for now. One of Miss Emma's tonics. Beatrice is quite concerned.'

'As she should be.'

Brandon rubbed the back of his aching neck. What a horrid night it had been.

'Have some men bring up the larger items from Fiona's old chamber, and ask the maids to gather the smaller things as well. Once they are settled in tonight, you will lock them in. You shall be the only one to have the key.'

Brandon pressed a large iron key into Hugh's palm.

'Are you sure, my laird?' Hugh furrowed his brow.

'Aye. I am,' Brandon answered. 'I know what happened earlier will not happen again.'

'Nay. It will not. Only Daniel or I shall be outside this door, standing guard.'

'Then take the key,' Brandon replied. ''Tis best for everyone—including me.'

Hearing the sound of a key turning, Fiona rushed to the door and yanked on the handle. It didn't open.

'Have you dared lock me in?' she called.

'Aye. By the Laird's command,' Hugh answered.

'Bastard…' Fiona muttered as she paced the room.

Brandon could be a fool when he'd set his mind upon something, and this was a fine example of it. She and her son were in more danger here, *in* this castle, than they'd ever be out in the Highlands alone—yet he ignored that truth and denied the possibility that he might be unable to keep them safe.

Arrogant man.

She was a mere doe, waiting for a bow and arrow to cleave her chest. Fiona had no allies. And no locked door was going to keep her alive for long. Rowan's attack this evening was a prime example. Surely fate mocked her?

She plopped onto the bed and scanned the room, scrunching up her nose. Where was she? She had never been in this chamber before. The furnishings were of a higher quality compared to the other chamber. A painting of women working in a field and a portrait of a woman who seemed oddly familiar hung on the walls. Then she came upon a painting of the mountains along the borderlands, and paused. She knew that place. It was the view from this very window.

Upon a closer look, she could see initials at the bottom: *EAC*. She drew back and sucked in a breath. *Emilia Abigail Campbell.* Brandon's mother had painted it. He'd said painting had been one of the few things in her final years to bring joy to her in her chamber, floors below.

'How did it get up here?' she asked aloud.

She stepped back and started searching the room. She had to know who'd slept in this room.

'Hugh, whose chamber was this?' Fiona called through the doorway.

She could almost hear him considering whether to answer. Impatience ruled her, and she asked once more.

'I know you are there. Brandon would not have entrusted my care to anyone else. Just tell me whose chamber this was.'

A sigh and a shifting of boots on the floor made her smile. He would answer her. It was only a matter of how long it would take for him to give in.

'Lady Emilia's,' he said.

Fiona furrowed her brow. 'I thought the chamber downstairs was Emilia's?'

'It was. She lived up here before...'

'Before she was taken ill?'

'Aye. Then she was moved down to a lower level to ease her.'

Fiona scoffed. Or perhaps because the Laird had wished her further away from his exploits. She had a keen idea of what that might have felt like, for it was exactly the way she felt now. Locked in a room, caring for the son they shared, while Brandon made other plans.

'Thank you, Hugh,' she murmured.

'The rest of your belongings shall be brought to you as soon as the maids can ready them.'

'I shall be happy to assist them, if you'll allow me.'

She thought she heard Hugh curse under his breath.

'Nay. You shall stay here. We've had enough disputes this eve.'

Fiona pouted at her inability to move Hugh towards freeing her and paced about the room. Despite her weariness, she was too awake to sleep.

She approached the window and stared out of it—for how long she didn't know. Only the sound of scraping upon the chamber floor jarred her from her stupor.

She turned to see a panel on the far wall sliding forward and opening into her room. Panicked, she tugged the dagger from her sleeve, rushed forward, and poised herself to defend her son.

Rowan would not surprise her again—not this time.

When Brandon stepped through the panelling that acted as a secret door, Fiona sagged in relief, her hand relaxing over the dagger and falling to her side.

'You gave me a fright…' she said, and pressed a hand to her mouth to prevent a sob.

A woman could only take so much in one day, and this last fright was her undoing, it seemed. Her hands shook and she could do nothing to stop the flood of relief escaping her.

Brandon lifted his hands in apology. 'I'm sorry. I wasn't thinking. I just wanted you to know that I am here, that these chambers are connected…'

He started towards her, but faltered—as if a part of him wished to comfort her, while another part of him demanded he keep his distance. He stopped in the middle of the room, fisting his hands by his sides.

His confusion mirrored her own. She was torn between her past and her present feelings for him.

Her dagger clattered to the floor and she began to tremble. *Blast.*

She willed him to come closer and comfort her.

Rowan's attack had stirred a fear deep within her. It had thrust her back into her childhood at Glenhaven Castle. She'd been the wee uncertain and fearful Fiona once more, awaiting whatever the next cruelty or attack from her father might be, unable to stop it. Once that little girl in her had been awakened, it was hard to soothe her and put her back in the past.

Brandon, of all people, knew this. No doubt he could

see it in her face now, despite how much she wished to hide the shame of it.

He approached her slowly, as he might a wounded animal, but once he stood within arm's reach he opened his palms to her in an offering she could accept or refuse.

To her own surprise she walked straight into his arms, crying against his shoulder.

He lifted her from the floor, cradling her against him, and settled her on the small bed. When she wouldn't let go, he climbed next to her, pulling her back tight against his chest just as he'd used to. Just as she wished he would, even as much as she loathed herself for wanting it.

The feel of his solid, warm strength wrapped around her soothed her. He ran his fingers along her temple, brushing tendrils of hair away from her face, and they remained with one another in the quiet candlelight cast by the lit wall sconces for long minutes before either of them spoke.

'When I saw you there,' Brandon began, his voice low and husky, 'in Rowan's hold…his blade a whisper away from your neck… I cannot describe to you what I felt. It was as if the ground had been pulled from beneath my feet. I'm sorry for what I said before. I was angry.'

She sucked in a breath and squeezed his forearm. 'Brandon, you do not have to—'

'Nay,' he continued. 'Nothing else mattered but keeping you alive, despite everything—' He halted on the word.

She turned in his arms, running a hand over his jaw, feeling a tremble skitter along his body as she had a hundred times before. Her body sang under his touch. She'd had no comfort in all the time they'd been apart. Was it wrong to take a bit of comfort now? To revel in the feel of him once more before she fled his castle, his touch and his life?

Before she could command herself against it, she leaned in and kissed him lightly on the corner of his mouth, felt his lips parting to greet her. He ran his palm over her hair and along the column of her neck as he pulled her closer. She didn't resist, but let gravity bring them back to one another in kiss after kiss, until she felt out of breath and just a whisper away from the abyss.

'Brandon,' she murmured as he feathered light kisses along her collarbone. 'We must cease.'

'Must we?' he asked. 'I had forgotten what it feels like to hold you. To be kissed by you. It is heaven,' he murmured, running a hand under her skirts, gliding his warm palm up her thigh, cupping her backside, pressing her tightly against him.

Her resolve was loosening, along with the tie of her skirts. The blasted man had that way about him.

His kisses deepened and she matched his hunger for her, scraping her teeth against his lips, clutching his broad shoulders in her palms. He groaned and toppled her back onto the furs covering the bed...

William's squall snatched her from the moment, and the awareness of what she'd almost done stung her.

She pressed a hand to Brandon's chest, thankful for her son's interruption and unnerved by her own weakness. She'd nearly lost her senses to Brandon's touch, and she dared not risk her heart once more. There was too much at stake and far too much uncertainty.

'Now we truly must cease. Your son is hungry and commands my attention.'

Brandon sighed and rested his face in the crook of her neck. His breathing was uneven, which pleased her. He was just as affected as she.

'Aye,' he agreed, and his voice was low and husky with desire.

He rolled off her and she climbed from the bed. Pulling William from his crib, she cooed to him and rocked him back and forth in her arms before settling back on the edge of the bed.

Brandon slid over and propped himself up on an elbow as William greedily began to take the milk Fiona offered him.

'He is beautiful, is he not?' Brandon whispered.

'By far the most beautiful and handsome in all the Highlands. He is the best of me,' she said.

Brandon paused, his lips parted as if he were about to speak. Then he clamped his mouth shut and rose, moving away.

At the threshold of the open panel door he stopped and faced her, meeting her gaze. 'I believe he is the best of both of us.'

Her breath hitched in her chest.

'Sleep well,' he called, before sealing the door between them.

Fiona let out a shaky sigh. She needed to keep her distance or she'd find her heart a prisoner to him once more.

Chapter Thirteen

Dark grey clouds hung low and menacing in the sky—a true reflection of Brandon's mood as he rode alongside Hugh towards the eastern edge of their border with the MacDonalds.

Yesterday had been pure disaster. His announcement to the clan that William was his son and that he and Fiona were to be protected as their own had only put them in more danger, and if he'd been but moments later his own brother might have killed both of them... He was making a muck of being a laird and a father.

As hard as he tried, Brandon couldn't concentrate on the task at hand. Instead of being focused on explorations and resources for the future, his thoughts were consumed by Fi, William, and the fact that if his son hadn't cried when he had last night Brandon would have bedded her—the last thing he should be doing right now.

But seeing her there, with Rowan's knife at her throat, fearing he would lose her for ever, had shaken him more deeply than he had expected. Despite his anger, and all the times he had wished her dead for her role in the MacDonald attack on Argyll Castle, and despite all his clan had lost, he realised losing her was the last thing he wanted.

Part of him still cared for her, and his body craved her touch. He'd almost ruined everything by once again bedding a woman who was not intended to be his bride.

Thunder rumbled past the mountains and Brandon studied the clouds building in the distance. They'd have one more hour of exploring, but no more. The weather had other ideas for this day. He could only hope that the fields they'd identified for future harvesting and the alternative trench location for easier irrigation would yield some dividends in the future. The clan funds were running dangerously low, and taxes would be due by year's end. He'd have to stay the course in his plan to marry a lass with a handsome dowry unless he found another more promising and immediate solution.

'I thought we'd explore the edge of the last pass along the mountains before we return,' Brandon stated, scanning the dark horizon. 'It's one of the few areas we've left to document as holding possible resources, and if it can be turned into a slate mine, like some of the surrounding mountains have been, it could easily fill our coffers for a while.'

Hugh frowned. 'There's a reason it has not been explored.'

'Oh?'

Hugh wrapped the reins about his hand so tightly that his skin whitened under the pressure. 'Does Rowan know your plans?'

'Of course not. He has no interest in agriculture or resources within the land. He only wishes to unseat me and rage against the past. His goal is power alone. Why does it matter?'

'The mountain does hold slate. And it used to be a mine, generations back, but it's been closed since your grandfather's time.'

'How would you know about such a mine when I do not?'

Brandon slowed his horse and paused, grabbing a ledger from his saddle bag. He opened the new map he was creating from his daily explorations and rolled out the small piece of hide across his lap.

'It isn't noted on any of the old maps, and I've seen every map in my father's study. This area is blank, as if it doesn't exist, which I found odd. It's why I wished to come here.'

A muscle ticked in Hugh's jaw and unease skittered along Brandon's limbs. Warning lit through him.

Hugh relaxed his grip on the reins and faced him. 'The mine is on no map because it was meant to be forgotten. This is where your father and Rowan found me when I was a boy. I spent weeks living in it and scavenging along the cottages beyond the grove. Rowan saw me thieving there one morn and followed me back into the mine. He nearly got himself trapped, reaching me. Both of us almost died that day due to a small cave-in. Stubborn as they come, your brother. But I'm grateful he came, otherwise I would be dead.' He paused. 'You know the rest.'

Hugh had hidden in a mine? Alone? He could only have been but a boy of eight.

'Why did you never tell me?'

Hugh shrugged and gazed far off into the distance. 'I prefer to leave the past where it is. Since you and

Beatrice were away then, we saw no need to tell you the ugly truth of it.'

Brandon knew enough to know that Hugh had good reason to leave his past there. His family had been murdered by the English in a raid along the borderlands when he was a boy. That was all Brandon had ever known. Hugh had never told him anything else of his past, but loss shimmered off him when he thought no one was looking.

'I can tell you the mine was unstable then, and it will not have improved with age.'

'But if it's full of slate, aren't we throwing away coin it could fetch if our crops don't yield a harvest? Coin we could use to pay our yearly taxes?'

'Not if you find there's no more slate to be had and you lose ten good men trying to unearth what isn't there. What good would it be then?'

'What good is it now, sitting empty?'

Hugh laughed. 'You oft complain how hard-headed your brother is, yet you are alike.'

Brandon couldn't help but smile. 'Perhaps it is the one good quality we share.'

He gently pulled the reins and his stallion began a slow walk once more. He'd have to visit his brother later today, to talk over yesterday's attack, but he dreaded it almost as much as speaking with Fiona about his actions with *her* last night. He'd put it off as long as possible.

Shaking his head, Hugh followed him. 'When we are buried in a pile of rubble you may rethink your choice. But I cannot allow you to go in alone. You are a new father after all.'

Father.

Gooseflesh rippled along Brandon's skin. Even now it seemed odd to hear the word in the air, especially as it now defined him, his life, and his choices.

Going into a mine known to have collapsed *shouldn't* be his first choice. Even Hugh had noted as much. Yet Brandon hadn't even thought of the danger. He was all his son and Fiona had, and yet he had to explore the area, didn't he? Even if he risked his life? Proving his worth as Laird to Rowan and the elders might be one of the only ways to get his brother and his people to trust him again and allow him to remain Laird.

But despite his desire to win favour by gathering new information, Brandon didn't wish to put his life at risk. Without him, who knew what would befall Fiona and their son? He seemed the only barrier between them and certain death.

Brandon gave in. 'Aye, you are right. The mine shall wait till another day. Eastern wall it is. Perhaps the soil has rested enough there to be good for a crop to be planted next year to increase our harvest.'

Hugh looked doubtful.

'Or perhaps good enough for a herd to graze,' Brandon added.

He knew the land on Campbell grounds had not been rested well enough along the border wall. The loch was close, the sun set upon it most of the day, and it had often yielded fine harvests...until the soil had been leeched of all its nutrients. If they didn't let it be, the soil would never be replenished.

It was a fitting comparison to his relationship with his brother. They had to let each other be for a while if they had any hope of becoming brothers again one day—real brothers outside of their link by blood.

Rain began in a slow, steady mist. 'Perhaps we should hurry,' he said.

Hugh nodded, and they increased their pace.

Brandon took the lead and headed over the last gentle slope. He frowned and scanned the area. No Campbell soldiers were in sight.

Odd.

Soldiers were always along this glen, to guard the border and watch for any approaching enemies. He slowed his canter and lifted a fist in the air to warn Hugh to slow down behind him. His friend settled his mount beside Brandon's.

'Where are the scouts?' Brandon asked in low tones.

Squaring his shoulders, Hugh silently scanned the area with Brandon. The wind rippled the edges of the trees and the tall grass bent and yielded in the rain. No birds sang. No animals called to one another.

The silence threatened to swallow them whole.

Holding his breath, Brandon listened.

Finally a pair of mounted Campbell soldiers appeared from around the mountain. They'd been patrolling *behind* the mountain pass. Relief should have coursed through him, yet Brandon could not shake the sense that something was wrong.

His gut hardened.

He studied the soldiers as they continued on their path along the rock wall marking the edge of Campbell lands and the beginning of MacDonald territory. Perhaps realising he was a father was making him temporarily paranoid.

Glancing to Hugh, he noted his friend's jaw was still tight. His brow was creased as his eyes continued to rest on the horizon.

'Seems it was nothing,' Brandon stated, trying to convince himself all was well. 'Two soldiers come upon us now.'

Hugh shook his head. 'Nay. Something *is* wrong,' he murmured, pulling a blade slowly from its sheath along his waist belt. 'I added to the watch after your announcement last night. There should be four.'

Fiona paced her room like a cornered animal, desperate for escape, which was exactly how she felt.

She *was* locked in a chamber, after all.

Darkness had fallen hours ago, yet Brandon had not returned. She knew he was out exploring with Hugh—Beatrice had come to see her and William and told her so—but after last night, and not being able to speak with him this morning, Fiona felt as if she had been walking on thistles all day.

When she had awoken this morning she had been hopeful, even eager, to speak with him. She needed to be clear. They could have no future together; their past and William's safety wouldn't allow for it. Nor would her heart. Even though he hadn't truly abandoned her, as she'd believed, just the idea of what might happen if she allowed him into her life once more was too much to risk. All her decisions needed to be for the betterment of her son. She needed to focus on him and nothing else.

William slept peacefully in his crib while Fiona's mind swam with worry. She had fully expected Brandon to be back by now—if only to see his son. The pitch-black calm of night that had descended upon them following the afternoon's storm mocked her.

Where was he?

She froze and dread crept icily along her skin. Had Rowan killed him?

Stop, she commanded herself. An unexpected duty or an extraordinary find had delayed him—nothing more. Sitting on the bed, she rested her head in her hands and took a few deep breaths to steady herself.

Panic would do her no good. Nor would it help her son.

'Settle yerself, child.'

The memory of Aunt Seana's sweet tones echoed in Fiona's ears. Her aunt was right—just as she always had been. How Fiona missed her. She had to settle herself if she hoped to work anything out. Worry did nothing but complicate her thoughts and make her nerves as tight as a drawn bow.

'Settle yerself in yer mind, in a place no one can reach ye.'

Her aunt had spoken such words before the lashings and during the birth of William, when Fiona had been consumed by pain and fear. What would Aunt Seana say to her now?

That she could survive anything.

That she needed to regain her wits and her reason.

That she would make it through this as she had every other dark moment of her life.

Her aunt had taught her that. So Fiona did what she had learned. Tried to be present and to settle in the moment of what was, and not worry over what might be. And since Fiona could not escape this room, this castle, this place, she would escape in her mind and go to a memory she had selected long ago, that represented peace, hope and happiness. A memory no one could take away from her.

A memory of the love she'd once had with Brandon.

Closing her eyes, she attempted to settle her thoughts by counting her breaths in and out, just as she had in those moments before the whip had come down again and again upon her skin. And soon the memory formed in her mind and her breathing slowed in a smooth, rhythmic pattern...

The bright summer sun shone in a blue sky, shone on the cliffside at the edge of the Campbell lands that over-looked the dark grey sea. The waves rose and crashed against the shores below, over and over again.

She felt the warmth of the golden sun on her face, smelled the new grass in the air and felt the cool smooth blades beneath her bare feet.

Brandon's strong, callused fingers were trailing over her neck as his lips hovered above her own be-fore claiming them in earnest. She could feel his body pressing against her as she clutched his tartan and tugged him closer...

Such a first kiss had led to a love unexpected. To more kisses that had left her without breath and with-out reason.

When life had been perfection and anything had seemed possible.

And it would be again—but she had to believe it.

All was not lost, was it?

Opening her eyes, she looked at the room that no longer felt so small and hopeless. No matter what, she still had her son. All was not lost—no matter what had happened.

She smiled. Nothing would have happened at all. Her past had made her finely tuned to worry, but she needed to be ready for good news too, didn't she?

The deep bellowing shouts and commands of soldiers sounded outside the castle walls and startled her from her wool-gathering. The moments of peace she had worked so hard to muster drifted away in the wind.

Fiona rushed to the small arrow slit windows with her heart thundering in alarm. These were not the eager and joyous shouts of happy men, but commands of urgency. Something was wrong—but what? Squinting below, she could see little in the darkness, for there were not many torches still lit this late. Only those needed for the nightly watch.

Curses.

It was too dark to see anything other than large shadowy figures and horses. There seemed to be about ten warriors in total, but only half the number of horses. The last of the party were coming across the bridge that spanned the small moat around the castle walls. As they entered the small ring of light given off by the torches she gasped.

Two soldiers were draped over the back of one of the larger stallions. *Dead.* The lifeless and eerie sway of their shadowy arms and lolling heads told her so.

It was a scene known to her. Highland warriors always brought their dead back for burial, unless there were no men left standing to carry them.

Her breath hitched in her chest. She gripped the cold stone below the window. As the soldier guiding the laden horse walked into direct torchlight Hugh's grim, shadowed face came into view.

She clamped a hand over her mouth to stifle the scream building in her throat. Brandon should be with him. What had happened? They had left for exploration, nothing more.

Chapter Fourteen

Steady.

Brandon reminded himself to hold fast as he climbed the stairs to his brother's chamber. After the strains of the day he didn't know if seeing him now was the best idea, but he knew putting it off would only add to his worries. And he needed more distractions as he needed a hogweed rash.

Seeing those two dead soldiers had gifted him some perspective. You could never know what time you had left in this world, and making amends with Rowan was important to him, despite his attack on Fiona yesterday. Rowan was still his brother—no matter what had happened, and no matter what grief consumed him.

'How is he?' Brandon asked the guard stationed outside his brother's door—a necessary evil to protect his kin and the others within the castle walls.

The soldier shrugged. 'Same as last eve, my laird. Your sister has been tending to him most of the day.'

'Thank you,' Brandon answered.

He opened the door and prepared himself for the worst. His brother looked small—fragile, even—in his large bed, covered in furs, and Brandon's chest ached at the sight of it. How the last year had changed the brother and Laird he had once known.

'Brother…' Rowan said weakly as he tried to move to a sitting position and faltered. 'I am sorry,' he added. Sadness pulled at the end of his words.

Brandon stilled. Had his brother just apologised? Had his mood turned once more to kindness and logic, away from the blinding grief and emotion of the night before?

He glanced to Beatrice, and she nodded. 'It is all right, brother. Come in.'

Brandon went and sat in the chair beside Rowan's bed. He said nothing, confused as he usually was by the changefulness of his older brother. He didn't wish to jostle whatever calm had settled upon him.

'I'll give you two time to speak with one another.' Beatrice stood, but Rowan reached out to her.

'Nay, please stay, sister. I need to speak to both of you,' he pleaded.

'Aye, I have news to share as well, Trice. Please sit,' Brandon concurred.

It would be easier if he could tell them both about the attack along the border. Plans would need to be agreed upon about how to respond. And quickly.

His sister eyed Brandon with hesitation but settled back in her chair, guiding her long plait over her shoulder before smoothing out her skirts—a nervous habit she'd had since she was a wee girl. He smiled a bit at the sight of it.

'I have thought much during the night and day, when I have not been sleeping off Miss Emma's tonic.' Rowan chuckled, attempting to sit up.

Brandon rose, propped an extra pillow behind his brother's head, and helped him settle back against it. Beatrice fussed with the furs and bedding around him until Rowan stilled her hands with his own.

She nodded and sat back in her chair.

'I realise now that I am unfit to rule. I will give you no further challenge as Laird,' Rowan stated, staring at Brandon.

Beatrice's surprise no doubt mirrored Brandon's own. He waited to see if this was a ruse, to be followed by a hearty laugh, but no laugh came.

'Last night I wanted to kill her...' Rowan swallowed hard, but pressed on. 'And your son, if I am honest with myself.'

Shock roiled through Brandon and he leaned heavily against the back of the chair. Only the feel of the hard wood against him helped remind him that this moment was real.

'You wished to kill my son? Your nephew? An innocent babe?' Hurt and rage duelled in Brandon's body. He fisted his hands and his throat tightened with emotion. 'Why?'

'Grief. Rage.' Rowan wiped his eyes. 'I do not know... But I do not trust myself.' He met Brandon's gaze. 'Nor should you trust me. Guards need to be placed upon me at all times, until I am sure I am myself again.'

Tears welled in Beatrice's eyes. 'Brother,' she sobbed, 'he is but a babe. I cannot imagine it.'

Rowan squeezed her hand. 'It is the truth. You cannot trust me. Even with my Rosa. I worry I will hurt even her.' His hand shook and he wiped a tear from his cheek. 'Until I am better, please care for her. Will you do that?'

She nodded, unable to speak.

'We will all care for her. And for you, brother. You will be well again, whole again. You will see.'

Brandon gripped their hands in his own and tried to smile, even though his soul felt shredded by his brother's revelations. At least the threat of Rowan turning on him and the clan was over. Now he just needed to get the other threat to them in hand…

'What is your news?' Rowan asked as he scrubbed a hand through his hair. 'Did you and Hugh find something while out scouting today?'

Brandon nodded. 'We did find something today—but it was horrid. Two of our soldiers on watch along the borderlands were killed.'

Rowan pushed himself up fully. 'What? We haven't had any attacks along the border for months now. What happened to them?'

Brandon glanced to Beatrice. Should he say exactly how bad it was in front of his sister?

'Go on,' she insisted. 'I need to know the truth of it.'

'They had been mortally wounded, and their deaths had been slow…intentional. We believe they'd been left alive for hours in agony before Hugh and I found them. They couldn't move and they were bleeding. Notes had been pinned to their chests with daggers. Notes of warning.' Brandon sucked in a breath.

'From whom?' Rowan asked.

'The MacDonalds. They know Fi and William are here. They wish them to return home.'

'Mother Mary…' Trice whispered.

'And if we don't comply?' Rowan countered.

'I imagine they will attempt to come and take her by force or attack more of our men.'

'What do you wish to do, brother?' Rowan asked. 'I will support you in whatever you decide.'

His brother's allegiance startled Brandon. It took him a moment to recover and answer.

'I wish for them to stay here. If they return to the MacDonalds they will be killed...or worse. And I cannot abandon them. Not again.'

'Then do what you must to keep them safe. There needs to be no more suffering in this castle.' Rowan rested back on his pillows. His colour was drawn and it seemed weariness washed over him.

'I will, brother. Get some rest.' Brandon squeezed Rowan's shoulder.

His brother nodded and Beatrice stood, wrapping Brandon in a fierce hug. 'I am so glad you were not harmed. I cannot bear to lose anyone else. Please be safe. Keep them all safe.'

He kissed her cheek. 'I will. Don't worry yourself.'

Heading to Fiona's quarters, Brandon felt weariness tug at his limbs. An aching sense of loss for the dead soldiers, a draining unease caused by his brother's illness and worry over Fiona and William pulled at him like quicksand.

'Thank you, Hugh. That will be all,' Brandon stated.

Hugh nodded and took his leave. Standing at the threshold of her chamber, Brandon knocked softly. He needed to tell her of his new plan, despite how foolish it was. He'd need her help for it to be a success.

'Fi?' he whispered, unsure if she was even awake.

The latch lifted and the door swung open as if she had been standing on the other side waiting for him.

Perhaps she had.

* * *

Another woman might have waited. Might have stepped aside and let Brandon enter the room and have a seat. Offered him consolation or asked if he needed a moment to rinse the dirt from his face after a difficult day.

Fiona wasn't that woman. She never had been.

As soon as Brandon entered her chamber she threw her arms about his neck and hugged the very life out of him. She didn't even wait for him to close the door for privacy. She could scarcely stand one moment longer before being near him.

'I thought… I thought at first that you were dead. When I realised you were alive…'

Pressed from head to toe along his body, she felt safe for the first time since she'd seen him in the shadows of the torchlight, with those dead soldiers in tow. Her body quaked against his.

What had been her plan—to tell him they needed to maintain their distance for the sake of William—had shifted hard into relief at seeing him alive. She didn't care if he didn't want to hold her or no longer loved her; she just needed to hold him and be near him. The fear of losing him had overshadowed her reason.

She'd thought she'd never see him again, hold him again, and that all was lost—but he was alive. He was here.

William hadn't lost his father.

She hadn't lost the man she had loved more than any other in her life.

When he wrapped his strong hands about her waist, the world disappeared beneath her feet. He kicked the door closed, dropped the latch, and crushed her to him, pinning her between him and the wall. Hard muscle, strength, and the earthly feel of him consumed her.

'When I saw you in the window earlier and realised you were safe…' he murmured.

He said nothing more. Nor did he need to. She had felt that exact pull of relief settle within her soul when she'd seen him emerge from the dark swarm of soldiers alive and unharmed. It was a feeling that could not be explained with mere words.

'So much…' he continued with unsteady breaths. 'There is so much to discuss but first…'

He gently released her and guided her quaking limbs to the floor. He pressed a kiss to her hair, took her hand in his own, and guided her over to William. For moments he stood just staring down upon their son, holding her hand in his own.

The tension she'd felt in her limbs all night loosened and eased from her body. Quiet settled between them.

She glanced up at him. His gaze was still locked upon their son. Was he memorising every curve of the boy's face? Or imagining him years from now as a strong lad, training as a warrior and lifting his first blade? Did it matter?

'It has been a strange and sad day. Not only has Rowan apologised for what happened yesterday, he has vowed to relinquish his quest to regain power. He realises he is unwell with grief. He has even confessed to wanting to kill our son last night.'

A coldness settled through her body and she shivered. She couldn't muster words at first. Then, 'I find myself surprised not to be more enraged by his confession. I'm stunned by it, I think.'

'I understand. I felt a similar unease and shock.

Rowan has been cruel at times, but I never thought him capable of killing an innocent…a babe—especially not his own flesh and blood. But when he told me I saw the truth…and the fear in his eyes. He is afraid of himself. He has asked us to care for Rosa and place additional guards around his chamber until he is himself once more.'

'I'm sorry, Brandon. I know you love him, despite all he has done. He is your brother.'

She rested her head upon his shoulder. She did feel sorry for him. She feared that one day he might be forced to make a far more horrid decision regarding Rowan's future in the clan, but she hoped it would never come to that.

He sighed. 'And then there were those two Campbell soldiers found. They were attacked along the border,' he said tightly. 'Brutal killings. Their horses seized, the men stabbed and hidden from view. It took Hugh and I along with the two other mounted soldiers on patrol a quarter-hour to find them. By then it was far too late.'

Her palms tingled and her heart raced. 'What…?'

'Killed by the MacDonalds, from what we can tell.'

Alarm budded in her.

'When we found them…' He paused, and a muscle ticked in his jaw. 'Daggers pierced notes of warning to their chests. They had been left to die a slow and painful death, Fi. It was horrible.'

She waited for him to continue. Her pulse quickened.

'The MacDonalds know you are here. Alive and with our son. They command your return.'

Fiona released his hand and paced the room. Hysteria bubbled in her chest. She almost laughed aloud.

'*Command* my return? They tried to kill me and our son. Why do they wish me back now?'

Brandon turned to her. 'For William, I suspect, now that they know he lives.'

'I don't understand. They wanted me to die—for me to lose him in my womb.' She ran a hand through her hair.

'But now that they know he is alive they want him. The notes said as much.' His gaze focused on a point far away from her. 'One of the notes was a warning that they were coming for you. For me. For our son.'

'Merely to possess, humiliate, or kill us?' She fisted her hands by her sides. 'I will die first.'

'We will find a plan, I promise—' he began.

A knock sounded on the door. 'Yer bath water, my lady.' Jenny's quiet, unsure voice resonated in the room.

'Thank you. Come in,' Fiona answered.

Jenny came in, faltered, and dipped in a curtsey at the sight of Brandon. 'My laird,' she whispered, her face flushing. 'I was not aware ye were in here. Do ye have need of anything? If I had known ye were here, I would have—' She slammed to a stop as he interrupted.

'Nay. Thank you.'

She poured the water she carried into the tub near the hearth, where the fire flickered with subtle warmth, then bobbed another haphazard curtsey and left, closing the door behind her.

'You put the poor girl on thistles,' Fiona muttered.

The sweet, promising scent of lavender rose into the air.

'Now, strip,' she commanded him as she dropped the latch on the door.

He didn't move.

Rolling her eyes, she pushed him towards the tub. 'Allow me to wash you before you collapse where you stand,' she whispered. 'I will listen to your ideas for this plan of yours as I go. Busying my hands will ease my worries.'

He removed his tunic and then released his tartan in one movement. The heavy fabric pooled on the floor as he stepped into the tub.

'This may be torture of a far different kind, Fi,' he answered in a low growl.

She chuckled. 'I can only hope so, after all you've put me through.'

The dark, haunted shift in his eyes made her regret the words. She had not intended to hurt him.

He clutched at her hand, which held a damp cloth in the air. 'I never meant to abandon you and our son, Fi. If I'd known…'

His gaze pleaded with her and her breath hitched.

'Aye, I know…'

She walked around him and began to wash the dirt and grime from his shoulders. A strong plane of muscle rippled under her touch as the cloth glided over his skin. He sucked in a breath as she wiped along the notches of his spine down to the crease of his buttocks. A finer male form she had not seen. Nor did she wish to. And she had seen many a warrior half clothed in battle, or bathing in the loch.

There was no finer man in her heart either, but that did not mean she had forgotten the sorrow she'd felt at his abandonment and his absence, even if it had been borne of ignorance of her situation.

Rinsing the cloth in the tub, she had an idea. 'Perhaps this shall symbolise the rinsing away of the last year,' she said. 'Every horrid moment when we imagined the worst of each other can be wiped away and put in this bath water. It can be tossed out and we can begin anew.'

Would he think it foolish? Too simple a resolution of the hurt that rested between them?

He said nothing, and she washed another strip of dirt from his side, which caused his breath to hitch.

'Only if I have the same rights this eve,' he whispered, and wrapped a hand over her own.

Her throat closed and she gripped the cloth tightly, making the warm water trickle down his back. Could she endure such intimacy, such kindness, and not crumble into sobbing bits upon the floor?

'Fi?' he asked. 'Please?'

She bit her lower lip. Uncertainty spiralled in her belly. Was she strong enough not to bend like a willow under his touch? Nay, but to deny his desire to make amends seemed cruel.

'Allow me to finish bathing you first,' she said.

Her voice quivered in the air. He would know she was hedging and uncertain.

He did not answer, but released her hand.

Was he angry? Disappointed?

She blinked away the hot tears burning the backs of her eyes. Had she hesitated long enough to break the fragile thread of connection they had only just woven between them? Why did she need him desperately one minute and then fear intimacy with him the next?

It made no sense to her, so how could she attempt to explain it to him?

She blew out a breath and rinsed the cloth once more. Moving before him, she brushed his shoulder-length

hair from his face and began to wipe away the heavy
dirt staining his cheeks. His heady gaze followed her
movements, and her face heated at his assessment.

'I will wait until you are ready, Fi.'

She hesitated and furrowed her brow. 'Ready for
what?'

He didn't answer, but smirked and stepped from the
tub, naked, slick, glistening like a mythical Celtic warrior from one of her childhood stories.

He hurriedly dried himself and grabbed an extra
plaid from the bed to wrap around his waist. Then he
paced the room with his hands resting on his hips.

She smiled at this familiar sight of him planning.
Many a night she had seen him doing exactly this as
he'd discussed his agricultural ideas for the clan. Being
included in them had always brought her joy, and she
had been deemed worthy to share her own ideas as
well. Something that had never happened with her father and brother.

'Shall I get your bound journal and some charcoal?'
she risked, nibbling along her lip.

He paused and smiled at her. 'Aye. It shall be like
old times. You can record our ideas and we may hatch
a well-conceived plan to thwart your family and keep
you and William safe.'

'Is it in the same place?' she asked.

'Aye,' he answered quietly, and gestured for her to
enter his room through the secret panel.

She nodded and left him, pressing upon the wall
panel and nudging it easily from its spot.

His room was warm and inviting, and his familiar smell—the musky, spicy scent only he had—sent a
trickle of desire through her to her toes. For a moment

she stared at the familiar furnishings about her and the flickering fire in the wall beside her. Memories of a happier time flooded her. A time when she had imagined herself as the lady of this chamber, climbing into this bed each eve to greet her loving husband, and then sharing secrets of body, soul and mind with one another.

She rubbed the chill from her arms and shook her head. The mussed bedcovers, the familiar fur rugs and the colourful landscape paintings that graced the room were exactly the same. His father's sword still hung at the back of the door, winking at her in the faint light.

On a windowsill sat a sketch, which she walked towards. His art had always drawn her like a moth to a flame.

When the image came into full view, her chest tightened.

William.

Brandon had drawn his son—*their* son—and it could not have been a finer reflection of him.

'I have realised I need some clothes,' Brandon murmured from behind her.

She didn't know how long she'd been standing there, or how long he had seen her transfixed by the sight of their son's face on parchment. 'It is quite remarkable,' she whispered, gesturing to the sketch and finally risking a glance at him.

'Aye. He was all I could think of that night after finding you both at the loch. His image filled my head and I had to sketch him. I couldn't rest until I had. I worried that somehow I would forget his face, or that he would disappear altogether.' He paused, standing behind her. 'A foolish thought, but a true one.'

She nibbled at her lip. 'Perhaps not so ridiculous.'

Her heart picked up speed and she risked a truth with him. 'I had been scheming ways to escape that night.'

He rested a hand on her shoulder and turned her to face him. 'And now?'

She risked a chuckle and dared another truth. 'Now I only think of it every other day.'

He studied her and tucked a lock of loose hair behind her ear. 'You have always had to run, haven't you, Fi? From your father, your family, your duty...' The back of his hand skimmed her cheek. 'One day I hope you will realise you've no need to run from me.'

Chapter Fifteen

Fiona deftly ignored his statement, walked around him, and gathered his bound journal and some charcoal. She curled up barefoot and cross-legged on his bed among the furs, and the normality of the action shook him. She had done this very thing so many times before, and here she was now, with him again, working out a plan with him despite everything that had happened between them.

He walked over and stabbed the poker at the smouldering fire in the hearth, to help coax it back to life. A few sparks kicked out and he smothered the embers on the floor before turning to face her.

'So, how do you believe William and I can stay safe?' she asked. She had marked two columns on a fresh page and now paused before setting her full attention on him.

'By killing your father.'

She frowned at him. 'While that *is* an option, I think that would only incite more problems between the clans, don't you?'

'Aye. But it *is* an idea, and remember—'

She waved her hand at him. 'Aye, I know... "All ideas are to be written down, no matter how daft they may seem at first."'

He grinned at her exaggerated impression of him. 'Your turn, lass.'

'You could allow me to continue on my journey to the MacNabs,' Fiona suggested.

It was his turn to frown. 'Not bloody likely.'

'It is no worse an idea than killing my father.'

'Fine,' he bit out, and rubbed his aching shoulder. These last few days had worn him out, body and soul.

She paused. 'Sit, before you pass out,' she urged, patting the spot on the bed next to her.

He hesitated, knowing full well that being closer to her might not be the best of decisions. He'd already abandoned his self-control the day before. He needed not to lose it again. Even if a part of him wondered if they could begin anew, another more logical part of him knew that he needed to follow through on his plan to marry another. His clan was in dire need of an infusion of wealth, power and allies—especially now the MacDonalds were riled once more and Fiona and William were in danger.

He gave in to his body's weariness and sank onto the softness of the bed, leaning back into the lush furs and shielding his eyes with his forearm. He sighed aloud. Her fingertips skimmed down his arm, sending tendrils of desire as well as comfort through him. It was a touch he had dearly missed.

'We can discuss this in the morn, if you like,' she said.

'Nay,' he answered, moving his forearm from his eyes and staring up at the timbered ceiling. 'Carry on.

We must make a list, even if we come to no true conclusion. My mind is too alert for sleep, despite the fatigue of my limbs.'

'Aye.' She shifted back to her spot on the bed and tapped the charcoal on the page. 'What of allies? Do you have any?'

He chuckled and met her gaze. 'Not any that I would currently trust with the lives of my people.' He paused, and his throat tightened. 'It is why I must marry another. Such a union will give me an ally as strong as any.'

Fiona stilled, dropped her gaze, and scribbled down some additional ideas. She was barefoot and wearing only her shift, with a shawl wrapped loosely about her shoulders. Her hair hung like liquid fire about her face. His stomach dropped and he fisted his hands at his sides. His body responded at the sight of her, betraying him once more.

'What do we have so far?' he asked, longing for a distraction from the need rushing through his body.

'I've made two columns. Here is the list in mine. One: continue my journey to the MacNabs. Two: begin a new life in Aberdeen or Glasgow. Three: flee to one of the smaller surrounding clans. Four: contact my brother for help.'

She met his gaze. Brandon balked at the ideas she'd listed. All of them related to her leaving here with their son, which was exactly what he wanted to avoid. The thought of being separated from William, whom he'd only just found, and even from Fiona, sent anxiety hammering through his veins. Who would protect them if he didn't? And did he even want anyone else protecting them? William was his son. Fiona was the mother of his child.

He rubbed his eyes, willing patience as he uttered his next words. 'Your list does not include the idea of you staying.'

She shrugged. 'Why should it? Why would I wish to stay here, underfoot, with a sea of people who hate me and William and wish us dead, while you marry another?'

He was so tired he couldn't think clearly, but still his mind raced and wouldn't settle. And, knowing himself, he knew it wouldn't until he'd written down all his thoughts, his concerns and his plans.

He pushed himself to sit up, so he could write. 'The journal?' he asked, extending his hand for it.

She rolled her eyes but handed it to him, along with the charcoal. The touch of her fingertips against his own sent a crackle of awareness through his arm.

He read over the first column on the page and added his own ideas to the second.

1. Kill Laird Audric
2. Keep Fiona and William here in the upstairs chamber, guarded at all times
3. Settle Fiona and William in their own small cottage in the village, with regular guards to protect them
4. Marry her

The last one seemed to write itself, and Brandon felt startled to see that he'd added it to the page and not just thought it.

Did some part of him truly believe that this was an

option? Did he really want to marry her after all that had happened between them? How would the clan react if he even proposed such an idea to them?

He knew the answer: not well. Most likely the elders would remove him and claim that both the Campbell brothers had lost their ability to rule—which perhaps was true. Marrying Fiona now would be lunacy, even if it hadn't been deemed so a year ago.

Hell. He'd never sleep at this rate. Perhaps he was too tired even to think clearly.

He rose from the bed and paced about the room.

Fiona picked up the journal from the edge of the bed. Her brow lifted in surprise as she read what he'd added. 'Marry me? Of all the things I thought I might see on this list, it wasn't that.' The journal closed with a snap before she set it down. 'I would have predicted *Kill Fiona* as a possibility before a union with me.'

She crossed her arms against her chest. Distrust registered in her pinched features.

Did he blame her?

Nay, he didn't.

'Perhaps an unlikely option, but an option all the same.' He turned from her, unwilling to give away any more of his feelings on the matter, and not trusting the way his body responded to her nearness.

'Is that something you actually want? You and I to be together once more?'

She was standing beside him now, not allowing him the escape he wanted. It was just like Fi to demand an answer. To poke at a wound before it had scabbed over.

'I don't know,' he answered, facing her.

It was the truth. He didn't know. Not really. He couldn't think clearly with his body raging and his mind flooded with images of dead soldiers, his grief-stricken brother, and her and William's lives in danger. He didn't know what he wanted other than to keep her and William alive.

She quirked a smile. 'Nor do I.'

'Finally we agree upon something,' he said, returning her smile.

'Then let us focus on William's safety. Perhaps the rest will work itself out in time. Agreed?' she asked, extending her hand to his.

He held her gaze. Her bright green eyes were rich with emotion…and something else he couldn't quite recognise.

He grasped her hand in his own. 'Agreed.'

As if on cue, William whimpered, and then began to cry in earnest. She smiled and turned away.

He grasped her wrist. 'Let me,' he pleaded.

She hesitated, and then nodded. 'Go on, then. Let us see if you can calm your son.'

Eager for the challenge, he walked into her room through the secret door and lifted his son into his arms.

William's eyes widened, and his gaze fixed on Brandon's face. 'There, there, son. What is it you desire? A story, perhaps? Of soldiers and battle?'

His son gurgled at him and let out a little cry, as if he listened.

'Soldiers it is,' Brandon whispered as he walked around the room, carrying his son against his chest and telling him the stories his father and grandfather had used to tell him as a boy.

And suddenly he found the strains of the day melting off him with every step, every word, and every moment with his son.

* * *

Fiona's chest tightened at the sight of Brandon caring for their boy. The softness she had always loved about him burned even brighter now he was a father. Breathlessness seized her as she watched, and a deep longing low in her gut banked and burned.

Was this what it could be? What they could have as a family?

Fool.

They might be able to remain peaceful and content in this chamber, but what about out there in the main castle? In the village and in the fields? She and William would be targets for death, at worst, and the recipients of insults at best.

The clan would always blame her for what had happened, despite how much she regretted her careless telling of the secret passageways within Argyll Castle to Eloise. If she'd known the horrible lass would tell her father and lead to the attack she would never even have thought it—let alone said it within the Glenhaven Castle walls.

Brandon turned and faced her. He grinned like the devil. 'He sleeps,' he whispered.

'You can put him back in his crib, then. Just don't jostle him too much or he might wake once more.'

He nodded and tiptoed over to the crib, slipping William into it as carefully as he might handle a wounded bird. He walked silently back into his chamber, pleased with his accomplishment. 'I'd say I did well, wouldn't you?'

His eyes sought her approval, so she gave it.

'Well done for a first try. Perhaps you'll be on bedtime duty more often?' she teased.

'I'd like that. I would. I've time to make up for. I want him to know that I'm here for him. Always.'

'Always?'

'For now, then. Why don't we try for a few days? Why not, Fi?'

He grabbed her hands within his own and the strong, calm certainty of his voice and his touch weakened her defences and her pledge to be clear-headed and logical about what was best for William.

She squeezed his hands within her own. 'Try what? Pretending we are a family? Seeing if I can get through a day without being threatened or stoned by your fellow clansmen?'

He squared his shoulders. 'Aye. That is exactly what I want us to do. Why not just see if it's possible before we declare it impossible?'

Her mind clamoured for her to refuse, in order to protect her heart from more pain when it didn't work, while the rest of her clamoured to try for the sake of William and herself. While failure and rejection were horrible, not taking the risk and not trying was ultimately worse, wasn't it?

So she nodded. 'Two days,' she agreed. 'I'll give you two days.'

'That shall be enough. You'll see, Fi.'

And she hoped she would.

Chapter Sixteen

Brandon frowned as he glanced out through his chamber window. He needed to stop wool-gathering. Hugh would be awaiting him at the stables for their next exploration of the borderlands already, as the sun had risen an hour ago.

After checking on William in his crib, and gifting his son a kiss to the cheek, Brandon returned to his chamber through the open panel, leaving Fiona to her sound sleep in her own bed.

He donned a fresh tunic and tartan, rubbed some salt over his teeth with a rough rag, and splashed water upon his face before jogging down the stairs to the Great Hall. Optimism buzzed through him and he was eager to break his fast and begin his day.

He and Fiona had come to a truce in order to focus on their son's wellness and safety. He'd also convinced her at least to consider the idea of them marrying, of seeing if they could be a family. If she could imagine herself living here, rather than the other options she'd entertained—all of which involved her and William leaving—it would be a step forward for them. Maybe…

just maybe…some hope from the past could be dusted off and put back on the shelf of possibility.

'Seems we have a small change in plans, my laird.' Hugh greeted him in the doorway of the Great Hall and gestured to the elders, who sat at the large table, breaking their fast for most likely the second time this morn.

Bollocks. Or maybe not…

'And they are here because…?' Brandon asked.

Hugh scoffed. 'You cannot be surprised. You know exactly why they are here: Fiona. You have not selected a bride and Fiona remains here, protected by you. No doubt they question your loyalty and your duty to do right by the clan.'

His friend's directness cut him. But Brandon knew it was the truth. He should have made a decision by now. Rowan would have.

'Nay. Not surprised, but irritated. Can I not have one day without a crisis pressing upon me?'

'It seems not.' Hugh smirked. 'Shall I send them to the study?'

'Aye. Once they finish filling their stomachs, send them in. Please ask one of the servants to bring me something to eat in the study before they arrive. If I do not break my fast before speaking with them I cannot predict a positive outcome.'

'Aye, my laird.' Hugh slapped him on the shoulder and left to carry out his orders.

Brandon slipped down the back corridor to the study. He settled in and enjoyed a few minutes of eating in silence before the elders came and joined him.

The three clan elders arrived and sank into the large chairs before the fire. Anson Campbell, his younger brother Douglass Campbell, and Sebastian Stewart sat like stoic mirror images of one another, silent and unmoving, with their hands laced together, resting along their stomachs.

As Brandon had feared, they were not pleased to have been kept waiting. Even if they had been enjoying food and drink, they were now in poor spirits—which was not unusual. He braced himself, waiting to see which man might be the first to speak.

'My laird…' began Anson, the oldest and most senior of the men.

His pale blue eyes studied Brandon and he attempted pleasantries.

'To what do I owe this unexpected visit?' Brandon rose from his father's desk and sat in the one large empty chair remaining amongst them. Hugh stood off to one side.

'Our visit should not be wholly unexpected,' Douglass said, settling further into the cushions.

Brandon waited.

'Some of the soldiers have informed us that you have not selected a bride, nor set a date for the banns to be read, despite what was previously agreed upon.' Anson sat up straight, his weathered hand gripped the arm of the chair.

'Aye,' Brandon answered, leaning forward.

'And they say that you have decided not to have Fiona MacDonald answer for her crimes against us.'

Sebastian spoke quietly, but his words hit Brandon's sense of calm like spikes.

'Aye.' Brandon gritted his teeth.

'We placed you in this position because we believed

ye were up to the task and more...*capable* than your brother.'

Douglass's gaze drifted away and then back to him.

'But, as of late, we are questioning such a decision. You are further dividing our people with your continued involvement with the MacDonald woman.'

Brandon shook his head. 'You have been misinformed, elders. I have made each and every decision to strengthen us, not weaken us. And I cannot help but be involved with Fiona MacDonald as she is the mother of my child.'

'And then there are the dead soldiers,' Anson said, his voice increasing in speed, and agitation rattling through his words. 'We have heard it said that they were killed by the MacDonalds because they know you are protecting her and her babe here. How many more men shall die before you return her to where she belongs?'

'I know what it must seem, but it is not so. I am not putting her wishes ahead of the clan. If Fiona and I marry it would help to unite our two clans, not further divide them. Do you not see that, Anson?'

'Or perhaps you grow soft, letting that woman lead you to ruin?' Sebastian asked.

Brandon swallowed hard, struggling to control his temper. 'Nay. I do not.'

'Then you shall not mind the hastening of your selection of a bride and your marriage,' Douglass added, standing with great effort. 'As soon as you receive agreement from the Laird for the bride you choose, you will announce it, set the banns and be wed. And the

MacDonald lass shall be sent away. The boy shall stay, of course, but she will go. It is for the sake of the clan.'

Brandon attempted to speak, but Anson put up his hand.

'There will be no discussion upon it if you wish to continue to be Laird,' he stated.

The other elders nodded to him and left the room.

At the open doorway stood Beatrice, her face stoic and unreadable. 'Brother?' she called.

'Aye,' Brandon answered wearily.

She walked into the study and squared her shoulders. 'Is that to be it, then?'

He glanced to Hugh and then back to her. '"It"?'

'When they arrived I thought surely they would remove you from your position as Laird. Is that not what they have done?'

Brandon squeezed her arm. 'Nay, Trice. I am still in charge…for now. But those against us are planning, and I think it best to pretend to go along with what the elders have requested.'

'And what is that?'

'That I announce my engagement to another lass, keep William here, and cast Fiona out.'

Cast me out?

Fiona slid quietly along the stone wall back around the corner. She'd almost walked headlong into Brandon and Beatrice's conversation, and she was glad she had tarried a bit on her way. At least now she knew what would be coming.

Betrayal. And abandonment once more.

Or at least it sounded that way. Granted, she'd only heard the very end of their conversation, so perhaps she was mistaken. But a small part of her whispered that what he'd said was the truth. And why shouldn't she accept something she'd long known would come to pass? She was seen as the enemy now. Unless the clan viewed her as an asset, rather than a traitor, she'd never be happy here, and nor would William.

Should she continue walking and ask Beatrice what they had spoken of? Or pretend she'd not heard anything? Then, if Brandon mentioned it to her later, she'd know that he wasn't planning on betraying her. That he wanted to continue with their plan of seeing if they could repair the past and move forward together into a brighter future for William's sake.

She stepped out to follow Beatrice, but then lost her nerve. She needed to see if Brandon would tell her. Only then would she know if she could trust him enough to stay here with William.

Taking a steadying breath, she pivoted and went back up to her room.

'Jenny,' Fiona said, as she passed her maid in the corridor, 'I will be eating within my chambers this morn. Can you have the kitchens send up a plate for me?'

'Of course, miss.' Jenny bobbed her head and travelled on.

Fiona smiled. She would eat, plan her day, and cast her doubts aside. Brandon would tell her tonight of his meeting with the elders and all they had discussed. Then the matter would be settled. And if he didn't tell her, she would also have her answer.

After breaking her fast, Fiona sat studying the chamber she'd stayed in these past few days. The irony of being in Brandon's mother's private chamber pressed heavily on her. For as long as she could remember the Laird's wife had resided in the room two floors below this one. Fiona had never known the woman had lived up on this level too.

Brandon had confirmed that the rumours of the old Laird's indiscretions and inclinations for other women were true... Such a strange reality to have known as a boy that his father cared so little for his mother. And such a fine, caring, capable woman Emilia had been. Fiona had spent many an afternoon with her when her illness had begun to overtake her and she'd needed assistance.

As children, she and Brandon had been allowed to spend time together; it had only been when they were older, and had formed an attachment to one another that threatened their future arranged marriages and the economic security of the clans, that they had been ordered by their fathers no longer to see one another. Thus their secret meetings and the true intensity of their love affair had begun.

Emilia would have adored the thought of their clandestine affair... Such a romantic she had been, despite how her own marriage had turned out. She had spun fairy tales and stories of old for Fiona, of love and happiness. Fiona could still remember standing on an old book, brushing out Emilia's long raven hair while she sang. The woman's fine silky hair had streamed through Fiona's fingers, and Emilia's eyes had shone bright as bluebells.

Her own mother had never been so warm, and after she'd left her and her brother one afternoon, never to return, Emilia had oft been the mother Fiona had longed for. When she'd died, Brandon's tears had blended with

Fiona's own, and being here in Emilia's room with her grandchild brought Fiona an unexpected comfort amidst the chaos—even though the woman's things had been removed from here long ago, from what she could tell.

I wonder...

Fiona studied the chamber. Emilia had been clever. Would she have hidden things here, away from the prying eyes of her husband? Now that she understood Emilia's situation far better, she realised such scheming might have had other purposes altogether: a means to ensure her own survival if needed.

Since she had no plans this day, and William was fast asleep after eating, now would be a fine time for Fiona to see if this room held any other secrets besides the hidden door.

Beginning at the door, she ran her hands up and down the walls, poked behind pictures and felt for any odd surfaces or draughts. After an extensive search, she found nothing. Her shoulders sagged in defeat. Where else would someone hide things? She tapped her foot, and then smiled. The floor—of course! She walked slowly, forcing her feet to roll toe to heel to help discover any oddities beneath.

A slight dip in one of the rugs stopped her. Smiling, she knelt, rolled back the rug with one hand, and examined the stone floor. A small round hole beckoned her, so she put her fingers in and tugged out a loose limestone slab. Shocked by the ease at which she'd removed it, she sat and stared dumbfounded for a moment. Then she dared peer into the hole.

In the crevice, she saw a black pouch. Removing it from its hold, Fiona placed it on the bed. Her fingers itched to open the pouch, but did she have any right to? She wasn't a Campbell. It wasn't hers.

Fiona swallowed hard. 'What would you do?' she whispered to William, picking him up from his crib as he woke.

To his credit, he merely babbled back at her.

'That is of no help,' she teased, and ran her hand over his tousled hair. 'Let us see what treasure awaits,' she told him.

Opening the drawstring of the pouch, she poured the contents onto the tartan on the bed.

She gasped.

'Emilia, what have you done...?' Fiona murmured.

A handful of jewels—some in settings for jewellery, others uncut and loose—shone back at her, glistening in the sunlight.

She'd never thought there would actually be treasure. Not here, buried under a floor.

William reached out a hand to grab for a bright ruby brooch and recognition bloomed.

'I saw her wear the ruby brooch and this pair of emerald earrings, but these others... I have never seen them before. What say you, William? Are they not beautiful?'

Her fingers skimmed over the fine precious gems that glimmered like freedom, hope and redemption. If she could but escape with these, she might have a chance to begin a new life, a grander life than she could ever have imagined. A life free of this place...free of the Highlands. A safe future away from here with her son.

Her stomach tightened. But they weren't hers, were they? Could she truly steal from Brandon and his family even if it was for the sake of their son?

'That I announce my engagement to another lass, keep William here, and cast Fiona out.'

His words from earlier echoed in her head.

She closed her fingers around the jewels. If he didn't tell her of his meeting with the elders and that he would not be following their plans, then, yes…yes, she could.

Chapter Seventeen

Brandon threw another dagger across the glade to the target set in the distance. It hit the edge of its centre and bounced off into the grass. He cursed under his breath.

'What's got you troubled? The demands of the elders, perhaps?' Hugh asked.

He shot Hugh a glare and threw another blade. It hit the edge of the wooden stump that served as a target. 'My bloody aim, at the moment.'

Hugh smirked and shook his head. 'I'd wager a few coin it might be a bit more than that.'

'You'd think that after all I have done to help support and protect this clan—all I've done to keep it from unravelling into bits—the elders would be a wee bit grateful. But, nay, they complain of my decision to protect my own son and the mother of my child. Why can they not allow me to try to mend what has come between us? Why can I not have more time? They command me to choose another wife and cast Fiona out. Otherwise I will be removed and replaced by whomever they choose, she will be hanged, and who knows what shall become of my boy?'

Hugh said nothing.

'And, aye, I know you know all this. You were there at the meeting. But I am so angry. I have no options. Why do I have no options when *I* am Laird?' Brandon grumbled.

He took a breath, and released it along with his blade. Though it landed closer to the centre mark, it was well outside his usual skill.

He turned to find Hugh studying him. Irritation continued to course unbidden beneath his skin. 'Say what you must,' Brandon uttered, knowing he'd most likely not enjoy whatever truth Hugh was about to speak.

'It would have been easier to let her leave,' he said.

'Aye, but I'll not abandon my son.' Brandon set his chin.

'You know as I do that you could have claimed him and forced her from these lands. Or ordered her hanging. Hell, the people would have applauded it. You are Laird. No one would have questioned such a decision.'

I would have.

The next blade Brandon threw landed in the grass, below the target. He scrubbed a hand through his hair. 'Would *you* cast out the mother of your child? Or order her death? Make your son grow up without her?'

He faced Hugh and the blank expression on his friend's face confirmed what he thought.

'Aye. I didn't think so.'

Brandon began to walk to retrieve his daggers and Hugh fell into step alongside him.

'I'm not saying it would have been right to cast her out,' he said. 'Merely that it would have been easier for you as Laird.'

Brandon chuckled. 'That is exactly something you

would say, and I agree with you—which is why I wish to send one of these blades into her father's chest. It is *he* who drove us to this place. If he'd let us marry long ago we'd not have been sneaking around and there would have been no need to use that secret tunnel. And then she would not have spoken of it out of turn.'

He bent and yanked the daggers from the ground, then pulled the other two from the target.

Hugh lifted a brow at him.

'Very well. Nor would I have been such a lovesick fool as to show it to her,' Brandon conceded as he wiped the dirt from the blades on his kilt. 'I know my part in it. I know hers. And now that I find myself wedged between two worlds I find it angers me as if the attack on the castle happened but yesterday.'

'That is why your aim is off.' Hugh gathered his own daggers and they began to walk back to throw another round. 'No man can throw well when driven by emotion.'

'I will either throw these daggers at a target or a person, and I choose no murder today.' Brandon chuckled, rolled his shoulders, and threw another blade. It landed on the target, left of centre.

'Your aim improves,' said Hugh. 'Perhaps you should imagine your enemy upon the target, as I do? It often helps me to envisage British soldiers before me upon my throw.'

Hugh's blade sailed through the air and struck the target dead centre. Brandon nodded and imagined the white-bearded bastard who was Fiona's father. The man who had caused all this. The man who had tried to lash Fiona to death and also to kill Brandon's son.

He let out a growl and sent the dagger free. It hit the

centre of the target hard and vibrated with the force of the impact.

'See? Use your emotion to fuel you, not distract you,' said Hugh. ''Tis a trick I learned long ago, when I was a lad. You either let pain eat you alive or you use it to propel you forward.'

'I choose forward, then.'

A group of soldiers walked by. Their scowling gazes reflected their displeasure, but Brandon didn't care. They had no understanding of his situation as Laird and as the father of a small boy born betwixt two rival clans. Brandon would command their obedience until they accepted his logic and reason, one way or another. He just needed to decide what to do.

Hugh waited him out, as he always did.

Brandon sighed and rubbed the back of his neck. 'I will not be my father. I will not do wrong by Fiona and William in order to do right by the clan.'

Hugh nodded. 'But do not let your desire *not* to be like him make you a fool in an altogether different way. Sometimes by trying to please all you please none—including yourself.'

As always, Hugh had a point, but it was not one Brandon wished to discuss. He stared out at the horizon.

Hugh spoke again. 'You cannot be blind to the clan's rage. Nor can you deny what we lost that day. All of us lost someone—even you.'

'Aye,' Brandon began, 'and I know many of them rally against me even now.'

'That is part of it, but grief and rage will engulf them—especially when they see Fiona every day, walking these grounds. Her presence drives the dagger of their loss deeper. They cannot see past it, and nor do they wish to walk through it.'

'And so they are consumed by it, just as Rowan was?'

Hugh nodded. 'To the point of rage, I fear. Or the destruction of this clan.'

Brandon scrubbed a hand down his face. What could he do?

'Why do you always dare to put yourself betwixt me and them?' he asked Hugh. ''Tis a dangerous spot to be in.'

Hugh shrugged. 'You took me in when I had nothing as a boy. You are my family, each of you, and I choose not to see you shred one another to dust.'

Brandon laughed and nodded ahead. 'Just in time. The lads bring our mounts. Let's be on our way to explore the rest of the area we had intended to reach before we discovered those soldiers the other day.'

'Let's hope this is a far less exciting outing. I can do with no more of it.'

'Nor I,' Brandon grumbled, guiding himself easily upon his stallion.

He fell into stride by Hugh and they rode together in silence until they were well out of the village.

'So, shall you select one?' Hugh asked.

'One what?'

'A wife.'

Brandon allowed his head to fall forward dramatically. 'Nay. Nor do I wish to. Just because the elders demand it, it does not mean I shall do it.'

Hugh chuckled with the hearty, carefree laugh of a man who never planned to wed. 'That does not mean you shouldn't consider it. You and I both know how badly the clan needs an infusion of wealth and power, and an additional ally.'

'I do know it.' Brandon scrutinised his friend. 'Why does it sound as if you have already given this some thought?'

'Because I have. Your brother and I pared down the list of potential matches weeks ago—even before Fiona returned. We selected three possible brides. I fear that if you do decide to marry another, and don't pick one soon, your options shall be...'

'Even worse?'

'Aye. So, as a way to help you better weigh your options, why don't you tell me what qualities you require in your bride?'

While there were many things Brandon had once hoped for in his bride-to-be, it no longer seemed to matter. 'Which one has the largest dowry and will provide the most powerful alliance for our clan?' he asked.

Hugh thought for a moment. 'That would be Susanna Cameron from the North.'

'Then that's my choice...if I choose to follow the elders' demands.'

His friend balked. 'You wish to know nothing of her at all?'

'Nay. If I marry anyone other than Fiona the union shall be an agreement, nothing more. My wife shall bring strength to our people by providing us with a strong alliance, heirs, and coin. If I am lucky, we might even like one another on occasion.'

Hugh frowned. 'And if you choose the Cameron lass what will you do with Fiona and your son?'

'That shall be a decision for a different day. I must think on whether I wish to risk losing everything and marry Fiona, or marry another to save the clan and end any chance I may have at happiness. But for now let us explore this area, so we can decide what can be done with this land and the mountains that border it. Surely that decision shall be a far simpler one?'

Fiona had busied herself with chores for the rest of the morn. Now, desperate to be out of doors in the warm afternoon sun, she pleaded with Daniel and Jenny to accompany her and allow her to take William for a walk, to burn off the energy and anxiety thrumming through her body.

Finally Daniel relented, and shadowed her and Jenny as they walked in the sunshine through the glen towards the barn. Jenny fiddled with the edges of her blouse sleeve and Fiona continued in silence beside her. William slept soundly in the tartan wrapped and tied skilfully around her torso so he was positioned securely against her chest.

'I am grateful for your kindness, Jenny,' Fiona stated. 'I know it has been hard for you to serve me upon my return.'

A blush pinked her maid's cheeks. 'I hated ye at first. I cannot deny such. But I know ye are the same woman I used to call friend. Ye are still incredibly kind to me, as ye have always been.'

'Because I did not tell Brandon of how you did not make me a fire those first two morns, or refill my pitcher and basin with fresh water?' Fiona chuckled. 'I actually quite admired your ire.' She grew sombre. 'I also understood it. I am truly sorry for what you lost because of my family. Because of me.'

'It shall take time, but it will sting less... I hope.'

'I hope so too,' Fiona answered, falling into step beside Jenny as they climbed the final hillside.

She hoped in time her hurts would sting less too, but she wondered how long such a time would be...

Fiona awaited Brandon's return and attempted to reconcile herself to the existence of the bag of jewels worth a fortune now hidden in her son's crib. It seemed the safest place to keep them until she decided exactly what she needed to do, and whether she should tell Brandon of her discovery.

She wanted desperately to believe that the conversation she'd overheard that morning had been a fragmented part of a larger discussion and had seemed more malicious and ominous than it was. Brandon wouldn't marry another and cast her out without her son after all they had begun to mend between them these last few days, would he? They'd grown closer in body and soul, and they'd pledged to each other to try to see if a future together as a family was possible.

She paced her chamber. She'd already taken supper in her room, and outside the sunset loomed in bright oranges and pinks. Staring out through the window, she saw Brandon ride up to the castle. He dismounted, removed his saddlebags and slung them over his shoulder, and handed the reins of his stallion to the stable boy who waited nearby.

Brandon glanced up to her window and she waved to him. Although she could have sworn he saw her, and he paused, he didn't wave back. Her smile faded and a pit opened in her stomach.

Perhaps I heard correctly after all. Maybe he does plan on marrying another and casting me from here.

She commanded herself to stop jumping to conclusions and letting her imagination and her fear run away with her reason. Nothing was certain. He would tell her all about his day when he came up to visit William. Everything would be fine.

After convincing herself of this for a good quarter-hour, she heard Brandon knock on her chamber door as he opened it to come in. Relief threaded through her.

'How is our son?' he asked, walking over to William, who lay awake in his crib.

'He fights his sleep. I believe he was waiting for you. Busy day?' she asked. Her attempt at making her tone light had made her words come out breathy and low. She cleared her throat.

'Aye, a busy one indeed. Hugh and I finished our explorations along the border and the mountain pass. There's still some land in good condition that could be used for crops. Good news all round.'

He squatted and ran a hand along William's cheek before picking him up.

Fiona stood watching him cradle William in his arms, murmuring to his son, and her heart thundered in impatience. Why would he not just tell her?

'Anything else of import? Any visitors?' She nibbled her lip in nervousness as she attempted to prod him towards what she longed to hear: the truth.

He stilled, kissed William's cheek, and placed the boy back in his crib to sleep. 'Nay. Just a usual day.'

He gifted her a smile, but it didn't reach his eyes. Her stomach dropped.

'I am exhausted. I shall retire to my chambers now. Have a nice sleep, Fi.'

Drat.

Before she could even answer him he was gone from the room, having already closed the door behind him.

She sat down on the bed with a thump and flopped back into the furs. Was that how it was to be, then? A sea of secrets? Had he learned nothing from before?

Tears threatened for a moment, but she blinked them back. It didn't have to mean anything. He truly might just be tired.

Fool.

She knew him well enough to know he was hiding something from her. Something had changed within him. Perhaps it had everything to do with the elders' visit…maybe it had absolutely nothing to do with it. She wouldn't know if she didn't ask— but she didn't want to know the answer if it had anything to do with him stealing her son from her and casting her out, abandoning her. Again.

She sat at the small dresser and began to loosen the pins holding back her hair. She hummed as she brushed it out, trying to smother the worry budding in her chest. What could she do? She couldn't compel a confidence from him, but she'd also not wait to be cast out.

Setting down her brush, she rose, removing her shawl. She folded it, placed it upon the chair, and readied herself for bed, knowing full well she wouldn't be able to sleep.

Before she could contemplate any further, the panel door between their chambers slid open and Brandon re-entered the room. He slid the panel closed behind him and simply stared at her…through her…his gaze focused on her and her alone.

The space between them buzzed like the charged air near the loch after a thunderstorm. He was bare-chested and barefoot, wearing only dark trews, which hung low about his waist. His eyes burned with desire and longing as they caught the light from the flickering torch on the wall.

He made his way halfway across the room and faltered, agony rippling through his face, his chest rising and falling as if he were out of breath. She watched him, frozen by the bedside, feeling her heart pick up pace in her chest and desire beginning a slow, uneasy ripple within her.

He wanted her—as she did him. There was no denying it.

Without a word, he closed the space between them and stood but a whisper away from her. The heat from his body flushed her own skin, sending gooseflesh skittering along her body in anticipation. His musky, spicy scent filled her nostrils, and a tendril of need budded in her. It had been so long…so very long…and she felt her body thrum to a fever pitch, wishing, willing, needing his touch.

She knew she shouldn't give in. He would be promised to another soon, and she would be alone once more.

'Brandon,' she murmured. 'I—'

He reached for her then. A feathering hint of his fingertips along her shoulders and down her bare arms. A trailing torturous dance of his touch along her body. She swallowed hard, her breaths becoming uneven as his fingers lingered on the inside of her wrists before disappearing, leaving her breathless and wanting more.

She couldn't move, despite the raging need coursing through her. She didn't trust herself or her desire.

He stepped around her and brushed her hair to the side of her neck. His hands continued a slow and steady assault along the scars puckering her back, gently nudging her shift lower, slipping the straps down from her shoulders, the heat of his breath bringing more gooseflesh along her neck. Soon his lips followed, their warmth brushing gently along the raised pink flesh where every horrid lash had fallen.

Tears heated her eyes. Such gentleness she had not felt in so long. To be touched out of love and not hate… To remember how they had once been together… The love they had once had… The intimacy they had once shared…

Before she could catch her breath, or even speak a word, Brandon stepped before her, clutching her face within his hands. He kissed her with a tender urgency and thoroughness that made her feel as if she were floating on the loch. The heat and pressure of his warm lips and tongue coupled with the strength of his body pressed full against her made her sigh. He answered back with a groan of his own.

Soon his lips moved lower, nipping along her jaw and slowly easing down to her collarbone. She wove her hands into his hair, the feel of the soft strands awakening memories of the past as they caressed her bare skin. His thumbs nudged again at the thin, loose straps of her shift and the material slid down her body, pooling at her feet. She stepped out of it and skimmed her palms along his hard-muscled shoulders and back before wrapping her arms around him.

The moment she pressed her bare skin fully to his, she gasped. Desire flooded her. He lifted her from the floor and she wrapped her legs around his waist as she had so many times before. He carried her to the bed, his desire matching her own. She was bound to him.

No matter what happened after this moment, she could not deny that part of her would always be his...just as part of him would always be hers.

Brandon gripped Fiona tighter to his body. His blood pounded through his limbs, demanding he have her. Had he ever felt such need, such desire to bed a woman before? Nay, he hadn't. *Ever.* He knew every curve and line of her lush flesh, and yet he couldn't get enough of her. Even pressed fully and tightly to her body, he wanted Fiona closer, nearer, as if her nearness could thrust them into the past or into a different future. One where they could be together without complication.

She fisted his hair in her hands and returned his kisses as fiercely as she always had, pulling him from his thoughts and from all attempts at reason. He met each and every silent demand she made with her caresses along his back and neck.

She yanked upon the side of his trews and he smiled against her temple, knowing and understanding full well her desire to be one with him, as he wished to be one with her. He struggled to slow his own need. He commanded himself to be patient and to savour the moment they were one, as he knew it would be their last.

Chapter Eighteen

Brandon woke feeling like the selfish bastard he was. What had he been thinking? He sighed. He hadn't been thinking. Desire and longing had ruled him.

He groaned and rolled onto his side. Instead of keeping his distance from Fiona, as he'd promised himself last night, so he could make a logical and sound decision about his future, he'd marched into her chamber and made love to her.

He wanted to hate himself for it, but he couldn't. Not when he knew in his heart that it had been their last time together. He had to marry the Cameron lass. It was his duty.

At least he'd woken with clarity on that issue. The rest he'd worked into a fine mess and Fiona would hate him for it. As she should. But maybe her hatred of him would make it easier in the end.

He skimmed his fingertips along her neck, shoulder and collarbone as she slept, trying to memorise each beautiful curve of her body. To his delight, she didn't stir, allowing him to soak in this moment, this memory, while he could.

It would have to serve him for the rest of his life. He was not foolish enough to believe that love would be a part of his impending alliance and union. A man could never be so lucky as to have love twice in one lifetime.

Desire flared in his body, but he tamped it down. Resigned to his decision as Laird, he kissed her gently one last time, allowing his lips to linger on hers, and then slid from the bed. He had to love her enough to let her go, even if it threatened to destroy him from within.

His bare feet padded along the cool floor and he retreated to his chamber, sealing the panel to her room. There he donned his clothes and readied himself for the difficult day ahead.

As he opened the door, Hugh was there, waiting for him, his hand in mid-air, preparing to knock. The flat look in his friend's gaze sent alarm through Brandon. He didn't have to wait long for Hugh to tell him what was amiss.

'They've left us another message, my laird.'

Brandon didn't need to know who 'they' were. It was the MacDonalds. Always. 'What was it this time?'

'Another dead soldier.'

'Bloody hell,' Brandon cursed. 'Where?'

'Other side of the border we share with them at Glencoe Pass. Right near the loch where we found Fiona. They say they will keep killing until she is returned to them…along with your son.'

'Walk with me,' Brandon commanded, fearing that Fiona might overhear their conversation if they stayed in the corridor.

Hugh fell in step behind him as he descended the stairs and entered the study. Slamming the door behind them, he paced the room. 'Tell me everything. Leave out nothing. Now.'

'Daniel was out with a group of soldiers this morn, merely following your orders from yesterday. He was teaching them how to set the grid lines for each family once the time comes for planting that area. When they reached the edge that overlooked the loch, and Glencoe Pass just beyond it, one of the soldiers called out to him, having spotted a drowned man at the water's edge.' Hugh paused, and a muscle in his jaw flexed. 'He'd been stabbed and then drowned, by the looks of it. A note was pinned to his chest, just like the others.'

He handed a crumpled, bloodstained note to Brandon.

The longer we wait for ye to return Fiona and her bastard to us, the more of yer men will die.

'Well, that's clear enough, isn't it?' Brandon spat, and crumpled the note into a ball and tossed it into the smouldering fire in the hearth.

The parchment caught and burned brightly, quickly, shrivelling into a charred curl within seconds. It had been easily destroyed, just like his soldier's life.

'And our soldier?' Brandon asked in a softer tone. 'Where is he?'

'He's been brought here. I thought you might wish to look upon him before we return him to his family in the village.'

There was something Hugh wasn't telling him that the slight hitch in his voice did. Brandon narrowed his brows at his friend and waited. 'And…?'

Hugh shifted on his feet and scrubbed a hand

through his hair, avoiding Brandon's gaze. 'It was Joseph's father who was killed.'

Brandon cursed and pounded the wall with his fist. Joseph. One of Brandon's favourite young lads in the village. A boy he hoped his son would match in eagerness to learn and serve his clan. Now this? How would he keep the boy from losing trust in his laird and in life after losing his father this way when he was merely nine years of age?

Whatever remaining hesitations Brandon might have harboured about what he had to do as Laird to protect his people and the future of his clan faded away, disappearing into smoke and ash like the MacDonald note in the fire. He had to marry another to keep the peace and infuse his clan with enough coin and resources to keep the MacDonalds at bay.

Once he crossed that hurdle and felt his people were protected, he could begin to think about how to handle Fiona. He wanted her to agree to stay here with their son—perhaps he could persuade the elders to such a compromise. He worried that Fi would not agree to such, since she'd been ready to flee this castle from the moment she'd been brought here. But he needed to tend to one crisis at a time today.

'It is decided, then.'

Brandon went to his desk and pulled out a piece of parchment, his ink pot, a quill, and a stick of crimson wax for his seal.

'I will go with you to speak to Joseph and his family about their loss. But first I must draft a letter and have it sent by messenger as soon as possible. Gather the freshest and fastest horse and rider and ready them for immediate departure. This letter must be delivered before sunset, no matter what. It cannot wait.'

'What is so urgent?' Hugh asked, resting his hands on his waist.

'I must write to the Laird of Clan Cameron and secure my union with his eldest daughter Susanna as soon as possible. It has become clear to me that such an alliance is the only way I can protect us all. The MacDonalds will never cease until they know they have no chance at overtaking us or reclaiming Fiona and my son.'

William's morning cries for milk stirred Fiona from her slumber, and she blinked her eyes open to see the sun streaming in across the bed. She ran her hand over the bedding next to her, only to find Brandon gone.

She covered her eyes, groaning aloud. What had she done? Why had she allowed herself to make love to the very man who would be marrying another and possibly casting her out? Was she truly so weak?

Aye. She was.

She forced herself to rise and greet her son, who was eager to eat. As she gathered him to her breast she glanced out through the arrow slit window, noticing the sun was high in the sky.

'I am sorry, my boy,' she cooed. 'It *is* late. No wonder you are so hungry.' She wiped the small tears from the corners of his eyes and he almost smiled.

She'd overslept. She and Brandon had been awake into the wee hours of the morning, as they often had been before, exploring each other's bodies and taking their fill of one another. So much had changed between them, and yet in other ways so little. Their dormant passion for one another had been awakened and rekindled.

Her limbs still remembered his touch from the night before, and she tried to hate herself for it but couldn't. When she'd seen him there across the room, his eyes hungry and full, she'd given in to her desire and longing for him. She'd no one to blame but herself. Well... and him. If he hadn't come into her chambers looking so handsome and half naked...

Noise and a flurry of activity outside the castle drew her attention, and she scanned the area.

Several horses were being led off to the stables to be rubbed down. Perhaps the elders had returned for further talks with Brandon? Goods were being unloaded from carts, and Beatrice was helping to sort them and determine where they were to be taken. Daniel was leading a group of soldiers in practice in the sparring ring off to the west, and a messenger was being sent out with haste, the dust from his stallion's hooves rising up behind him as he disappeared over the hill with speed.

Something had happened while she'd slept—she'd bet her life on it. But what? She frowned. Scanning the grounds again, she did not spy Brandon or Hugh. Perhaps they had left early, to scout out more of the borderlands.

Before she could think upon it further, they both crested the hill, walking side by side towards the castle. Fiona did not need to see their faces to know that they were angry. It registered in the tightness of their gait and the rigidity of their shoulders, which sent a warning down her spine.

Brandon was intercepted by Beatrice upon his approach, and whatever she told him only deepened his scowl. He rested his hand on the hilt of his weapons belt and increased his pace, running up the stairs that led to the castle door.

It was time she took matters into her own hands and found out what was going on. She opened her chamber door slowly and peered outside. Since no guards stood outside her door to stop her, she took William with her and travelled as quietly as she could down the corridor and a set of stairs.

She nestled herself in an alcove off the Great Hall. No one took any notice of her as she murmured softly to William in the shadows. She watched as Brandon went into the study. To her added benefit, the door was left ajar after he entered. And, since all the men inside seemed equally displeased with each other, their voices carried easily out through the door and down the corridor to her ready and willing ears.

'Thank ye for gracing us with yer presence, my laird,' one of the elders said, his tone icy and biting.

'Anson, you were not intentionally left waiting,' Brandon answered firmly. 'I have had much to contend with this day. Another soldier was found killed this morn, and I wished to speak directly with the family to offer my condolences. The man's son is one of my stable boys.'

'That is why we are here,' said Douglass. 'We've heard news of the killing. The MacDonalds grow bolder with each passing day. There is no more time for you to consider your options. A decision will be made today for the well-being of this clan.'

'A decision *has* been made. I have already sent a letter by messenger this morn, to the Laird of Clan Cameron. It includes my offer of marriage to his eldest daughter along with an opening discussion of terms to be agreed upon to confirm the union.'

What?

The blood in Fiona's veins went from fire to ice. A feeling of lightness in her body made her limbs tingle. White-hot rage and the fear of what his decision meant to her and William battled within her, along with the familiar cold sting of abandonment. How could he do this? What of all his pretty words to her? Words about beginning anew and weaving trust between them? About loving William more than all else?

Lies. They were all lies. And she'd fallen for each and every one of them, just as she'd done before. He had merely slaked his lust with her. Their lovemaking had meant nothing to him even if it had meant everything to her.

She'd been a fool. Again.

At that moment she wished to cry her eyes out about it. But she had no time for it. She focused her energy on listening to the rest of the conversation. The more she knew about Brandon's plans the better. It might just aid in her escape—which now seemed the only option.

She sat down in a chair near the alcove before her legs gave out from the shock of her new situation. Blinking back tears and swallowing a steadying breath, she honed in on their words.

'I am pleased to hear that ye have come to some sense of reason finally,' Anson chimed in. ''Tis about time. Now ye must decide what to do with the Mac-Donald. Yer son will stay here, of course, but her... She cannot be allowed to stay. It will only incite more violence from her father and his men.'

'You will not command anything further of me. *I*

will decide what is to become of Fiona and my son, not any of you.' Brandon's words were sharp and brittle.

'You forget that you can still be replaced,' one of the elders answered him.

'By whom? My brother is unable to lead, and there are no other Campbells of noble blood lingering about. You have no options to threaten me with.'

A long pause ensued. Then, 'We can seek out your second cousin.'

'Sean?' Brandon scoffed. 'He left this clan of his own choice. He won't return after what you did to his mother. That is an empty threat and you know it, Douglass.'

Fiona froze. Was it such an empty threat? There were plenty of men willing to crawl over the dead bodies of other men to seize power when they saw an opening, no matter the past. Fiona knew that, and Brandon did as well, despite his haughty words. Sean might have left because of the way the elders had shamed and isolated his mother, but revenge could be a hearty pull to a man…and to a woman.

''Tis no empty threat. The promise of power can ease a man's memories of the past.' Douglass shrugged. 'He may have grown tired of living with his wife's people. And his mother made the decisions that led to her treatment. She'd no one to blame but herself.'

'Nay. A boy does not forgive sins against his mother so easily. Trust my words upon that.' Brandon's tone tightened.

Silence stretched out between them and Fiona held her breath.

'Our visits will continue until changes are made, my

laird,' Anson stated. 'We do not expect to have to wait when we arrive next time.'

'And I do not expect to be commanded about *"next time"*,' Brandon answered.

His words were cool, biting, and left no room for misinterpretation.

Fiona stilled, hiding herself behind a large tapestry as she heard the men leaving the study and travelling through the Great Hall. The large castle doors slammed closed behind the elders after they'd left. Although William's eyes flickered open for a moment at the sound, he only gurgled and drifted back to sleep.

Brandon was speaking to Hugh in the study in tones too low to hear. Fiona had half a mind to sneak along the wall, so she could hear more clearly, but she wasn't entirely sure she wished to hear any more. The man she'd thought had begun to love her once more, and plan a life for her and their son, was crafting a future with another.

Straightening her spine, she lifted her chin and walked back to her chamber. She'd had enough of waiting. Instead of crying and awaiting the moment of his betrayal, she would outwit him. He didn't know that she was aware of his plan to abandon them, so she'd use this time to make plans of her own to escape. With the jewels, she had the means to make a new life elsewhere. Now she just needed to discern the best time to disappear and the best route to take.

She frowned. A secondary plan was also in order— for when had anything she'd planned gone as expected?

Chapter Nineteen

Brandon dragged himself up to Fiona's chamber. After a horrid day, he needed to see his son. If he were honest, he also needed to see Fi. But the idea of pretending he wasn't miserable and that he wasn't about to betray her after making love to her the night before soured his stomach.

Summoning strength he didn't have, he didn't knock—just opened her chamber door.

Fiona turned to face him and stopped the soft tune she had been singing to William. He was wrapped in a fur and slept snuggled against her chest. She sat on the edge of the bed and settled him in her arms.

Brandon sat beside her without a word. For moments, he merely studied his son's peaceful face and let his heart settle into a more regular rhythm. They were alive and they were safe—for now. What he was doing by marrying another would help keep them that way... even if he was miserable.

He shoved the thought away. He'd been a fool to believe they could seize the love they'd once had between them and be happy. Lairds were not intended to be happy, it seemed. His father had been proof of it, and now so was he. He could only hope his son fared better than them both.

'I hear you are to marry,' she said, quietly staring down upon William.

Damn. How had she found out already?

She traced a finger over William's small hand. He opened his tiny fist and seized her petite finger in his grip before sighing and settling back into sleep.

Brandon's chest tightened and he squeezed his eyes shut. He hesitated before answering, wondering exactly how much she knew and how she knew it. 'Aye.'

'And you thought not to tell me? Preferred for me to find out from another?'

She whispered the words, and when her gaze set upon him pain was evident in her green eyes. He felt as small as a mustard seed.

'I thought it a kindness not to until I was certain of it. And this morning it was obvious to me that it had to be done, despite what I may wish.'

The words sounded hollow and ridiculous even in his own ears. He'd always been a rather poor liar. Something he'd used to believe was a virtue.

Fiona chuckled. 'A kindness? Nay. You were a coward. It seems you are a different man from the one who left my bed this morning.'

'Perhaps you are right.'

She lifted her brows.

'Surprised that I agree with you?' he asked, amused by her expression.

'Aye. Very much so.'

A hint of lightness had entered her serious tone, and he seized upon it. He had to try to make her understand.

He reached over and took her hand in his own, the cool light weight of it a familiar anchor for his weary soul. 'It is the only way I know to keep you both safe and save this clan and my people from further chaos and ruin. It will please them to know I am not marrying you, and it will bring wealth and added power to the clan—which we desperately need to defend ourselves.' *Against your father.*

Fiona slid her hand away and shook her head. 'You are a fool if you believe such. It will only make the elders feel more empowered that you are following *their* command instead of them following *yours* as Laird.'

He frowned. 'You twist my words. This is what I want.'

She scoffed and stood, holding William in her arms. 'Is it? Have you changed so much over the last few hours that you wish to marry a stranger? I don't believe you.'

'Nay,' he said loudly, anger bubbling in his gut. He stood and approached her. 'I marry for the future of my clan and my son. It is my duty as Laird to protect my people, and I cannot do that alone. Another soldier was found murdered this morn. By your father's command, no less. Would you rather I give in to his demands and return you and William to him, to suffer whatever horrible punishment he has for you? Is that what you wish?'

For a moment she froze, clearly taking in the horror of his words as if she finally understood the severity of the situation.

Brandon nodded at her silence. 'I thought not,' he said. 'So what other solution is there? I must marry to protect not only the clan but you and William. Do you not understand?'

'Nay, I do not!' she cried. 'You are weak. You resign yourself to marrying a woman you don't know to please the elders and the clan. The union will turn your soul to ash.'

'No bride shall make me half as miserable as you have made me,' he ground out.

She stilled and her mouth gaped open. Tears brightened her eyes, and he regretted what he'd said—even if it had been the clear, unburdened truth of his heart and exactly how he'd felt when she'd betrayed him last year.

He thought to reach out to touch her, but held fast.

'And you think I...*we*...have not suffered because of you? If my aunt had not crafted our escape from Glenhaven, with the help of a few trusted guards, William and I would already be dead. We were fine before you captured us and brought us here. We were on our way to a new life elsewhere. You keep me here by claiming William, and you place us in unfettered danger by surrounding us with people who want nothing more than for us both to be dead. We are targets who will be caught in the fray between you and my father, and you know that. Set us free, so we may be safe and unburden one another. It is far too late for us. I know such now, and so do you.'

Did he?

He knew that some part of her was a seed that would always remain in him, ready to blossom with hope if she would just say the word. Perhaps it was time he squashed it, for his sake as well as her own. But his son... He couldn't take the boy from his mother, nor her from him. He was trapped in misery. Perhaps when he was wed to the Cameron lass he would be able to see a clearer solution.

'I will be married. Best you get used to the idea of it. You and William will remain here...even if I must make you my prisoners. I will *not* lose my child.' He turned and headed for the door.

'It's finally happened,' she argued.

He faced her. 'And what is that?'

'You've become a laird—just like your father.'

Her words hit him hard, like a kick to the stomach, and he paused. But he commanded himself to say nothing more and leave.

Bastard.

Fiona had been a fool. Why had she ever believed Brandon would build a future with her and their son? He'd proved time and again that when things got too hard or complicated he sought the easiest solution and folded at the demand of others. As much as he'd always said he'd not turn into his father, here he was doing just that. He was sacrificing her and William, just as his father had sacrificed his wife and his children's happiness for the clan.

If it hadn't been so tragic and she hadn't been so heartbroken, she might have laughed at the irony.

So here she was, abandoned once more just as she'd feared.

The only difference was that she would not accept such a fate, even if it was thrust upon her. She and William would craft their own future from the ruins of the past and seize a better life for themselves. She needed no man for that. She merely needed her wit, her strength and her creativity to plan her escape from here.

Settling William into his crib, she began to craft such a plan. Pacing the room, she thought of what she

Chapter Twenty

The celebration to announce his official engagement to Susanna Cameron was but a day away—which plagued Brandon to his core. He leaned against one of his bedchamber windows, staring out at the dark night sky. The quiet peace of the Glencoe Mountains before him offered no solutions, as it usually did.

Dread churned within his gut. What had seemed a clear-cut scheme but two weeks ago, to protect Fiona and his son, glimmered false to Brandon now. With every day his heart had squeezed tighter. He knew he had to marry the Cameron lass, but it was the last thing he wished to do.

Tomorrow he would be sealing his fate to a woman he didn't even know.

He stared upon the secret panelling that separated his chamber from Fiona's. They had been civil to one another, and he'd visited her chamber each night to see William, but a coolness had settled between them, and although he was glad to have peace, he missed the friendship and the rekindled care that had grown before their argument about his decision to marry another.

He also missed her touch—and he hated himself for it.

He stood for minutes with his fingertips resting on the panel, trying to stop himself from sliding it open, but he couldn't. He wanted to see her, even if he had no right to. He pushed the panel back.

Fiona sat on the edge of her bed, humming and brushing her wet hair. His body stirred at the sight of her, and longing pushed through his logic. They would never be together, she would never be his wife, but his body could not squelch the memory of her touch and it betrayed him.

'William sleeps,' she murmured, not even turning to face him.

He said nothing, but watched her, drawn to her.

She turned to him and ceased brushing her hair. 'What is it? You look as if you've swallowed one of Miss Emma's tonics.'

He chuckled. 'Nay. Nothing quite so dire. I just wished to see you and William. All shall change tomorrow at the announcement.' He scratched his jaw and crossed his arms against his chest. Guilt and confusion won him over. 'I also wanted to make sure you fared well. I don't want you to worry over your future here. You will never be banished. You and William will always have a home here. I want you to understand that.'

'Not even if the elders command it?' she asked, still perching on the edge of the bed. She pulled her hair to one side and began a small braid, now that it was long enough to do so. She fumbled with the loose strands.

'Let me,' he offered, before he could stop himself.

Her hands stilled and her uncertainty reflected in her gaze. He understood. He didn't know what he was doing either. He just longed to touch her one last time before he promised himself to another. If it was only her hair, then that would have to be enough.

He moved to her, settling in behind her closely on the bed. She smelled of lavender and mint, and he inhaled deeply as his fingers slid into her silky damp hair. Part of him—the logical, more reasonable part of him—knew he was lurking along a dangerous boundary between them, one misstep away from falling headlong into the past. But another part of him—the baser part of him—craved her smell, her touch, her voice, and to relive the memories that had once bound them to each other body and soul, the dreams that had nestled alongside them.

He couldn't stop himself from being a fool this one last time...

He trailed his fingertips along her scalp and around her perfectly shaped petite ears to gather her hair. She sucked in a breath when his thumb brushed below the soft lobe of her ear, letting him know he was not the only one who would miss this closeness.

'Since when did you learn how to braid hair?' she asked, her voice high and tight.

He chuckled, savouring the moment of ease between them. 'You forget that I have an older sister, and that I have a rather demanding niece to tend to. I learned quickly under wee Rosa's tutelage, and her praise of my skill warmed my spirit.'

He pulled gently, dividing her fine hair into sections before weaving them together in a single braid. Before he even had to ask, she held a blue ribbon in the air before him, for him to use to tie it.

As he nudged it free from her fingers, she asked

quietly, 'Why were you so sure I had betrayed you on purpose after the attack? I've always wanted to know why such an idea was so easy for you to latch on to. Why did you never believe it wasn't an accident, borne of carelessness and nothing else?'

He hesitated and cleared his throat. Tying off her hair, he mustered what courage remained. 'It was easy for me to believe that you had betrayed me. I never quite felt I deserved your love. It frightened me at times.'

She turned to face him, resting her hand along his thigh. Her touch elicited a warm buzzing beneath his skin.

'Frightened you? Why?' she scoffed, her brow furrowed.

He held her gaze. Her fiery green eyes were bright and searching for the truth, so he dared give it to her. 'Frightened of what it meant. No one had ever loved me with their whole being except for my mother, and when I lost her I was afraid to love that much again. It was easier and safer to believe that you had never truly loved me and that you'd merely used me to further the MacDonald hold over the Highlands.'

'Part of me understands your reasoning,' she answered. 'Perhaps that was why I was so very sure you had abandoned me. I always blamed myself for my mother leaving. I thought if I had been but a better daughter she would have stayed. It was easy for me to believe that you had abandoned me too. That I was not good enough for you.'

He rested his hand upon her own, leaning forward. 'I promise you that I didn't then and I won't in the future. You and William will be protected here. Always.'

'Despite what Lady Susanna may want?'

'Aye. And if you have concerns you will come to me. Agreed?'

'Aye. But I may have to find subtle ways to plague her.' She smirked.

'Nay. Have pity upon her, Fi. She has done nothing other than follow her father's command by marrying me—just as I have fulfilled the duty my role as Laird requires. Neither of us shall be happy.'

He kissed her cheek and rose, willing himself away from her while he still had the power to leave.

Fiona shivered as the panel between their chambers slid closed. Her body was still thrumming from Brandon's gentle touches and she flopped back on the furs, taking deep, steadying breaths and trying to slow her heartbeat.

She could do this. She had a plan. Tomorrow evening during the engagement announcement would be the best time for her and William to escape. Everyone would be distracted, catering to the whims of Lady Susanna and her family.

She and Brandon had settled the rift between them after his brief and unexpected visit this eve, so she felt she was leaving with a clear conscience. They'd said all that needed to be said and there was no need to linger. It didn't matter that his mere touch sent her body into a fever. Her body didn't know what was good for her and William, but her mind did. They were leaving on the morrow.

Until then she'd need to play the part of a defeated woman who was weak and accepting of the terms of her new station in life. It would be hard, but she'd do it. This time tomorrow she'd be on a new adventure, seeking out a better life for her and her son. Soon Brandon would forget them, as he'd have a new family to contend with. She and William would be a distant memory.

Tomorrow she'd sneak into Brandon's chamber for his knapsack, along with the map of the Highlands she knew would be inside it. She'd also find an extra tartan to drape around herself and William to keep them both warm on their travels. She'd already taken some hunks of dried beef and some oats from the kitchens—an easy feat once she'd got the cook talking about what she was preparing for the large celebration tomorrow, for the Laird and his future bride.

She'd tuck the jewels into a small pouch tied around her waist under her dress. That way it would have the greatest chance of not being found if she was ambushed on her travels. She'd also take Emilia's dirk—the one Brandon had gifted her—for protection, as well as an extra one from his chamber when she gathered his knapsack.

It all seemed too easy—which made her stomach turn. All she needed was a full moon to guide her steps and a bit of luck for a clear escape. If she could get those two things in her favour, and perhaps even a tiny diversion, she would be on her way to a new future and free of this place. A place she'd never dreamt of leaving a year ago, but a place where she could remain no longer.

Brandon sat in one of the large chairs in the study, staring into the fire smouldering within it. He'd given up on sleep an hour ago and come down to the study in an attempt to occupy his mind. He'd tried to make plans for the new section of farmland near the border, but soon given up on that endeavour as well. Concentration eluded him. He was announcing his official union with Susanna Cameron tomorrow and he was a bloody mess.

A light knock sounded on the study door, and Brandon's gaze flicked over to the large grandfather clock that stood against the opposite wall. It was past midnight. His heart hitched at the thought that it might be Fiona in search of him.

'Enter,' he replied.

When his brother Rowan poked his head into the room disappointment flooded him.

'Not who you expected, I'd wager, by the look on your face,' Rowan teased as he came in and closed the door behind him.

'Nay. I'm glad to see you. How are you feeling?' Brandon asked. He was pleased to see his brother up and looking better than he had in ages.

'Well. Sleep occasionally still eludes me, but I see I am not the only one to suffer in that area. What keeps you up, brother?' Rowan settled into the chair opposite him.

'The future—what else?' Brandon ran his index finger over a worn patch of leather on the chair. He wondered if his father or Rowan had worried at the spot in a similar fashion. Perhaps both had.

'The MacDonalds or your future marriage?'

'Are they not one and the same?' Brandon said, frustration pushing through his attempts to keep it at bay.

'You know…' Rowan began and then paused. 'You do not have to marry the Cameron lass. Not if you're willing to fight for Fiona…if you want to and if you still love her.'

Brandon blinked at his brother and shook his head.

Rowan lifted his hand. 'I know that I must be the last person you would expect to say such, but hear me out. Listen for a moment. Please.'

When his brother said 'please' Brandon stilled. 'I'm listening.'

'This…this grief has given me much time to think and mull over my many mistakes. It has allowed me a clarity that I did not have before. It seems it took me almost losing my mind in grief and rage to regain my reason.' Rowan cleared his throat and continued. 'This is your life, Brandon, and you are Laird. You must make your own choice about who to marry.'

'But you know that if I do not do something to bring us power and stability we will be swallowed up by the MacDonalds. I cannot allow it.'

'You do not *know* it, Brandon—you *fear* it. Those are two separate things.'

'And the clan hates Fiona. If I marry her there will be an uprising, and such unrest after all we have been through will only further weaken us.'

'But we would survive it, brother, if that is your choice. And I am not sure you will survive and be happy without her.' Rowan risked a smile. 'I have seen you together. There is love there. The past is the past. You cannot undo it, but you also cannot be enslaved by it.'

Brandon couldn't believe what he was hearing. 'Have I gone mad? You are encouraging me to marry her? After all that you lost because of her family? After all we have lost as a clan?'

'Aye. I am. I believe it will make you happy. And I believe if I can forgive her, and hope for the best in the future, so can you.' Rowan rose from the chair. 'I'll let you think on it.'

When Rowan reached the door he turned and faced Brandon once more. 'Do not give her up if you love her. You never know when she may be gone.'

His brother's words landed on Brandon's chest like an anvil. Pain was evident in every syllable. If there was a man who knew what loss and regret felt like, it was Rowan.

As the door closed, Brandon let his head fall back against the chair and cursed. It didn't matter if his brother was right. Brandon's future had already been decided. He was announcing his engagement to the Cameron lass tomorrow, and nothing would change that.

Chapter Twenty-One

Fiona nibbled her lip for the mere thousandth time and attempted to remind herself that there was little to worry about. She had everything ready for her escape. The knapsack was filled with her supplies and hidden in the back of Emilia's wardrobe, along with the simple dress and boots she planned to change into as soon as she could manage a well-timed exit from the celebration this eve.

She'd have to put in her required appearance and see Susanna Cameron and Brandon presented as future husband and wife.

She swallowed hard. It would be one of the longest evenings of her life.

'How are you coming along?' Jenny asked from the other side of the chamber as she folded some of William's clean blankets.

Fiona adjusted her gown's sleeves, turned from the mirror and faced her maid.

Jenny smiled and sighed. 'You look beautiful, miss.'

To be truthful, Fiona felt she had lost some of the brazen nerve and edge she'd once possessed. With William sleeping steps away, it was hard not to fret over all she risked this eve. She worried if she was making the best or the worst decision of her life.

'Do I?' Fiona asked.

Everything about this felt wrong. Seemed wrong. To be dressing for the announcement of Brandon's banns of marriage to another, and pretending to be happy for him… It was ridiculous.

Jenny turned her to face the long mirror once more. 'Look for yourself, if ye don't believe me. Beautiful, I tell ye. The Laird may just rethink his announcement.' The maid winked at her.

Fiona stood staring back at her reflection.

Jenny was right. She was beautiful.

And horrid.

All at the same time.

Pressing a flat palm on the emerald-green gown where it cinched her waist, Fiona stood in awe of the woman blinking back at her. The whale bone corset was finely made and had been laced with precision by Jenny. And now the sight of this gorgeous dress— Anna's dress—placed atop it, buttoned to perfection, made Fiona's eyes well.

Perhaps I am a traitor. I stand here in your dress when it was my actions that got you killed, Anna.

Fiona shook her head and wiped her eyes. She was being ridiculous. Anna would not blame her for what had happened, even though others did.

But what could come of such shame? Nothing but distraction this eve.

She blinked back her tears. Her auburn tresses had been styled into a smooth knot at her nape, with those strands too short to be bound falling into loose waves, scarcely touching her exposed collarbone. Glass bobs of green hung from her lobes, and a ribbon with a matching glass charm hung tightly about her throat.

She *was* gorgeous—until she turned a fraction. Her smile fell at the sight of the pronounced pink scars that would always be reminders of the past—*her* past. Memories she would never escape.

They could not be covered by a dress such as this. Ever. It was a reminder that they would always be a mark upon her, to make her damaged, undesirable, and hideous. Perhaps that was why her father had done it. Made his mark to ensure she never forgot his power over her.

She swallowed hard and wrapped a wispy shawl about her shoulders to cover them. 'I do not believe he will rethink his choice, but I am grateful for your help this eve, Jenny. And for all the other things you have done for me and William.' Fiona smiled.

Jenny tilted her head. 'Always happy to be of service to you. And don't worry—Lady Susanna shall not steal me from ye, if that is what ye fear. I hear she has some fancy collection of maids she shall be bringing with her.'

'Oh, aye, that is a relief.'

Fiona smiled again. She'd almost given herself away, but Jenny's misinterpretation of what she'd meant offered her a reasonable excuse.

'Sorry for being so sentimental this eve. I fear Anna's dress has turned my thoughts.'

'Anyone would understand, miss. I believe it is admirable for ye to hold yer head up and attend. It cannot be easy to be in yer position.'

To see the father of your child choose another bride.

'Nay, it is not. But William and I are strong and we shall be fine in the end.' Fiona reached out and squeezed Jenny's hands. 'I shall show myself for a while and then retreat here to be with William.'

'Of course.' Jenny started to tidy up the room. 'Better hurry yerself along. I believe they plan to make the announcement in but a few minutes.'

Fiona nodded, smoothed her skirts, and sucked in a steadying breath. 'I am as ready as I shall ever be. If you could plan to bring some willow bark tea to my room in an hour, I'd be eternally grateful.'

'Aye. I'll put William down in a few minutes, and then leave to get you some tea, so it will be here upon your return,' Jenny replied. 'Best of luck.'

'Thank you, Jenny. I'll need it.'

Fiona glanced back at her son and then left the room, knowing it would be their last night here. She opened the door and stepped out into the corridor.

Brandon was there. He had his back to her and was staring down over the railing to the Great Hall, which was bustling with noise and celebration below. She closed the door behind her and he turned.

'Are you ready...?' he asked, but the words died on his lips as he gazed upon her.

It was as if every fibre of him had stilled at the sight of her, and for the briefest of moments she wondered if the scars upon her back were too hideous, too horrible even when she tried to hide them. Perhaps seeing them in contrast to the beauty of the dress she wore was too much for even a man as good and decent as he.

But then his eyes softened in a way that revealed deep appreciation, affection, and...something else. Something she did not care to acknowledge.

'You…' He paused and there was a hitch in his voice. 'You are more beautiful than I imagined a woman could ever be.'

She worried her hands under his assessment. Her cheeks heated.

He smiled and approached her. 'Have I, after all these years, finally made you blush properly, Fiona MacDonald?'

'Aye,' she answered. His praise warmed her down to her toes, which she wriggled in her soft petite slippers. *And on the eve you are to promise yourself to another.*

The irony was not lost upon her but she shoved it aside, along with the butterflies in her stomach. She'd made her decision and so had he.

Hugh arrived then, severing the moment between them.

'Hugh will watch over you this eve. I must be off for the announcement,' said Brandon, then hesitated as if he wished to say more, but faltered. He nodded and turned to leave.

'Come, then.'

Hugh offered her his arm and led her down the corridor and the stairs to the lower balcony, where the announcement would be made to the crowd below, gathered in the Great Hall.

It was then that Fiona's ears finally tuned in to the revelry below. Harps and pipes echoed through the large open room and the buzzing of voices and singing permeated through the air. A feast had been planned and prepared over the last two days.

A small voice budded, deep in her chest. *This is for the best. You must let him go…let this go.*

Fiona squared her shoulders, casting away her selfish

desires. There was only one way through if she truly wished to protect her son. She'd smile, grit her teeth, and endure the announcement and some idle conversation. Then she would return to her chamber, gather her son and her supplies, and begin a new life without Brandon—as he would begin his new life without them.

Brandon looked over the Great Hall, awaiting the arrival of his future bride. It was a moment that should have been joyful. The space brimmed with clansmen, soldiers, and women dressed in their best finery. Music shook the rafters, merriment filled the air, and the smells of a feast greeted him. In a corner, a group of soldiers who seemed already rather deep in their cups laughed and joked with the lasses filling their tankards.

But this was the last place he wished to be. He was in no mood to celebrate. His heart felt cleaved in two.

He'd been a fool to believe he and Fiona could slip back into each other's lives without consequence. He'd begun to care for her, to trust her, of all things, over the time she'd been here, and the longing he had shut off long ago had begun to return in full force. He'd all but forgotten his duty as Laird. He'd all but forgotten that he had no right to choose his future—not any more. It had taken a handful of dead soldiers at the border to remind him of that.

Brandon lifted his chin and pulled back his shoulders, straightening to his full height as he reached the centre of the balcony, awaiting his brother's announcement of his arrival. Clearing his throat, he prayed his mind would do the same. Distraction this eve would breed disaster. He needed to impress his future bride and her soldiers to ensure a happy union and further protection for Fiona, William and the entire clan.

Hugh approached him and Brandon spied Fiona at the other end of the balcony chatting with his sister. 'How do you fare this eve?' he asked.

'As well as you might expect.' Brandon's words sounded as flat as he felt.

'Well, put on your best mask. Your future bride and her men have arrived and will be entering shortly. They have been quite demanding so far, which should make the evening interesting...' Hugh rubbed the back of his neck.

Before Brandon could enquire further, Rowan's loud, booming voice commanded the musicians to cease their tune.

'Friends,' Rowan began, addressing the full room of revellers and clansmen. 'As you know, we are here tonight to celebrate my brother, your laird's, engagement to Lady Susanna Cameron. Thank you for coming. Please join me in welcoming our guests and the future lady of Clan Campbell.'

He gestured to the other side of the Great Hall. A woman in a black cloak emerged from an alcove with four Cameron clansmen in tow, and Brandon felt his blood boil beneath his skin.

'Bloody hell,' Brandon murmured in a low growl. 'Why is she down there? Wasn't the plan for us to be presented together up here? To show our unity and equity?'

'That was what I was about to warn you of,' said Hugh. 'She has made her own adjustments to the announcement. I only learned of it minutes ago. I wished to tell you but I couldn't find you. She has demanded her own separate entrance on her own terms.'

Brandon cursed again through gritted teeth.

'Brother, may I present to you Susanna Cameron,' Rowan called, 'your future bride.'

Brandon nodded and bowed to Susanna below. It was the required show of respect to his betrothed. Anything else would have been deemed a slight, even though she had just slighted *him* by not following his wish for them to be presented together on the balcony.

'My lady,' he bellowed down to her, in the most sincere voice he could muster. 'Welcome to Argyll Castle—your future home.'

His heart thundered in his chest and the muscles tightened along his neck. Now he would have to go down to her—an additional slash to his pride.

Susanna nodded and curtseyed to him, before allowing the hood of her cloak to fall back from her head. The dark, haunting features against pale skin held him transfixed for a moment, and a hush fell over the crowd. The woman was stunning, in a rather shocking, unsettling way. But when her ice blue eyes met his, the coldness in them registered within him immediately.

He walked briskly down the last staircase to greet his future bride, all the while searching and scanning the room, eager to see how his clansmen—especially the elders—were responding to the announcement.

Everyone seemed pleased. Everyone but him.

Deep down, Brandon knew that had he announced his engagement to Fiona instead, she and William and perhaps he himself would have been dead within hours. Not only would the elders and those loyal to them have been enraged by his choice, but the Camerons would have attacked him and his people on sight for such a slight to Susanna, the daughter of their laird, after making such a show in offering for her hand.

Despite what Rowan had said to him last night, Brandon didn't have choices. He was Laird.

Upon the last step, Brandon gathered a deep breath and prepared himself to be charming…even if his heart was filled with dread.

'My lady,' he offered, meeting the unflinching gaze of Susanna Cameron.

She offered her hand and he bowed over it, pressing a chaste kiss to her cold ring-covered fingers.

Releasing her hand, he noted surprise in her features. 'Would you care to dance?' he asked.

'Perhaps,' she answered, scanning the area behind him. 'For now, I'd like you to take me on a tour of my future home. Then I'd like to meet the rest of your family. It will help me to prepare for what is to come.'

Her words rang with resignation and for a moment Brandon almost smiled. He knew exactly how she felt. All he wanted was to be with Fiona. To protect her. Yet here he was, acting the part of guide at a party in his honour that he didn't even wish to be at.

He cast a glance at Hugh, who nodded to him. Fiona would be safe. Hugh would make sure of it.

'Of course,' Brandon answered, with a measured smile.

He guided Susanna through the throng of people towards the alcove opposite the one from where she had made her grand entrance. Soon the noise of revelry faded into the background and became a dull thrum as he led her towards the library.

At the doorway she paused, released his arm, and

then entered the room. After a moment she settled on a selection of poetry books near the back wall, running her fingertips slowly across the spines of several volumes as she scanned the titles.

He watched her smooth, catlike movements from the doorway, waiting for whatever game she wished to play to begin.

'I have heard many things about you, my laird,' she said.

'Oh, and what might those be?' he asked, following her deeper into the room.

She stopped cold and faced him. 'Among other things that you have usurped your brother's rule and that you have a child and the woman who bore him living under your roof.'

Surprise rippled through him at her statement, and his steps faltered. They studied one another, and he tried to decide if he despised her or was intrigued by her directness. Unable to make up his mind, he waited, interested to observe her next move.

'Did you not hear me?' she asked, coming closer to him.

'Aye, my hearing is quite good.' He crossed his arms against his chest.

'And are the rumours true, then?' She approached him, her eyes growing colder with every step.

'They are all true,' he answered, with a chill to match her own.

As he stared at her he lifted a wavy lock of her long raven-dark hair and let it slide through his fingers like gossamer. Her eyes widened and she stepped away from him as if stunned. Whether it was from his words or his actions, he couldn't tell. Perhaps she expected him to lose his temper. The woman was unreadable.

'I have seen enough,' she stated, brushing past him and leading the way back to the Great Hall.

He fell in step behind her, in time with the serpent-like swish of the fabric of her dark gown.

As they reached the edge of the dance floor she faced him. 'A dance won't be necessary, my laird. I know all I need to...for now.'

She settled in between two of the Cameron soldiers and stared off into the distance, looking at no one in particular.

Or so it seemed.

As he followed her gaze he felt his skin tingle with unease. Fiona was in her sights. The last thing Fiona needed was yet another enemy. He also didn't wish for his first disagreement with his future wife to be about the mother of his child.

'As you wish, my lady. I do hope you enjoy the celebration. I'll return to you shortly.'

Brandon nodded and took his leave, eager to be anywhere other than with his future wife.

Chapter Twenty-Two

Who knew one could be bored to bits and yet also feel as if one stood on nettles?

Fiona released another strained laugh as a few of the women whom she was quite sure had lobbed curses at her upon her initial arrival weeks ago prattled on about the latest crops to come in, the herbs that needed to be dried, and the latest news about their children and grandchildren—of which there seemed to be many, based on the difficulty Fiona was having in keeping up with their conversation.

At the earliest opening she excused herself. Nodding to them, and slipping through the crowd like a salmon swimming upstream, Fiona headed through the crowd of revellers who were celebrating Brandon's pending union with Susanna Cameron.

Her heart squeezed at the reminder of the purpose of this eve: to celebrate relinquishing Brandon to another. She forced a smile, ignoring the glares Susanna had been gifting her most of the evening, then spied Brandon and approached him. He looked as pained by the evening as she, which was little consolation. One of them should be pleased, shouldn't they?

'You may wish to smile a bit, my laird,' she whispered beside him. 'This is your engagement celebration after all.'

He chuckled and gazed down at her. 'I'm trying. But I already find my future wife to be quite…' He paused and released a sigh. 'Challenging.'

Fiona pressed her lips together to stifle a chuckle. 'Marriage is about compromise. Do not give up quite so easily.'

He shook his head and scoffed. 'Says the person not marrying a stranger.'

'Nay,' she answered quietly, shifting away from him. 'I am not.' His words stung like a barb.

He scrubbed a hand down his face. 'I'm sorry. I didn't mean—'

She rested a hand on his forearm. 'I know. It's fine. I just wanted to bid you good eve. I'm going to check on William and retire. Enjoy your celebration.'

He started to say something, perhaps to convince her to stay, but must have realised the cruelty in such a request. 'Thank you for being here,' he said instead. 'Give him a kiss for me.'

'I will,' she replied, squeezing his arm and taking one long last look at him. The man she'd once loved… the one she was letting go. The man who belonged to someone else now.

She turned away and headed up the stairs to her chamber for the last time.

As much as she despised Susanna Cameron for being the one to live the life *she* had wanted at one time, Fiona couldn't deny the impressive picture they would make together, side by side. Watching them at the gathering had reminded her of the force their two clans would muster, and what prosperity they would bring to a vast number of people in the Highlands. The union of their clans would also bring a formidable challenge to her father and her own clan.

Remaining here with Brandon would only hamper that future, and watching them forge a new path together from the shadows would be near impossible. It would destroy Fiona's happiness…and their son's. Just as she'd long known, leaving Brandon and Clan Campbell was the best option for everyone, despite how much she still cared for him.

As Fiona had hoped, only one guard—and a green one at that—stood in the corridor near her chamber door, due to the demands of their guests that eve. She would easily find a way to distract him and be on her way. She sighed in relief. Step one complete.

Then she opened her chamber door and found Jenny there, waiting and singing quietly to William. She'd brought Fiona the tea she'd requested before the gathering began, and would be able to help her out of this painfully complicated gown. Despite how beautiful it was, it required assistance to get in and out of it. Jenny would be a helpful part of Fiona's escape plan, for no woman could go on the run with so much fabric gathering around her ankles. Step two complete.

Jenny rose to greet her. 'How was it?' she asked, biting her lip, likely knowing full well how it had been.

Fiona chuckled. 'As awkward and horrid as one might imagine—but I smiled and made idle conversation as best I could, and then, I bade Brandon goodnight.'

'How ye managed it this eve, I do not know,' Jenny said in a low voice.

'I have had my share of pretending, I suppose. At least it was a blessing this night.'

Fiona removed her shawl, as well as the glass bobs in her ears and the necklace from her throat. She tucked them away neatly on the dressing table.

Jenny began undoing the endless column of buttons and clasps along the back of Anna's beautiful emerald gown. Fiona released a sigh when the gown gave way, falling in a smooth liquid wave to the floor.

When Jenny removed the whalebone corset that had been beneath it, Fiona rubbed at her side. 'While it has served its purpose of providing me with a more pleasing form, I am glad to be rid of it,' she murmured, taking her first full deep breath since Jenny had laced her into it hours ago.

'Do you wish to put on another gown or remain in yer shift only, miss?' Jenny asked, holding the gown carefully in her arms.

'The shift is fine. I will have some tea and sing William to sleep. That is all I require of you this eve. I'm sure you will enjoy watching some of the celebration from the balcony—even sneak down to grab a few of the pastries and cakes, if you wish. The berry ones are especially delicious. Cook outdid herself this eve.'

Jenny's eyes lit up. 'Perhaps I will, after I return Miss Anna's dress to her old room.'

'Please do. And thank you, Jenny.'

'Tomorrow will be a new day and a better one,' she said.

Fiona nodded as Jenny opened the door to leave. 'Aye. I believe it will be.'

As soon as Jenny had disappeared down the corridor Fiona changed quickly, gathered the knapsack, and situated William inside a tartan wrapped tightly about her body to ensure his safety as they travelled. No one would even suspect her son was with her unless they heard him cry.

She slid the secret panel back and entered Brandon's chamber, breathing in the spicy musk of his scent one last time. She grabbed a dagger from his drawer and replaced it with a note to say goodbye, along with the jewels that she could not bear to steal. She'd find another way to provide for herself and William.

She had kept one lone emerald from the pouch of jewels, and planned to gift it to William when he was of age, as a reminder of the Campbells and the grandmother he'd never known. Fiona would never part with it. She wanted to have some memory of Brandon and his family to give their son when the time came.

She closed the drawer with a shaky hand, reminding herself that this was the best decision and the best course of action for everyone.

The clock had almost reached ten—time for the change in the guard, which would be her best chance of sneaking out sight unseen through the servants' passageway that led out through the back of the castle.

She opened Brandon's chamber door slowly, peering out into the corridor with William tucked closely to her chest. The lone guard had moved away from the threshold and waited for his replacement to arrive at the end of the main stairway. The young soldier was casting eager glances to the Great Hall below, where the din of music and conversation sounded.

Thankful for the distraction, she tiptoed out onto the

landing, closed the door quietly behind her, and headed to the opposite stairway. The one that the servants used to pass unseen among the castle floors. While she knew she took a risk in travelling the staircase, many of the servants were still bustling about among the guests and in the kitchens below. They would not be attending to the family rooms or the guest rooms above stairs until much later in the evening.

This was the best option for escape she had. The secret tunnels had all been sealed after the attack. Her heart pounded in her chest as she made each silent step closer to the stairs. Once there, she released a breath and began a quick descent.

She made steady progress down the winding stone stairs. Soon she was at the base of the stairs and only a step away from the landing.

'Alison!' the cook called from the door leading to the kitchens.

Fiona ducked into the shadows and bit her lip.

'Aye!' the girl answered from the opposite direction. 'Don't lose yer cap!'

'That lass will be the end of me,' the cook muttered, tramping back inside.

The young girl crossed dangerously close to the stair where Fiona and William hid. After she had passed, Fiona peered around. She was alone. Without hesitation, she darted out. Soon she reached the outside, and the first breath of air tasted like the freedom she had craved all her life.

'Are you ready, my love?' she whispered to William.

He cooed, and she smiled.

'Here we go, my sweet,' she replied, ready to take

the first step on their new adventure to a life without Brandon Campbell.

She paused and listened. At ten the guards would cross paths on the outskirts of the castle. There would be two minutes when she could scurry out and make it to the nearby set of boulders. If she could make that stretch without being seen, they would be well on their way to freedom.

She peered around the edges of the castle wall, their smoothness a gift from centuries of weathering. The two guards outside started to move to her left—a sign that they were planning to change. No doubt they were eager to join in the festivities that were still in full swing, based on the music thrumming through the castle walls.

Fiona shifted into an all-out sprint for the boulders. Clouds hid the moon as she ran, for which she was grateful. But when the first plop of rain hit her face as she skidded behind the boulders she frowned. The rain would not be such a blessing. It would hamper their travel and leave them cold and soggy, which wouldn't be good for either of them.

She studied the choices before her.

While she'd hoped to travel through Glencoe Pass, as it was the shortest distance to the MacNabs, now she wondered if it would be safe with the coming rain. The pass would flood easily as the rain gathered along the valley on its way to reach Loch Leven.

Peering up into the clouds, she couldn't tell if the rain would be short-lived or a large, raging storm. As thunder sounded, she frowned. One could never tell in the springtime... Best she planned for the worst and travelled through the borderlands and the forest. At least there she could take cover if needed.

As long as she wasn't intercepted by her father's soldiers... He had long hidden men in the forest as a security measure. It didn't matter to him that he was oftentimes hiding his soldiers along a border shared with the Campbells and other clans. Her father had never been great at following the rules.

She began her trek across the field, using the pitch-black darkness of the pending storm to aid her stealthy progress. The clouds opened up and the soaking rain began almost as soon as she began her advance. She cursed under her breath.

The soles of her boots scarce touched the ground as Fiona charged across the landscape. Soon, mud splashed up her legs and rain nearly blinded her. But none of it mattered. None of it would keep her from seizing this one opportunity for escape.

She veered towards the most direct path to the border—a swath of open meadow and hillside with no cover or protection from the elements. But keeping to this dangerous and brazen line for as long as she could would save her time. At the last moment, she would shift into the dark woods on the edge of the border to hide her approach—otherwise she would be discovered by MacDonald soldiers and most likely cut down on sight. And she'd not die before she knew William was safe.

Her cloak grew heavier with each stride, soaking up the rain that fell so steadily she couldn't see more than a full stride ahead of her own step. She was eager to discard it, but needed it for cover and warmth for William. Soon she'd disappear into the woods like a nymph.

As the edge of the forest came into view, the dark, waving branches of the trees swayed in the harsh winds. She slowed as she made her way into the dense, musty evergreens, weaving in and around sticks and branches, making her advance as soundless as possible. If there was a place to be ambushed it would be here. And she'd need to find a place to hide for a while, until the rain subsided. It was becoming too dangerous to walk as the lightning crackled around her and the thunder boomed.

William shifted against her and she murmured assurances to him that all was well. To his credit, he never squalled once. Her boy was an angel.

Spying a small clearing surrounded by large evergreens, she tucked herself and William within it. She sighed in relief to be out of the driving rain, and settled them on a large boulder.

Scanning the area around them, she saw nothing out of the ordinary. Just rain, darkness, and the occasional flash of lightning to brighten their surroundings. The temperature had dropped over the last hour and she shivered in her wet cloak. Her breath came in spirals like smoke, and she mentally cursed. It would be impossible to disguise every aspect of their presence, but she would try.

Pulling the edge of the cloak around her mouth, she tried to stifle the puffs of air before they escaped.

A twig snapped ahead of her. She squinted in the darkness, willing herself to see who or what it was. Someone? Or something? It was hard to know with the pebbling rain and the rustling winds.

She closed her eyes and listened, forcing her breaths to slow. Perhaps her ears would tell her more. But she could hear nothing but the thunder and the rattle of rain upon the trees. She opened her eyes just as a lightning flash illuminated the sky, and gasped at the sight of the backside of the MacDonald soldier who stood two ells in front of her. Her gut turned at the sight of the familiar dark green, navy, and red plaid. She knew full well that the soldier wouldn't be out scouting alone.

Urgency hastened her. She needed to silence him while she could. She pulled her dagger from its sheath and sneaked up behind him, stabbing him in the gut before he could let out a shout of warning to the others.

Unfortunately, he fell hard.

The sound of him hitting the ground echoed as loud as a fallen tree in the area around her and the shouts of other MacDonald soldiers soon permeated the air.

Fiona charged away from the downed soldier, headlong into the darkness. Branches slapped against her arms and legs, and as she skidded down a small hill she heard shouts behind her.

Blast. She'd been spotted.

Fiona grabbed for a large boulder to steady her footing and rounded a tree—or at least what she thought was a tree. But hard, steely muscle twitched beneath the arm she'd grabbed, and the form whipped around, putting her in a choke hold so tight that she gasped for air and clawed at his forearm. William released a cry of alarm.

'Cease yer struggles,' the soldier commanded.

Knowing she was outmatched, and worried for the safety of her son, Fiona stilled.

'If ye and yer bastard wish to live ye will come with us. Quietly.'

He gripped her tighter, yanking her arm awkwardly behind her until she feared her arm might snap in two.

She sucked in a breath and stilled in his hold, her eyes focused on him.

'The boy?'

Another soldier approached, much larger than the one holding Fiona, panting from the chase. His eyes flashed in the moonlight, triggering no recognition within her, which struck her as odd. She knew all her father's men. Who were these warriors?

'He is here. I heard his cry. Take him,' he commanded.

The larger soldier made a move towards her and she twisted her body away as best she could. 'Nay,' Fiona snapped. 'He will stay with me, out of the cold and rain.'

Instead of being angry, the larger man smiled. 'Ah, I see that ye are the Lady Fiona I have heard talk of, then. No other woman would dare be so daft as to deny me a request.'

'Aye, I am one and the same. Who are you? You may wear the plaid of the MacDonalds, but you are not one of us. I have never seen you before and I know all of my father's men.'

'Let's go,' the shorter of the two soldiers ordered, tugging Fiona along. 'Think of us as your father's new recruits, eager to bring order to the Highlands. Capturing ye is a small, but necessary part of our plan.' He shoved her forward.

Mercenaries. There was no other explanation.

Minutes passed in silence as Fiona tried to plan her escape and discover exactly what was going on as the soldiers led her and William to Glenhaven. She was missing something important. If she was to be a part of his father's plan, what role would she play?

Slowly, the pieces began to slide together.

Brandon.

Was he to be attacked or killed?

Fiona's stomach flipped. Was that what her father's request for her and William's return had really been about? A way to punish Brandon and finally throw Clan Campbell into chaos, so her father and his men could attack them while their attentions were divided in trying to rescue her and her son?

She cursed, frustrated that she couldn't work out precisely what was to happen.

She cast aside her efforts and studied her current situation. Could she get away from her captors and fell these two soldiers without her boy being hurt? *Nay.* She was outnumbered, and these men were mercenaries. They'd not hesitate to kill her and William, and she'd do nothing to risk her son's life. Not after all she'd already been through.

She closed her eyes and prayed for help.

To her surprise, the image that floated before her was the face of Brandon—the man she'd just betrayed by kidnapping his son...the man least likely and willing to rescue her.

Chapter Twenty-Three

Fiona had retired, and Brandon watched the revelry continue. Contentment flooded his clansmen as they danced and celebrated the future, filling the Great Hall and spilling out into the surrounding area outside.

Their joy should have been contagious. Finally he'd made a decision that would ensure the future of his clan and protect Fiona and William at the same time. But instead of joy, dread crept along his skin. He wasn't looking forward to his marriage to Susanna Cameron. In fact, he wasn't looking forward to much of anything except seeing Fiona and William this eve.

It was late—half past eleven—but he still wished to sneak in and see them, bid them goodnight. Perhaps he'd do so now, before it became any later. If they were already asleep, which they most likely were, he would just sneak in through the panel and gaze upon them. That alone would fill his weary soul with a bit of happiness. It would remind him that he did this for them, and that their safe future was well worth his sacrifice.

He approached Hugh. 'I will return in a few minutes,

if anyone asks. I wish to check on Fiona and William. Make sure they are well.'

'Aye. I'll keep an eye on your future bride and her men.' Hugh sighed. 'I can only hope they make no further demands of us.'

Brandon clapped him on the back. 'Thank you.'

Eager to depart, he turned on his heel and climbed the stairs two at a time, until he reached Fiona's chamber. He nodded to the soldier stationed outside her door, and then knocked softly. There was no answer. He tried the door, but it was bolted from within.

He smiled, pleased to see she was protecting herself and their son by keeping the door bolted when he and Hugh were away. Then he continued on to his own chamber, went in, and pushed open the secret panel between their rooms. It slid open easily.

Her chamber was dark, quiet, and not even a single flame flickered in the hearth, despite the subtle chill in the air which made him shiver.

Odd.

He thought to call out to her, but didn't wish to wake her and William while they slept. Instead he gathered a lit torch from the wall in his room and entered her chamber once more. The flicker of light cast eerie shadows over the empty room. Where was Fiona? Where was William?

The hairs on Brandon's arms prickled to attention and his throat dried. Something was wrong—very wrong. It was close to midnight and they weren't here.

His mind raced with possible reasons, none of which seemed logical.

Brandon opened the wardrobe and noted that some of Fiona's belongings were gone. William's crib was also bare. His blankets and a Campbell plaid had been removed, along with the wooden horse Brandon had carved for his son.

His stomach rolled and his chest tingled.

His son and Fiona were missing.

Squeezing his eyes shut, Brandon commanded himself to be calm, to use reason, and to cast the panic flooding his body aside until he'd gathered more information about the situation.

He hurried back into his chamber through the panel and out into the corridor. Jenny was watching the revelry from the balcony and flirting with a soldier nearby.

Brandon hastened to her side and clutched her forearm. 'Where is Fiona? William?' he asked.

Jenny's eyes widened. 'In…in their room, my laird,' she stuttered. 'I helped Miss Fiona out of her gown, brought her tea, and helped her settle at half past nine. She said she had no further need of me and barred the door. I heard the latch drop myself.'

'I have been on watch since she came up to her room, my laird,' the soldier added. 'She never left her chamber.'

'Are you sure?' he asked. 'Did you step away for a moment?'

The soldier looked at Jenny and a flush grew along his cheeks. 'I may have stepped away for a moment to watch the celebration of your engagement, my laird…' He squared his shoulders and held Brandon's gaze.

Brandon cursed, knowing full well that 'a moment' was all a woman and warrior such as Fiona would need to escape. 'You will be dealt with—but for now begin searching for them immediately. I've got to check something.'

Jenny and the soldier hurried on their way, and Brandon stalked back to his chamber, with each footfall feeling as if he was stepping through the sucking mud of a bog that threatened to pull him under. Part of him knew what he would discover…another part of him wished to deny it as long as possible.

He gathered a steadying breath at the threshold and re-entered his room. The music below was dulled to nothing and there was deafening silence—the same kind he experienced before the moment of battle, when time slowed to nothing. She and William were gone. He knew it. He didn't know how she'd escaped, but she had.

'Give him a kiss for me,' he'd said.

'I will,' Fiona had answered.

He shuddered at the memory of the look she'd given him just hours ago at the banquet. It had been a last look. A goodbye. He cursed aloud. Why hadn't he noticed it? Why hadn't he paid more attention?

Because he was a fool. Because he had been distracted. And because he didn't wish to believe she was capable of doing this to him. Of betraying him by kidnapping his son.

'No one has seen her, my laird,' said the guard from the doorway.

Jenny joined him by his side. 'Nor has she been below with the servants,' she added.

Brandon sighed, settling his hands on his waist. 'Aye. She's run.'

Jenny gasped as a clap of thunder sounded. 'In this weather?'

Brandon shifted from the emotions of a father missing his son into those of a laird needing to lead a mission to recover him before it was too late.

'Jenny, put together some food and blankets for my son and bring them to me.' He faced the guard. 'Bring Hugh to me now, but don't raise any alarm in doing so. I'll not have anyone hampering my efforts to retrieve them this eve.'

After they'd left, Brandon stripped off his fussy jacket and kilt, opting for a woollen coat and trews and leather boots to fend off the dropping temperature and the rain that fell heavily outside.

He didn't want to think about what might have happened to either of them in the time that had already passed. Why hadn't he realised she would have gone? He was marrying another and she had never wanted to be here in the first place. The cover of his engagement party had been the perfect distraction.

He yanked open the drawer that held his weapons belt and reached in to grab them. The sight of Fiona's familiar curling script on parchment stopped him cold. A chill skittered up his body. He clutched the note greedily in his hand and sat on the bed to read it, opening it with trembling fingers.

Brandon,
By now you will know we are gone. Do not worry for us. I've taken care with our son, and we'll make the journey to the MacNabs in two days' time if the weather holds.
You know as I do that my not being here is for the best for everyone. You can build a new life with Susanna Cameron and the Campbell Clan can flourish once more and fend off any threats made by my father. My staying would only im-

*pede your ability to be the leader and laird your
clan deserves.*

*I also, selfishly, cannot bear to watch you build
a life with another...a life I had once dreamed to
share with you.*

*Do not come after us. Enjoy the new life you
have been given, and so will I.*
Fi

He let the note drift to the floor and sat hunched
over, his elbows digging into his thighs as he held his
head in his hands. How had he not foreseen this? Why
had he dared believe that he had all things under his
control and that everyone was pleased with his decisions? That everything would work out for the best?

Because he'd been a fool, that was why.

Glancing back into the drawer, he spied a small vel-
vet pouch he'd never seen before. It had been hidden
under Fi's letter, and he'd been so eager to read it he'd
not even noticed it there. He lifted it in his hand, pulled
the drawstring open and spilled the contents into his
palm. Bright, glittering jewels winked back at him.
He gasped.

Stuck in the pouch was a small note which he unfolded and read. It was also written by Fiona's hand.

*I found these in your mother's chamber. They
must have been hers, stored away for safekeep-
ing. I thought of taking them for our new life, but
couldn't bear to as they belonged to Emilia.*

*I'm sure she would have wished for you to have
them. They are as beautiful as she was.*

Emotion filled his chest. Jewels from his mother? Jewels that Fiona could have taken from him without him ever knowing to start her new life? But she'd left them for him, knowing how much they would mean.

He could scarcely breathe. His clumsy fingers faltered as he replaced the jewels in the pouch, along with the second small note, and shoved the drawer closed.

'My laird?' Hugh called from the open door. 'You have need of me?'

'Aye,' Brandon answered. 'I do. Close the door.'

Hugh did as he'd asked. 'What's happened?'

'Fiona has gone and she's taken William with her.'

Hugh blinked back at him. 'Gone?'

'Aye. She left a note. She's taken William and continued her journey to the MacNabs. She claims this is best for everyone, especially me.' Brandon stood, cupping the back of his neck with his hand, and began to pace the room.

'In this storm?' said Hugh.

'Aye.'

'What do you need?'

'To find them as quickly as possible. Before they are intercepted.'

Brandon didn't need to say more. Hugh knew as well as he what might befall Fiona travelling through Glencoe Pass at night, in the rain, with a babe in tow. Brandon banished the thoughts before they began to chip away at his reason.

His pulse throbbed, and his body buzzed with an urgency to leave and find them. *Now.* But he knew he needed to get supplies, leave without being seen, and have a plan. He couldn't risk upsetting his future bride or her men by openly leaving his engagement party in search of his son and the woman he…

He couldn't allow himself to continue that line of thought. He'd get Fiona and William back first. Then he'd worry about the clan and his future as Laird, just as he should have been doing in the first place.

He pounded his fist into the wall. If he hadn't been such a fool none of this would have happened. He'd been so focused on being a good laird that he'd forgotten how to be a good man and a good father. It was a lesson he should have learned long ago, when his own father had made the same mistake.

Fiona could only be angry with herself. Her impatience to get to the MacNabs and avoid the elements in Glencoe Pass had caused her to walk right into the MacDonald soldiers' path. She *knew* her father's men patrolled the edge of the forest, and yet she'd gone through anyway.

She should have waited in hiding for the weather to improve and then travelled down Glencoe Pass. If she'd merely followed her plans for travel she'd not be in this mess. But patience had never been one of her better qualities.

Fool.

She pulled at the ropes that bound her and dragged her legs and her boots through the brush and the mud— anything to slow their progress through the darkness. Even now Glenhaven—her childhood home and the castle of Clan MacDonald—stood like a towering albatross against the night sky, its flags flickering in the wind like a warning of what was to come.

She'd told herself long ago that she'd not come back

to this place unless she was dead, and even then she'd put up a fight. As soon as she knew her son was safe from harm she would rage against every soldier in her path to escape, but now?

William whimpered against her and she cooed to him. She dared not struggle with her sweet boy between her and the mercenaries who led her.

She spat on the ground as they neared the lit torches lining the path to the Glenhaven castle doors. MacDonald soldiers flanked both sides of the entrance, their faces grim and sombre. Not exactly the warm, welcoming return a daughter of the Laird should receive. She only recognised half of the men. Had so much changed since she'd been gone? Perhaps it was time to find out.

She shivered and tried to shake the wet strands of hair from her face. 'Take me to my father,' she shouted, glaring at the sea of grim-faced soldiers before her, some of whom she recognised. Some of them used to protect her. 'Seamus? Gordon? Tell him I am here and take me to him.'

The two soldiers she'd once known merely glared back at her without answering. She shoved against her captor and spat in his face. 'Brute—tell him!'

He slapped her hard in return.

Fiona struggled to keep her footing and tasted blood in her mouth. William squalled with alarm in her arms. Through her hair, she saw Gordon step forward to protect her—most likely a reflex he couldn't suppress—and Seamus push him back into line.

Perhaps not all the MacDonalds had turned upon her, she thought, and hope flared in her gut. If not all of them were as cold and heartless as these new recruits she might be able to turn them against one another, or at least plead for help in allowing her to escape before she and William were killed.

As she staggered back up to her full height she smiled, a new plan shaping in her mind.

'Ye dare smile at me, wench?' the brute asked.

'Aye. I do. Only cowards slap defenceless women.' She sniffed the air dramatically. 'And I smell a coward.'

Angered, he raised his hand to her once more. Fiona turned her shoulder to protect William and prepared herself for the blow.

'That won't be necessary,' a loud booming voice called from the castle doors. 'Bring her in. Now.'

Fiona lifted her face to meet the gaze of the man she'd hoped to never see again. Laird Audric MacDonald—her father.

Chapter Twenty-Four

'Fi! Fi!'

Brandon's throat burned as rain soaked his clothes. Thunder cracked down around him drowning out the attempts he made to call to her. Despite knowing she wouldn't be able to hear him, he couldn't help but continue. His heart would allow nothing else.

He called again and again, his pulse pounding and his lungs burning from the exertion of running all the way from the castle to Glencoe Pass, which would take her on the road that would lead to the MacNabs.

When he reached the edge of the cliff that led to the pass below he spied a river of water already raging down the ravine to Loch Leven—a common occurrence during the spring rains, and one that Fiona would have been aware of and considered before she travelled further. If she'd dared this route she would have risked being caught up in the current and drowned. It wouldn't take much water rushing along for one to lose one's footing.

Brandon swallowed hard. Fiona was no fool. She wouldn't have risked this even if she'd left hours before, when it had first started to rain. It would have been too dangerous for William and, despite all her failings, Fiona was a smart and savvy warrior and a protective mother to their son. She would have known it was too great a risk and chosen another path.

'She couldn't have travelled this way—not with William!' Brandon shouted to Hugh over the din of the driving rain. 'Too dangerous,' he continued, pointing to the rushing water below.

Hugh nodded in agreement. 'The forest is the only other way she might have ventured to reach the road to the MacNabs.' He gestured to the forest far off, the opposite way from the path they had just come.

They'd lost time coming to the pass, but Brandon had needed to know she wasn't there. In a sense, it was a relief to know she hadn't risked these rushing waters.

He turned and they headed back to where they'd come from. Soon they had circled back to the castle, and his legs pumped up the grassy hill, now slick with water, as they neared the barn. His boots failed to grip the wet earth and he grabbed a handful of wildflowers that blew from side to side in the whipping wind. Their sharp, clean scent was a reminder of Fi and all he might lose.

Reaching the crest of the hill, he stood wiping the wet hair from his eyes and stared down into the darkness of the valley below. Lightning lit the night sky and Loch Leven glistened briefly, far out in the distance to his left. He squinted to catch any glimmer of light or the sound of any movement, but there was nothing. The confidence he'd felt over an hour ago had been washed away. It wouldn't take them much longer to reach the forest's edge, and the border they shared with the Mac-Donalds, but so much could have happened in the time between when she'd left and now.

Brandon wondered if he should begin preparing himself for the worst.

Hugh reached his side, panting for breath. 'We'll find them.'

Will we?

The unspoken fear tightened his chest. Even if they did find them, would they be alive? Or would his greatest fear be realised, in a crumpled heap of plaid along a hillside? Fi and their son…dead. Cut down by the MacDonalds.

She'd run straight into danger because of *him*—because of *his* weakness. If he'd stood up to the elders sooner, been a stronger leader who could not be challenged, he would have followed his heart and chosen to protect his family.

But he'd put his clan before Fi and his son and bowed down to the demands of being the Laird.

Just as his father had done.

And his mother had paid the ultimate price—as had he and his siblings.

Even Rowan had tried to warn him off his engagement, but he hadn't listened. Now his brother and sister were acting as a distraction to Susanna Cameron and her men as the celebration dwindled and they readied themselves to stay overnight—another unwelcome development because of the horrid weather.

He wiped his drenched hair from his eyes again. He cursed and scanned the valley once more. 'How far could she have gone?'

Hugh faced him. 'You know the answer.'

'Aye, she could have already reached the border and cut down every man in her path.'

'You need to remember that. She is a fine warrior. And those men will be none the wiser. Indeed, you should feel sorry for *them*. They are as good as dead if they stand in her way or threaten her son.'

'Aye.' A small wisp of hope nestled against his fear. 'If she does not kill them first to protect our son, I will.'

He took a step off the hillside, and when his feet folded beneath him on the slick grass he slid down the rest of the hill, letting the rain and slippery brush ease his travel until he reached the bottom. Anything to make up the time he'd lost. Anything to find her before harm befell them.

Hugh was not far behind, and soon stood beside him in the pouring rain. 'Our plan?'

'I've no plan but to search the forest along the border until we find them and bring them back. There will be no other outcome.'

He pulled a dagger from his waist belt and wiped the rain from his brow before advancing into the pitch-black darkness.

They followed in the wake of the storm, struggling through rain that blew sideways and thunder that rumbled along the trees. Soon the rivers would be full, if not overflowing from the spring rain.

They would be wise to continue their approach under the cover of the darkness and the storm and seize any advantage they could. Just like on the night the Mac-Donalds had attacked them. Even now Brandon could hear the cries of battle, the clanging of swords, the sound of flesh meeting metal and the screams of women and children running and clamouring in fear.

He shook his head and blinked the water from his eyes. He needed to focus on the task at hand. Breathing in and out, he calmed the ragged pitch in his chest and settled into his surroundings. He knew this land as he knew his own: the best places to hide, the nooks that held danger, the parts of the forest to avoid.

Hugh followed Brandon's path a few lengths behind, allowing for a measurable gap to open up between them—one that might lure an unsuspecting guard into a false sense of safety. All they needed was one fool to fall into their trap. Then they would get all the answers they needed. Hugh was especially gifted in the art of making men give up their secrets.

They entered a dense section of woods. A portion intentionally left overgrown and thick to encourage lesser men to turn back. In a breath, one might lose one's bearings as the trees climbed high and full, creating a beautiful canopy in the night sky. A cloak of darkness thickened about them, and soon all Brandon could hear was the thunder and the rain. He could no longer even hear Hugh's advance behind him.

Taking a deep breath, he continued on past a large stone the size of a table. One he and Fi had used to meet at in order to lie back and watch the stars.

A stick cracked in the darkness, followed by a low moan. Brandon held his breath and closed his eyes, listening for another sound so he'd know the direction it came from.

Another moan sounded, followed by the shifting of leaves and earth, but he couldn't tell if it was a man or a woman. All he could know was that it was on his left and not too far away.

Brandon opened his mouth to call out, but hesitated. It could be a well-thought-out trap to lure them from the darkness to be attacked. He advanced two steps further towards the sound and stopped, waiting for another noise to signal a presence.

Nothing.

He stepped around the large tree trunk with his dagger drawn and faced a shadowed figure sprawled on the ground.

Rage flooded his veins as he saw the mass of MacDonald plaid and the wounded soldier within it. 'Where is my son? Where is Fiona?'

The soldier ignored him and clutched his gut.

Only then did Brandon see the blood oozing from the soldier's chest and abdomen. He'd been badly wounded.

Brandon pressed into the man's wound. 'You will tell me,' he shouted, ignoring the man's agony.

The soldier groaned. 'They took them,' he answered, choking and coughing, his eyes fluttering closed.

Hugh put pressure on the soldier's abdomen to staunch the flow of blood. 'My laird,' he muttered, 'he'll not last long. Be quick.'

Brandon didn't have such kindness left in him. He needed to find Fiona and his son. Alive.

'Who? Who took them? And where?' he shouted, already knowing what the answer might be.

The MacDonald soldier's eyes opened into slits. As he started to answer he coughed and spluttered once more. He pointed towards Glenhaven with an ugly smile on his face. 'Yer too late, my laird. They'll already be dead.'

* * *

Beyond the dull ache of Fiona's limbs coldness consumed her body, and she shivered against the damp, wet stone beneath her. She struggled to move in the darkness and her wrists chafed against the rope binding them against her waist. Her heart picked up speed and she tried to sit up but couldn't. Her whole body ached.

Where am I?

Where is William?

What has happened?

Cease, she commanded herself. *Breathe.*

Panic would do her little good. She took air in through her nose and out through her mouth over and over, until her heart slowed to a more natural rhythm. She focused her senses. Water dripped from behind her and a torch flickered down a darkened, shadowy corridor. A window beckoned ahead of her, near the torch, and she could see rain still cascading down outside in the darkness.

How had she ended up here—wherever here was?

She squeezed her eyes shut and focused on the sound of the rainfall. Anger and frustration roiled through her. No other noises echoed about her. It seemed she was alone. Alone without William. And in a dungeon, it seemed. There could be little other explanation.

But why had her father the Laird bothered to keep her alive at all? She knew that look of hate she'd seen his eyes before that brute of a soldier had punched her into unconsciousness. Her father wanted her dead.

A door above her strained open and then closed softly. Additional light streamed down the corridor from a small candle, but not enough to cast light on the face of the large warrior who held it and came towards her. Although she could see a glimpse of his plaid: MacDonald.

She gritted her teeth. Her own people held her prisoner.

'Sister?' a baritone voice whispered.

'Devlin?' Fiona asked, watching the man's approach, emotion coating her words.

Her younger brother had grown much since she'd last seen him. He no longer looked to be a young man, but a seasoned warrior. She struggled to gain purchase and move closer to the iron bars, like a fish stranded on the shore. She flopped once more and stilled as he bent down to the light cast upon his shadowed face. His auburn hair reached past his shoulders, and warrior ink donned his bare upper arms. Pain etched his furrowed brow and there were bruises and cuts along the corner of his left eye and lip.

'What has become of you?' she asked, worried over his wounds.

He smiled at her and wrapped his fingers around the bars. ''Tis I who should ask if *you* are well, sister. I am sorry...so sorry for all that has happened to you. I could not stop it then. And you almost lost your child because I could not protect you...' He choked upon the word.

'Nay, brother. There was nothing you could have done.' She reached her bound hands up to the bars to touch his. 'My son William—your nephew —he lives,' she whispered. 'He is strong, as handsome as you are. Look at you...' Her eyes filled with tears. 'But he was taken from me. Is he still here?'

'He is here, and he is safe for now. But I wish... I wish he was not here, Fi. I wish *you* were not here either. Father...he has lost all reason. And the new men—

these mercenaries he has hired—only feed his greed and lust for more power. He will bring us to ruin.'

Her brother's dark eyes narrowed in on her. She swallowed hard. The fear in his voice crawled through her and only amplified the cold consuming her limbs. She shivered and her teeth chattered.

He leaned closer. 'Why, after freeing yourself, would you dare venture back on to the very lands you fled from? Why, Fi? Those notes…those Campbell soldiers Father killed and left for Brandon to find…they should have warned you off, not brought you closer to us.'

A tremble edged into his voice, reminding her of the young scared boy of her youth.

'I was trying to continue on my escape to our cousin who lives with the MacNabs. Brandon is remarrying, and I didn't wish to remain there as anything other than his wife. It seems foolish now. We were cared for and safe under his protection, and I abandoned that out of my own pride and selfishness. Now William is in danger.' She rested her forehead against the cold iron bars. 'What is it Father wants from me and William? Why has he not killed us already?'

Devlin closed his eyes and leaned his forehead against her own through the bars. 'You are a part of his larger plan; so is William. A plan to end the Campbells once and for all.' He opened his eyes and squeezed her hands. 'I know not how to protect you, but I will do everything I can to try. I will not fail you again, sister. You've my word.'

'Free me,' she pleaded, straining against her bindings.

He shook his head. 'Nay. 'twould be a faulty plan. Even if I do, I know not how to help you escape alive.

There are soldiers posted everywhere, with orders to slay you upon sight outside of these castle walls. I only came to you now because Oric guards the door above.'

Oric. She smiled. The old soldier had known Fiona all her life and had helped her and her aunt to escape before wee William had been born.

A whistle echoed along the darkness.

Devlin started. 'That is Oric's signal. I will find a way to get you out. I promise, sister. I must go, but I will return with a plan.'

A glimmer of hope sparkled in his eyes, and Fiona prayed beyond measure that he would come up with a plan for her escape. Otherwise she was as good as dead, and so was William.

She must have dozed, for the next thing she knew the sound of a door opening stirred her to wakefulness. Sun streamed through the window before her and she blinked to focus on the looming figure approaching her, casting a large shadow in his wake.

She stiffened at the sight of him. Dread, rage, and fear coursed bright and hot through her, just as it always did.

'Father,' she said, unable to keep a tremble from her voice.

He nodded to a guard. The brute unlocked the cell and yanked her up from the ground. She stumbled and fell against the burly warrior, who was clutching her arm so tightly it made the blood throb within.

Laird Audric reached out and gently grasped her chin before turning her face towards him. A softness flickered in his grey eyes. 'You remind me so much of your mother.'

A small smile almost reached his lips before his hand fell away.

'We will wait.' He smirked at her. 'He will come, and then finally this shall be finished.'

'Who shall come?' she called out. 'Who?'

He laughed and left her struggling against the guard, who refused to release his hold on her.

But deep down she knew who would come. She knew she and William had only been kept alive to serve a greater purpose: to lure the Laird of Clan Campbell into a trap and bring their bitter clan rivalry to an abrupt and chaotic end.

And once Brandon was dead she would be as well.

As would their son.

Chapter Twenty-Five

'Brandon,' Hugh began in hushed tones beside him, resting a hand on his shoulder, 'what is our plan? We are but two men. There is no hope for us to storm a castle alone and have any chance of rescuing them alive.'

Brandon stopped at the edge of the forest, staring out at the glowing fortress of Glenhaven that tormented him in the distance. As usual, Hugh was right. They needed more men to breach the walls, to find his son and Fiona—if indeed the castle was where they were being held—and to escape alive.

It didn't matter how much Brandon needed to see and hold her and their son. To charge the castle now would be reckless and impulsive—which perhaps was what the MacDonalds were counting on—but it was not what Brandon would give them. He would do the very opposite of what they would expect.

'We're turning back.'

'What?' Hugh asked. 'Did you just say we're turning back?'

'Aye. I did.'

Until he could find out what the game was Brandon

would engage no more players. He'd been rash to rush out in pursuit of Fiona and William with only Hugh by his side. And if the MacDonalds had captured them for a reason, rather than murder Fiona and their son outright, then there must be a larger plan. And Brandon needed to find out what it was before he stepped further into MacDonald territory.

Taking one long, last look at Glenhaven, he prayed that he was making the right choice. If not, Fiona and his son were both dead.

Hours had passed since their return to Argyll Castle and they'd received no word from the MacDonalds.

Brandon paced the study, watching the sunrise and trying to guess what their game was.

Was it merely revenge for past deeds? Or did Laird Audric MacDonald hope to lure Brandon there and kill him in the hope of absorbing Clan Campbell within his own, as he had attempted over a year ago?

Brandon stilled, resting his hands on his weapons belt, and stared into the blazing fire. Rowan and Hugh were readying the men for an attack, but Brandon itched to be at Glenhaven already. The longer the MacDonalds held Fiona and William, the more danger they were in. He knew he'd taken a gamble by abandoning the plan to storm the castle and rescue Fiona and William when they'd first set out, but he had known the chances of success with only two men were slim, and he couldn't lose Fiona and their son.

Not now. Not ever.

How had he been such a fool?

A fool just like Father.

His gut twisted and he slammed his fist onto the desk.

Exactly as Fiona had warned.

He'd let her and William slip through his fingers by focusing on his duty as Laird. He'd been given everything he had ever wished and hoped for: love, a family and a future. Yet he'd been too scared to trust it, too scared to seize it, so he'd let it go. He'd lied to himself and decided that marrying another was his duty as Laird, that such an act would keep them all safe and well.

In truth, he had been protecting himself, and cowering behind his role and his duty to hide his fear of trusting Fiona once more and being hurt. He'd chosen half a life without Fiona, but he realised he wanted a whole one now. A life with Fiona and William and all the complications that would come from such a union, no matter what the elders or anyone else from the clan thought.

A knock sounded, and Brandon's heart raced as he rushed to the door of the study. He yanked it open and his shoulders drooped. The air rushed from his lungs. *Susanna Cameron.* Exactly what he didn't need right now: enquiries from his betrothed. He'd escaped conversation with her upon his return, but it seemed there was no escaping it now.

'May I have a word, my laird?' she asked in smooth velvety tones, her eyes sparkling with mischief. 'My men have apprised me of your…situation,' she added, 'and I believe we may be able to help one another.'

Something in the quirk of her smile pricked Brandon's interest as well as his hesitation. She clearly had a plan, but he'd no idea what it could possibly be.

Shrugging, he opened the door wider, gesturing for her to enter. Things couldn't be any worse, so why not entertain her ideas? 'Do come in. I'm surprised to see you still up. I thought you had retired long ago.'

He closed the door and watched her walk around the room. Only then did he notice that she still wore the exact gown she had the night before, which piqued his curiosity further.

'I don't sleep often, my laird, and with all the happenings since I've arrived I haven't even thought of it—much like you.'

She settled in a large chair before the hearth, where a fire flickered and glowed. She pulled her legs up beneath her, reminding him of a black cat Beatrice had once owned. The beast had bitten him on the finger.

'I'm sorry that your visit has been less than we had planned,' he said.

She waved a hand at him, as if to bat his apology away. 'Nay, that is of no concern to me. I believe we may benefit one another in an entirely different manner. One that will please both of us more than our previous arrangement, I suspect.'

She traced a thin fingertip along the arm of the chair and gestured for him to take the chair beside her. He hesitated, but then did so, not taking his eyes off her for a moment.

'You may not be aware, but the Camerons are a rather distrustful lot.'

Brandon leaned back, settling into the cushions as he listened. 'No more than most, I suspect.'

She chuckled. 'Do you also travel with fifty extra soldiers in secret?'

He balked, his nerves prickling in alarm. 'Nay... Are you telling me that there are fifty Cameron soldiers hidden within our walls?'

'Not *within* your castle walls, but within your borders. 'tis how we ensure our safety when we visit other clans—even those we call friends.'

He leaned forward, his irritation building. This was the last thing he needed this morn. 'Are you threatening me, my lady?'

'Nay. You misinterpret my meaning.' She smiled and her eyes flashed at him. 'I will offer them to you if needed...to help retrieve your son and his mother. I hear they have been taken by the MacDonalds.'

'For what in return, exactly?' He frowned, crossing his arms against his chest. No such offer would come without a condition, and he was afraid to hear what hers might be.

She fussed with the rumpled fabric of her gown for a moment and then released a breath. When she met his gaze again, a sad look hung heavy in her eyes. 'I know what is like to be disappointed in love. And I refuse to be a man's second choice for a wife.'

Brandon waited, uncertain as to what exactly she would be proposing.

'I wish for you to release me from this sham of an engagement—by your own fault, not mine, so I do not have to endure my father's wrath. That way we will be free to follow our own hearts, and my father will not see me as a disgrace to the clan. Only then will I promise you my men.'

Surely he'd misheard her? He shook his head and scrubbed his hands down his face. What he wanted and longed for—freedom from this engagement—was being offered to him. But he didn't trust it. It all seemed too easy.

'What is the catch, my lady? This seems too much in my benefit. What else do you require in return?'

She flashed a smile at him. 'You are perceptive, my laird. I shall require a favour. One to be granted upon my request, when I decide to use it, without any questions asked.'

'You want me to agree to grant you whatever you ask whenever you wish to claim it, having no idea what or how great a favour this might be?'

'Aye.' Susanna's lips pressed into a flat thin line. 'Those are my conditions.'

He held her gaze, knowing full well that this might be the greatest risk of his entire life, but also knowing he was willing to take it to save his son and the woman he loved.

'I believe we have an agreement, my lady.' Brandon stood. 'I shall draft a letter to be sent by messenger to your father this very morn.'

Smiling, she rose beside him. 'Wonderful. I had hoped we might come to such a mutually beneficial understanding.'

She whistled long and low. The door opened and two Cameron guards entered with Hugh beside them. They matched Hugh in size, as well as in their scowls. They looked irritated to be beckoned in the service of others, but perhaps Brandon could use their anger to his advantage.

'Lunn and Cynric, please do as Laird Brandon commands. He will have full use of our men and resources while we are here. As you know, his son has been taken. Do whatever needs to be done to ensure his safe return...along with the boy's mother.'

Susanna Cameron nodded to them and took her

leave. Brandon watched her disappear from the room, uncertain if he'd just made a deal with the devil or an angel.

'It has finally arrived, my laird,' said Hugh, appearing at the door of the study with Rowan in tow.

Brandon paused in his planning with Lunn and Cynric, stepping away from the large maps made of animal hide that they'd been studying for hours. They had a plan for the rescue—more than one, actually—so now that the letter from the MacDonalds had finally come they could do something.

'What do they demand?'

Rowan opened the note, and when he did so a wisp of hair fell from the parchment and drifted to the floor. The bright fiery strands were Fiona's, and Brandon recognised them instantly. The control he'd harnessed over the last few hours snapped, and he scooped the hair from the floor, clutching it tightly in his palm.

'Read it,' Brandon commanded.

Clearing his throat, Rowan read it aloud. *'"Laird of Campbell, if you wish to see your son and Fiona alive, you will come to Glenhaven before nightfall. Alone. Laird Audric MacDonald."'*

Lunn spoke, walking from the table to stare out of the window. 'Ye can't go alone, Laird Brandon.' He rested his hands on his waist belt. 'Ye will be cut down immediately. Ye need to counter his terms.'

Brandon balked, rubbing his neck. 'Counter? Have you lost all reason? The MacDonalds don't *counter*. Fiona and William would be as good as dead.'

'I agree,' Hugh weighed in. 'And there is no proof they are even still alive.'

'But such a gamble…' Brandon muttered.

'We have had our own issues with the MacDonalds,' Cynric offered. 'They can never be trusted; they cheat to win every time.'

Rowan nodded. 'He speaks the truth, brother. We all know it. If we don't think as ruthlessly as they, we don't stand a chance—even with the help of the Camerons this day.'

Part of Brandon knew that if it hadn't been his son and Fiona at stake he would have agreed with all they said. But it *was* his son. It *was* Fiona. He couldn't think with the cold, calculating mind of a soldier. He could only think like a father and like a man in love—a man in danger of losing his soul mate, the woman he'd loved and still loved more than any other, and the son they shared together.

Which is exactly what the bastard is counting on.

Brandon rolled his eyes and sighed. He'd almost fallen straight into the trap. 'You're right. I must be a laird and a soldier now, not a father. He wants me emotionally compromised, needs me to be distracted, but I won't be. Tell me your thoughts, men, I'm listening.'

'We counter and demand that they bring them here,' Lunn said quickly.

'Then he will refuse, and we will meet on neutral ground at the border,' Hugh added.

'The border has challenges, my laird. There are few places to hide ourselves other than the edge of the forest.' Cynric pointed to the map, adding pebbles to the areas where they might place their men. 'But they would have to hide their own men even further back, under the copse of trees on their land. If there came a full-out charge of men, ours would be first to the border.'

'Or...' Brandon smiled, his gut full of hope '...we send them nothing and breach their walls. Rescue Fiona and my son within Glenhaven before any additional terms or counters are even agreed to.'

'Now you're thinking like a MacDonald, brother,' Rowan clapped him on the back. 'A surprise such as that would be bloody perfect.'

The other men in the room agreed.

'We'll get our men ready and be prepared to leave before dusk. We'll give them time to wonder if we have received their note and if we will agree to their terms at all.'

Chapter Twenty-Six

Men lacked imagination in spades. Hour after hour had ticked by and Fiona remained imprisoned, waiting for something—anything—to happen. She'd counted the cobwebs and tried to wrestle free dozens of times, without success. Her ropes were bound far too tightly. She'd even learned the rotation schedule of the guards, which she knew would be helpful later to aid her escape.

And she *would* escape. She would not be dying in Glenhaven Castle—at least not without a fight.

Distraction alone would help her survive the present. To imagine anything other than a successful escape with her son would surely drive her to the brink of insanity, and she needed all her wits about her to improve her situation. Midday was fast approaching, based on the position of the sun, so she settled in against the damp walls about her and studied her surroundings. She needed to see what weapons were at hand, what diversions she could utilise, and what advantages she might be able to create for herself. She wished to be ready for escape when the moment came.

William, William, sweet boy, I miss you.

It was her prayer every moment in between her thoughts of escape. As if on cue, she heard a cry. *His* cry. She sprang up and pressed herself tightly to the bars, straining to hear. He was hungry, which caused her a slight tremble of relief. Not only was he alive, but he was about to deafen them with squalls for milk if he wasn't fed soon.

She couldn't be prouder of her strong son. He had survived so much, and he would survive this. So would she.

Minutes later she heard the squeak and strain of the dungeon door opening above, and heavy footfalls coming towards her cell. Soon Oric, once her most trusted guard and a soldier who had always been kind to her, appeared with William in his arms.

He gifted her a gruff smile from amidst his grey beard. 'The babe is hungry, miss. I was bade bring him to ye.'

Greedily, Fiona ran her palms down her dirty gown, eager to hold, smell and kiss her son. When Oric opened the cell door and handed the babe to her tears of relief fell down Fiona's cheeks. She checked over every inch of him quickly, happy to see no physical harm had befallen him. He was well, he was alive, and she would keep him that way.

Oric turned away as Fiona opened her bodice so that William could feed. Then she covered herself with the plaid wrapped around her son. The sight of the Mac-Donald plaid surprised her. She hadn't thought her father would allow them to swaddle her son in his plaid. He had hated her son long before he'd even been born because he had Campbell blood running through his veins.

'Thank you for bringing me my son, Oric.'

The old warrior faced her, and his features softened at the sight of her with her son. His long grey hair glistened in the light and he smiled at them both. 'Yer mother would have rejoiced to see ye this way,' he said, his words simmering with emotion and something that looked strangely like regret.

'Do you believe so?' She looked down at the dewy blue eyes of her boy and wondered if what Oric said could possibly be true. 'She abandoned me and Devlin, Oric. Left us with just a note of goodbye. She didn't love us enough to stay, or to try to protect us from our father. Why would she care a whit about my happiness or that of my child now?'

Fiona didn't bother to disguise the edge of bitterness in her voice. Such words fell from her lips easily. Her mother's leaving had always made her feel this way: equal parts anger, sadness and shame.

Oric had always been a friend to her, even as a wee girl trying to understand the ways of the Highlands and her part as the daughter of a laird. He'd been assigned to protect her for as long as she could remember.

Now he hesitated and studied his palms. 'Although I don't know for certain, I believe she did it to protect ye.'

'She left to protect me?' she asked, confused by his words. How had her distance offered her protection—especially under the care of Laird Audric MacDonald? She didn't understand.

The door squeaked above and Oric froze. 'I will return for the boy.'

He turned to leave her.

Fiona furrowed her brow. 'Protect me? Protect me from what, Oric?' she whispered after him.

Oric didn't answer and disappeared around the corner.

The uneven footfalls she heard warned her of her father's approach. She stepped far back into the confines of her cell, so he wouldn't be able to reach them with the horrid cane he used. The one she had learned early to fear and always to keep watch on. She had never known when Audric's temper would flare.

'How fares my daughter and her wee bastard of a boy?'

Her father's angry grey eyes flashed at her. Fiona held his gaze but didn't answer.

'Seems the father of your boy holds little regard for either of you. He does not respond to our request to meet. Perhaps he doesn't wish to bother to claim you after all. And if that is the case I must find other uses for you.'

She glared at him.

'You have until nightfall for him to claim you both. Until then, daughter.'

Nightfall came far too quickly, and Fiona worried at her lip. Only Oric had visited her, to retrieve William after he had eaten, and the old soldier had said not a word to her.

Where was Brandon? He wouldn't abandon her—not after all the trouble he'd taken to keep her when he'd still hated her. Not after all that had come to pass between them the last few days. Fiona knew he loved her, even if he was bound by duty to wed Susanna Cameron. He was too good a man to leave her and their son here to rot or be misused. And once he rescued her and William she'd not take his protection for granted as she had before.

She had been a selfish fool to throw away the life Brandon had offered her and her son. She would set up home quietly in a cottage in the village with William and allow her boy to be a part of the clan he belonged to. A clan that would love and cherish him in a way that she never had been. Her boy deserved such a life. He deserved to live and one day be Laird like his father.

The dungeon door squeaked open and relief threaded through Fiona. She clutched the iron bars, straining her ears to listen. Two sets of footsteps headed her way, and a twinge of worry scurried along her spine. As the men turned the corner, Fiona released the bars and put on her best warrior's mask. It was the two brutes from the forest. The mercenaries who'd captured her and brought her back to this horrid place.

'The Laird requires a word,' the tallest one said, his cold dark eyes trained on her while the other man held a length of rope.

'I'd rather not,' she answered.

He frowned. 'It isn't a request. It's an order. Ye will come with us even if it 'tis by force.'

She studied them, gauging how quick and impulsive they might be. These men seemed prone to violence, from what she'd witnessed so far, and she needed to stay alive as long as possible for her son.

She walked forward, waited for them to open the cell door, and then held her wrists out. Being secured at the front would allow her to run. If she looked weak and complicit, she might have a chance to fool them all and escape.

The smaller of the two men bound her wrists, gripped the rope hard—and tugged. She fell to her knees and elbows, unable to break her fall after the unexpected pull.

'That's for making us ask twice. Now, get up.'

Blowing the loose strands of hair from her face, she looked up at them and glared.

Bastards.

She moved between the two of them to the main level, and there a table, two chairs and a circle of guards awaited her.

Brandon was nowhere to be seen. Nor was her son. Her heart clamoured in her chest. *Where were they?*

Her father nodded, and the smaller soldier shoved her into one of the wooden chairs. She grappled with the back of it to keep from toppling to the floor. Sitting upright, she met her father's measured gaze.

'You need to speak with me, Father?' She smirked. 'I find these restraints a bit unnecessary, since I am surrounded by your men.' She lifted her bound wrists in the air.

Her father walked over to her and stared at her for a long minute—before slapping her face with such force that she flew from the chair to the floor, landing hard. Stunned, she wiped the blood from her lip and panted.

'Get up!' he shouted, pacing before her.

Rage flooded her veins. 'Why? So you may slap me to the ground again?'

He stopped pacing, walked to her, and grabbed her by the hair. 'I. Said. Get. Up.'

She winced and struggled to her feet with effort. She made her way to the chair and spat blood on the ground near her father's feet. She no longer cared if she lived, but her son—he *would* live. She had to find out where he was and distract her father for long enough to keep her boy alive until Brandon came. After that, she'd kill her father herself if she had to.

Scanning the room, she realised her brother wasn't there. 'Where is Devlin?'

'Ah, you wish to speak with your weak, useless brother? We can arrange that. Bring him in.'

The soldier who'd pulled her to the ground earlier nodded, left, and returned with Devlin leaning heavily upon his shoulder. Her brother had been beaten—badly. One of his eyes was swollen shut, and he dragged one of his legs behind him, struggling to remain upright.

'Brother!' she cried in alarm, moving from the chair on instinct.

A soldier punched her in the stomach and she crumpled to the ground. He'd knocked the air right out of her, and as she lay gasping for breath she heard Devlin cry out to her. Then she heard a scuffle, and he landed on the floor beside her, passing out.

Weaving her fingers through his mussed red hair, she whispered into his ear. 'They will come, Devlin. Stay alive for me. I love you, brother.'

A soldier grabbed her by the waist and yanked her up to stand. He held her tight, with her arms pressed flush against her body.

'You will tell me the answers to all the questions I ask, daughter. Or you will die. Slowly, I might add.'

'I care not what you do to me,' she bit out, her voice shaking in anger.

'That is what I thought. Bring him!' he called.

A maid carried William into the room.

Fiona's wide, fear-filled eyes glistened with unshed tears. 'You will not touch my son! Even you would not harm a babe...'

But even as Fiona spoke the words she knew they weren't true. Her father had tried to kill her and William before. Why wouldn't he try once more?

He laughed. 'You and I both know that isn't true.'

'But why, Father? Why is it you have always hated me? And why do you hate my son? He is an innocent. He has done nothing to you. Nothing!' Tears welled traitorously in her eyes.

''Tis because of me, miss.' Oric appeared from behind the soldiers.

She gasped at the sight of him. 'What have they done to you, Oric?'

Knife-cuts marred his face and arms, and a large wound bled on his leg.

None of this made sense. Oric had always been their friend, loyal to her and Devlin…and their mother. *Unfailingly* loyal to their mother.

Fiona sucked in a breath as she pieced it together.

'Because,' Oric whispered, his voice hoarse and raspy with emotion, 'ye are my daughter.'

'Your daughter?' Fiona murmured.

'Aye,' he answered. 'It is a relief to me that ye finally know. I have loved ye all this while as such.'

She thought back to memories of her childhood. Oric had been the one to teach her to shoot. He'd dried her tears when she'd fought with her father, and he'd given her advice on how to make her mother smile. He had been her true father all along.

The seed of anger that had always been in her belly over being rejected and hated by her father disappeared. Her true father hadn't hated her. He'd loved her with every fibre of his being in the only way he could. She realised now that Oric's soft green eyes were like mirrors of her own, and the knowledge wove an unexpected peace and calm through her own soul.

'And you have known all along?' Fiona asked the Laird of Clan MacDonald—the man she'd always thought was her father.

'Aye.' He spat in her face and the spittle ran down her cheek. 'I always knew you were not mine—that you were Oric's bastard.'

Finally she realised that *she* had done nothing wrong. All those failed attempts to earn and win her father's love hadn't been her fault. He had hated her from the beginning because she was the product of her mother's love for another man.

And now all Oric's efforts to protect her made sense. He'd risked his life to help her and her Aunt Seana to escape that fateful night because she was his daughter and William his grandson.

'Why did you allow him to stay? He is one of your most trusted guards,' Fiona asked.

Audric sneered and approached her. 'Because I wanted him to know that you and your mother would never be his. That you would only stay alive because *I* allowed it.'

He gripped her chin and wrenched it hard, so his eyes were only inches from her own. Hate resonated through his hold.

'But I don't feel that will be necessary any longer. Just as I didn't with your mother.'

Fiona froze and ice settled in her veins. For a moment she couldn't even speak. Then, 'Mother? You told me she left us...abandoned us.'

Audric released his hold and smiled at her. 'That is

what I told you, but she resides where she should have always been.'

Fiona thrashed against the soldier holding her back. 'What? You will explain yourself!' she seethed. Emotion pounded through her body and tears threatened. 'Where is she? *Where?*' She screamed the words and struggled.

'She is at the bottom of the bog, where I left her. She threatened to leave me and take you and your brother. To be with *him*. No one leaves me unless *I* allow it.'

Oric stared at her and then at her father. His eyes were desperate. He wrestled against the soldiers who held him back. 'Bastard!' he growled.

A pit of emptiness opened in Fiona, and she gasped, struggling for breath. Her mother had never abandoned her, as she'd thought. She'd loved her. She had tried to leave and give them a better life, but her father—nay, not her father, *Laird Audric*, had murdered her.

She screamed aloud in anger. 'I will kill you!'

Audric laughed. 'Nay. It is I who shall kill you— and your son.'

'My laird, leave her be. I beg ye,' Oric pleaded, pulling free from one of the guards before being punched hard in the face.

'Or what?' Audric answered.

'Or I'll kill you where you stand,' Brandon answered in smooth, dark tones from behind her.

Fiona felt weak in the knees at the sound of his voice—Brandon's voice. She turned, unsure if it was real or an imagining. Brandon and his men emerged from the back staircase of the castle almost as if they were ethereal creatures, melting through the stone walls. The sight of them stole her breath and relief flooded her body. He'd come, just as she'd known he would. William would be safe now and nothing else mattered.

She met his gaze. Together they would rescue their son and escape the mess she'd put them in.

'So you received my note after all, Campbell,' Audric said, then licked his lips and scanned the room.

The battle would be evenly matched with MacDonald and Campbell soldiers. They eyed one another.

Eager to get on with it, Fiona kicked her guard away, sending him staggering back to the floor. A brawl broke out between the soldiers and more poured in from the back entrance and up from the dungeon. Was that Cameron plaid she spied? Surely not.

She shook her head, confused. How they'd got in past the guards she didn't know, and nor did she care. All she wanted to do now was find her son and get him away from the danger of the battle that was brewing. She crawled along the floor, slithering like a snake to the opposite side of the room, where she'd last seen the maid holding her son. But she was gone. So was William. The woman must have fled when she saw the commotion.

William's high-pitched cries pricked Fiona's ears. Closing her eyes, she concentrated on the noise, trying to isolate it from the sounds of duelling metal, the shouts of soldiers and the groans of the wounded. She froze and frowned. It sounded as if William was above her. But how?

Rolling to her back, she stared up and spied the maid, climbing up the winding stone staircase that led to the Laird's bedchamber. Panic bubbled in her gut and she regained her footing. Running to the stairs, she felt a dagger hit her in the shoulder. The force of it knocked her down momentarily, but she climbed back up to stand and made her way to the stairs without further injury.

'Fi!' Brandon called from across the room, concern rippling in his voice.

'I'm fine,' she called. 'I must find our son.'

She wasn't sure he even heard her over the noise, but she continued on, despite the blood seeping from her wound. She loosened the knots of the ropes still on her wrists and let them fall away, taking the stairs two at a time. She left the dagger in her shoulder, knowing that to remove it would only cause greater blood loss as she continued up.

At the top of the staircase she panted for breath and leaned heavily against the railing. The maid stood in the Laird's chambers, near the large eastern-facing window, with her back to Fiona.

'If you give me my son I won't hurt you. I swear it,' Fiona stated, weaving her way into the room, trying to get her bearings as a wave a dizziness consumed her. She steadied herself against the back of a large chair near the left side of the room.

'I can't do that, miss,' the woman sobbed. 'The Laird will kill me if I do.'

'But I will kill you if you don't. I am his mother. You *will* return him to me,' Fiona demanded.

She gripped the woman's forearm, forcing her to face her. She gasped when she saw the woman held only a pillow nestled in plaid in her arms.

Fiona shook the woman, using all the remaining strength she possessed. 'Where is he? I heard his cries. I know you brought him up here.'

'Nay…' the woman answered, her voice trembling as her eyes darted about the room.

Just then William cried out again, from behind her. Fiona turned, staggering to the other side of the chamber. His cries came from a wardrobe. Opening it, she saw him there.

She clutched him to her chest. 'William, my boy,' she murmured, savouring the sweet smell and feel of him against her body.

'Ye will both die, then!' the woman cried.

Fiona turned in time to see the woman charging her with a blade in her hand. Before she reached Fiona a dagger hit the maid square in the chest and she collapsed to her knees before falling to the ground, her weapon clattering out of her hand onto the floor.

Fiona sucked in a breath and saw Brandon standing in the doorway, panting for breath. He rushed to her and William and crushed both of them in his arms, pressing kisses to her head as well as William's.

'I feared I'd lost you both,' he murmured, his voice husky with emotion. 'And here you are. Alive. Well.'

Fiona savoured the warmth and the strength of him, clinging to his tunic. But she couldn't keep her eyes open, and her body grew numb.

'Take him,' she murmured, trying to focus on Brandon, but the planes of his face had turned fuzzy and grey and she drifted away into darkness.

Chapter Twenty-Seven

'Fi? *Fi?*' Brandon shouted at her, trying to shake her back to wakefulness, but he couldn't. She lay lifeless in his arms, her head lolling to the side like a rag doll, a dagger wedged neatly in her shoulder.

Christ.

Blood stained the front of her gown and the plaid that was wrapped about their son. The son who stared up at him with such love and certainty.

'Don't worry. I'll keep your mother alive.'

He pressed a kiss to William and settled him in Fiona's lap as he ripped strips off his plaid and tucked them into her wound, trying to stop or at least slow the bleeding until he could get her back to the castle.

Footfalls sounded on the stairs and Brandon quickly tucked William back into the wardrobe, nudging Fiona behind him. Pulling his remaining dagger from its sheath, Brandon prepared to slaughter the next warrior to cross the threshold.

When his brother skidded into the room, Brandon relaxed and sighed in relief. 'I thought I told you all to stay downstairs,' he said.

'When you didn't return, I wanted to make sure—' Rowan ceased speaking as he took in the sight of Fiona, crumpled on the floor behind Brandon. Worry furrowed his brow.

'She is wounded, but William is fine. I must get her back to the castle, and quickly. She's lost a great deal of blood.'

'And Audric? He has escaped. Shall I go after him?' Eagerness echoed in Rowan's words, and his eyes were fixed with anticipation.

Brandon knew that going after Laird Audric was what his brother wished to do more than anything else in the world. To avenge his wife and son's death by killing the bastard himself. But... 'I need you for a more important purpose, brother.'

'What is that?'

'I need you to protect my son. Please. I cannot get him and Fiona to safety alone. I know what I ask of you.' Brandon gazed upon his brother, unsure of how he would answer.

Rowan's features softened. 'I will protect him with my life. He is my nephew, my blood. Audric can wait for another day.'

'Thank you,' Brandon said, startled by his brother's compassion and willingness to help him, despite all that had passed between them.

He gathered William from his hiding place in the wardrobe and handed his son over to his brother carefully.

Rowan secured the boy closely to his body by wrapping him in his plaid. 'I will not fail you.'

'I know that,' Brandon answered, grateful for his brother's help. 'Thank you.'

Rowan disappeared down the staircase, and Brandon prayed that he would be successful in escaping Glenhaven with Fiona.

He scanned the room, looking for additional weapons and ways of escape. He yanked the dagger from the dead woman's chest and tucked it back into his waist belt. At the open window of the chamber, he spied a length of rope, anchored into a cut notch in the stone floor. It led outside. Was that how the woman had planned to flee with William? He hurried over to the window and stared down. The thick rope reached almost to the ground, with knots spaced along the way to ease descent.

Brandon shook his head, pleased and startled by his own good fortune. Audric always had been a sneaky bastard, but this time Brandon and Fiona would benefit from the means of escape that he had provided.

Soldiers still battled below, so the rope seemed the best option for a timely escape. Racing through the sea of men still at arms in the Great Hall below would be a far riskier strategy, especially with Fiona unconscious, and he couldn't wait. Time was something he didn't have.

Fiona's pale, still body sent alarm through him. He hurried over to her, draping her beneath his plaid, attempting to disguise and protect her at the same time. Lifting a decorative wooden MacDonald-crested shield from the wall, he held it in front of them in an attempt to block any arrows or blades thrown their way upon their descent. Then he grabbed the rope that hung from the large chamber window and tied it around her waist and his own.

He could only hope Fiona wouldn't wake as he eased

them down the rope, as it would upset the delicate balance required to hold her, the rope, and the wooden shield. Easing out of the window, he moved as quietly as he could, his arms burning from the exertion of their controlled descent. The longer he could go unnoticed as the soldiers battled each other below, the better.

He slid down the sections of rope in between each knot in an attempt to aid their speed without much noise. They were halfway down the side of the castle wall before one of the MacDonalds spied them.

'The Laird escapes!' the MacDonald soldier shouted, before the Cameron battling him silenced him with a dagger.

'Bollocks,' Brandon grumbled, shifting the shield to cover them as he slid down to the next knot.

An arrow hissed by his ear. He slid down again, noting they were not far from the ground.

'Hold fast, Fi,' he murmured, clutching her tighter.

A dagger pierced the wooden shield protecting them, narrowly missing Brandon's shoulder, while another arrow hit its mark on his thigh, eliciting from him a groan and a slip in his hold as he slid down the rope. One more slide and they hit the ground, though harder than he would have liked. He grunted from the impact to his wounded leg.

He dared a glance around the shield, and was pleased to see only two MacDonald soldiers remained standing. The Camerons were holding their own, and Brandon was grateful to have had their aid.

Lunn finished off the MacDonald he battled and shouted over to him. 'A horse awaits ye, my laird. Once ye reach it, we will pull back.'

'Aye,' Brandon replied and dropped the rope, untying it from their waists with speed.

He had only a short distance to travel to reach the mounts they had brought and hidden along the edge of the forest for this very reason. Unfortunately, the distance between the castle and forest was all open field, making him and Fiona easy marks for any enemies who saw them, but he had no time to waste. He could only hope Rowan had already reached the protection of the trees with his son and begun the ride back to Argyll Castle. That way all Brandon would have to worry about was managing to carry Fiona.

Just then Brandon spied Rowan, sprinting across the field. *Bollocks.* His brother hadn't made it to the mounts yet. His son was still in danger. Two soldiers ran haphazardly alongside Rowan, trying to draw away arrows or daggers. One of them was Hugh, while the other wore the MacDonald plaid.

Brandon squinted in confusion. Was that Fiona's brother Devlin? Nay, he was too old...

Fearing it was a trick, Brandon hurried along into the open field, trying to yell a warning to Rowan and Hugh. As he did so the MacDonald soldier leaned in closer to Rowan, absorbing an arrow to his shoulder before it could hit his brother. The MacDonald stumbled to the ground. Then he crawled back up and continued running behind Brandon's brother, attempting to aid his escape.

He didn't know who the man was, but he was grateful. The stranger had just saved his son and his brother's lives.

Rowan made it into the cover of the evergreens and Brandon sighed in relief. His son was safe.

But he and Fiona weren't.

A band of MacDonald soldiers now gave chase, falling in behind Brandon as he ran. Pushing through the pain of the arrow still in his thigh, and the added effort of carrying Fiona, Brandon groaned. But no pain was too great to save her and he'd not give up. He'd take a thousand more arrows if it meant she and William would live. Nothing else mattered.

A battle ensued behind him, and he saw Lunn in a rolling struggle with a MacDonald. Two more enemy soldiers were closing in on them, and without aid Lunn would surely die. Brandon paused and threw his remaining dagger into the man who had his new-found friend in a choke-hold. The bastard gasped and flopped back on the ground, dead.

Lunn scrambled quickly to his feet, pulled two arrows from the quiver on his back and sent them in rapid succession into the approaching MacDonald soldiers. The men were hit square in the chest and fell to the ground like fallen trees.

'Go!' Lunn shouted at Brandon. 'I'll hold off any more that come this way.'

Brandon nodded and carried on with Fiona, reaching the cover of the forest without further incident. He dropped to his knees when he saw Hugh preparing the second mount.

'Rowan?' Brandon panted, clenching his jaw through the pain searing up his leg.

'On his way. I've sent men to run along ahead of them for some added protection.'

'Thank God,' Brandon murmured.

A flash of MacDonald plaid caught the corner of

his gaze, and he pulled a dagger from his belt while shielding Fiona.

The old soldier lifted his arms, one of which had an arrow protruding from it. 'I mean ye no harm, my laird,' he said, grimacing.

Hugh intervened. 'Don't be alarmed. This is Oric. He aided our escape.'

Brandon wouldn't sheath his blade just yet. 'He is a MacDonald. Is this some trickery? Why did he help you? Why is he helping us?'

The man put his hands down, gazing at Fiona. Her still, pale form was exposed in the loosened tartan still tied about Brandon like a sling. The softness in his eyes was unmistakable.

'She is my daughter. I would do anything for her and her son.'

Daughter?

Brandon couldn't believe he'd heard the words correctly.

Hugh continued readying the mount, glancing back to Glenhaven. 'All will be explained, but you must go. *Now!* More of them are coming.'

Urgency laced his words, slicing through Brandon's fatigue and confusion. He staggered to stand, still struggling from the shock of the man's words.

Oric came to assist Brandon as he struggled to walk and mount his horse with his wounded leg. As soon as he had Fiona secured carefully against him he pulled on the reins, sending the horse into a gallop deep within the darkened forest.

Water hit them as his body slapped at the branches still wet after the storm, and the heady musty air clung to his lungs. He brought his body low, to avoid as many hanging branches as he could and to protect Fi from any further injury. Her body jostled against him with every turn, and he wondered if he was running out of time to save her.

Digging his heels into his mount, Brandon spurred the horse on faster, despite the slick forest floor beneath them. Soon they emerged from the dense brush unscathed and he could see Argyll Castle off in the distance.

'Hang on, Fi, we're almost home. Please stay with me.' His words sounded as desperate as he felt.

Rowan wasn't far ahead. He could see his brother at the far hill, preparing to pass the barn and head to the safety of the castle. His son was almost safe within the stone walls of their home and Brandon's heart filled with gratitude.

He'd achieved one miracle: his son was safe and alive.

Now he needed but one more: he needed Fiona to live.

Chapter Twenty-Eight

Three days had passed since the successful rescue of Fiona and William from Glenhaven and their return to Argyll Castle. While William was safe and well, Fi would not wake, despite all that Miss Emma, Beatrice, and Brandon had done. They had talked to her, sung to her, and recounted stories to rouse her. All to no avail.

Fiona hadn't woken since she'd passed out in that Glenhaven tower with a dagger in her shoulder. She'd lost a great deal of blood, and Brandon worried that she would never wake again.

Susanna Cameron and her men had long gone, their aid a blessing he wouldn't soon forget. Without their assistance he and his men wouldn't have been able to storm Glenhaven and retrieve Fiona and his son in the first place.

Despite Miss Emma's cleaning and stitching of the wound, and several draughts of a healing tonic, Fiona lay listless and still. Brandon wished to shake her, to bring her back, but knew he couldn't. And now that he knew beyond a doubt what he should have done, as a man and as a laird, he feared it might be too late to make things right.

While he knew Fiona had lied to him, kept the jewels she'd found a secret, and fled with William, had he truly given her any reason not to plan such an escape? Not really. He'd promised he'd care for her and William after he married Susanna Cameron, but had he actually thought about how that would have played out?

He hadn't given her any assurances as to her safety. And could he, if roles had been reversed, have borne watching her build a life with another man while living within the same roof?

Nay, he couldn't have. He understood all her choices now, as well as his own failings. He wanted to put things right for he loved her, needed her, and he longed to tell her so. But she'd have to wake in order for him to do that. And of course Fiona wouldn't co-operate on that front.

'Stubborn as always,' he muttered, squeezing her warm, limp hand in his own.

Her chest rose only a whisper with each breath, and once more he fought the urge to shake her into wakefulness. An angry, spitting mad Fi he could accept and manage, but this pale, vulnerable creature who had lain in bed for days without any signs of life or improvement… He sucked in an uneven breath. The sight of her like this unnerved him more than he could say.

'Any change?' Oric asked, standing in the doorway of Brandon's chamber, where Fiona lay unconscious.

Brandon had posted himself by her bed in a chair like a sentry for the last three days. Oric had been just as persistent. He'd come by several times every day in the hope of seeing her awake.

'Nay…' Brandon answered with a sigh.

'Ye know, she's always been too scared to depend on anyone too much. Her family made her that way. Cruel man, Laird Audric was—but ye know such. And now that we know her mother did not leave, but was murdered by his hand… I know the loss cuts deeply. All that time she believed, as I did, that her mother had left us.'

Oric entered the room, still limping after the battle of three days ago. A battle that seemed to Brandon to have happened at some other time to some other man.

'Aye.' Brandon chuckled. 'But she has a softness to her under all those rough edges.' He rubbed her hand between his own.

'Aye. She does. Always has—ever since she was a wee girl.' Oric smiled, his features glowing as he spoke of his daughter.

The old soldier loved Fiona. Brandon could see it in his face and hear it in the warmth of his voice.

Oric leaned against the edge of the bed and pressed an aging hand to Fiona's foot. 'She did trust ye, though, depend on ye,' he continued. 'The way her face would brighten when she spoke of ye and the life she had planned for ye both… That was why she was so broken after Audric's betrayal and his attack on Argyll Castle, and yer separation before wee William was born. Ye taught her that she could lean on someone. And then…' he shrugged '…she thought ye had abandoned her like her mother had. But it was Audric. He told me he ordered Eloise to burn all of her letters to ye. They never left the castle walls. It's why ye never received them. If I'd known, I would have brought them to ye myself. Instead I also believed ye had abandoned her.'

His shoulders sagged and Brandon could hear the

regret in the man's voice. He felt it matched his own. 'You are right, Oric. I didn't know of the babe, but it shouldn't have mattered. I knew what Audric was like and what he was capable of. I should not have given up on her so easily. But I was reluctant to believe I could depend on her…on anyone. I too find it hard to trust fully.'

'It's never too late, ye know, to begin anew. It has been decades, but I finally have my daughter, and now she knows and understands that all the mistreatment she suffered in the past was never her fault. Never. It's not too late for the two of ye to find your way back to one another. And ye have that beautiful boy to guide ye.' He smiled over at William's crib, where the bairn slept soundly.

'Aye, Oric. Let us hope we have the chance that you speak of. And I know I've said it before, but thank you. If not for your help William and my brother would not have escaped alive. I owe you a great debt.'

'I owe ye for allowing me to live with my daughter and my grandson—something I never imagined possible. Consider such a debt repaid in full, my laird.'

Brandon smiled. 'Aye.'

Oric nodded and stepped out of the room.

Brandon rested his forehead upon the smooth, soft flesh of Fiona's forearm. He had been an utter fool. And now he had no idea how to fix what had happened. He couldn't control her healing even though he longed to.

For the first time in a long time he prayed to a power greater than himself for help. He let go of control.

'Fi,' he whispered, 'Please, *please* wake.'

'There's no need to beg it of me,' she answered weakly, moving her hand within his own.

Brandon's head lifted. Had he just imagined her words? When he met her foggy gaze, joy consumed him. Her smirk made him laugh. 'Have you been awake this whole time?' he asked.

She shifted her head slightly. 'Only for the good parts…such as learning that Eloise burned my letters to you, hearing you thank Oric—my real father—for his help, and knowing that you have offered him asylum here. I am grateful for your kindness to him. He risked a great deal to help me, and to help us escape.'

'Aye, he did. I am thankful to him and so grateful that you live. You gave all of us a scare.' Brandon chuckled, pressing a kiss to her forehead, then brushing back the small fine auburn wisps of hair from her face.

'Even Rowan?' she asked.

'Aye, even him.'

'Bloody hell, it must have been serious, then.'

He sobered quickly. 'It was. But now that you are awake…' He paused, eager to tell her all the many things he'd wanted to say over the last few days. The words pressed eagerly to his lips, begging for release.

'William?' she asked suddenly, looking past him to their son's crib in alarm.

'He sleeps. He is well. He has missed you.'

As I have missed you.

She smiled with relief, and slipped her hand out of his hold. She struggled to sit up and winced from the effort. He added a pillow behind her, and she sank back into it with a sigh.

'And Devlin?' she asked, alarm crinkling her features. 'Is he alive? Did Audric kill him?'

'Nay. He is also here, alive and on the mend. He has come every day to see you and to visit his nephew.'

Her brow relaxed and she nodded. 'Thank you for your kindness to him. He has been much abused.'

'Aye. He also aided Oric in our escape. I could not ignore such heroics, could I? But, Fi—' he began, eager to tell her how much he loved her and admit all the mistakes he had made. To tell her how he wanted the future between them to be different, how he'd been a fool, but she interrupted him again.

'I'm sorry,' she blurted, her eyes serious and fixed upon his chest.

'Fi, you do not—' he said, but she shushed him.

'Let me say this. Please,' she insisted, taking a deep breath and meeting his gaze. 'I want you to know that I will give you no further trouble. I will live in the village with William, as you asked. I appreciate and understand now what you offered us, and I was a fool to cast it aside because of my pride. William deserves to be raised here by you and those who love him. I want him to have that. Something I never had.'

What?

'I don't think you understand, Fi…' He shook his head at her.

'And the jewels,' she continued breathlessly. 'I should have told you about them the moment I found them. I'm sorry I lied to you…again.'

'Fi, I know, and—'

'Please let me say this before I lose my nerve.' She squeezed his hand, which silenced him. 'I kept one of the jewels, which I shouldn't have. I just wanted one thing of yours to give our son when he was older. It was an emerald.'

She dropped her gaze, perhaps fearing his rebuke.

'Aye. Miss Emma found it when she was tending to you. I know of it, and I understand.'

'And you are not angry with me?' She risked a glance at him.

'Nay.' He sighed. 'As I keep trying to tell you, I am happy that you are alive and that William is alive. Nothing else—'

A knock sounded and Brandon turned at the interruption.

Hugh entered the room. He smiled at Fiona. 'I'm pleased to see you awake. The elders are here, as you requested, my laird. They await you in the study.'

Even though it wasn't the best timing, Brandon wanted and needed to get this over with. The sooner he was clear about his path moving forward, the sooner he could begin his new life with his family: with Fiona and their son.

When Brandon left the chamber and closed the door behind him Fiona fought the urge to burst into tears. She knew she'd done the right thing in letting Brandon go and agreeing to raise William here, with a village full of people who would come to love and adore him, even if they never learned to care for or love her.

It had taken all the strength she had left to let their love and Brandon go. She still had no idea how she would manage not to die of heartache at the sight of him with Susanna Cameron as laird and lady of the clan, but she would learn how to deal with it one day at a time. If her father, Oric, had endured living in the castle and loving her and her mother from afar for years in silence, before Audric had had her mother killed, then Fiona could manage a life here in the clan that would provide her and William comfort, safety and, if she managed it right, eventually their acceptance.

It was something she'd never had as a child. At least now she knew why. But William would not endure such a fate. She had apologised to Brandon and agreed to his terms before she had lost the nerve to do so. As it was, she'd barely managed it. Brandon's handsome face and his kindness had almost made her wish for more again.

Hugh's interruption had saved her from being a fool and confessing her love for Brandon and her gratitude for all he'd risked to save her and William after her foolish attempt at escape. She'd almost got their son killed. She'd almost got them *all* killed, for that matter. Even though she didn't remember everything, she did remember how close they'd all come to dying because of her foolish pride and lack of trust. She'd not make such a mistake again.

Unable to keep her eyes open any longer, Fiona drifted back to sleep, knowing that she and William were finally safe—truly safe—for the first time since the day he'd been born.

For the first time since Brandon had been named Laird he was entirely confident in his decision and eager to share it with the elders. He strode down the corridor with Hugh close behind and entered the study with his shoulders pulled back and his confidence in place. Finally, on the day he was to give up his title, Brandon felt like a laird. The ridiculousness of it wasn't lost on him. Fate was having her way with him again, but for once he didn't mind her heavy-handedness.

'Rowan and Beatrice,' Brandon began, pleased to see his siblings were there, as he had requested, along

with his brother-in-law Daniel. 'And elders.' He nodded
to the trio of elderly leaders with deference.

Rather than sitting amongst them, Brandon stood,
leaning heavily on the hearty mantel. He took in the
room around him, savouring his last moments as Laird.

'I appreciate you joining me this afternoon.'

'We were surprised and pleased by your invitation,' Anson answered. 'Since your plans for wedding
the Cameron lass will not come to pass, we are eager
to meet with you to discuss additional...options.' He
folded his gnarled hands in his lap, his pale blue eyes
full of anticipation.

'Aye. I am also eager to discuss my plans for the future,' Brandon said. 'The first of which is my plan to
marry Fiona MacDonald. As soon as she is well enough,
of course. I am pleased to tell you that she finally shows
signs of improvement.'

His grin didn't match the expressions on the shocked
faces of those around him. Poor Douglass fared the
worst, seeming to choke on the air as it entered his feeble lungs. Anson clapped his brother on the back until
he regained his bearings.

The old man frowned. 'That is not exactly what I
meant about options for you as Laird.'

'That is where you are misinformed. I am stepping
down from my duties as Laird as of this moment. I am
no longer needed, and nor do I wish to remain Laird.
My brother is well enough to rule the clan once more.
I have seen his clarity of reason.'

Rowan gasped. 'Brother, I don't understand. This is
not what we discussed.'

Brandon stepped away from the mantel and faced
him. 'You are meant to be Laird, Rowan. You always

have been. And while your grief sent you off-course for a time, you are of sound reason once more. I have seen it. During our rescue at the MacDonalds I asked you to bring my son to safety, instead of chasing after Audric in revenge, and you did not hesitate to care for William, your nephew. Only a selfless and sane man would put aside his own desire for revenge to bring a small boy to safety for his brother, his family and his people. I will not forget such an action for as long as I live.' He cleared his throat. 'You saved my son's life.'

He pressed his lips together to suppress the emotion tightening his chest.

Rowan nodded, his eyes softening in understanding.

'I cannot know or understand what that choice, that sacrifice of self, cost you, brother, and I hope I never do.' Brandon paused. 'But I pray I can repay such a debt to you one day.'

Beatrice covered her mouth with her hand and leaned against Rowan's shoulder, gripping his upper arm in support. She had not known what Brandon had asked of Rowan, nor had anyone else, but Brandon wanted everyone to know the selfless strong leader his brother could be, not the enraged and grief-stricken man he had been.

'We have much to discuss,' Anson replied, forming a steeple with his hands and then bringing them to his lips.

'Perhaps we can give you our decision tomorrow, my laird,' Douglass chimed in.

'Oh, you misunderstand me,' Brandon stated. 'This is not a request for permission. My decision has already been made. I am merely telling you about it before I in-form the clan of my decision on the morrow. Until then,' he said, and left the room before anyone could respond.

There was no point in their trying to persuade him. He had never felt more certain of anything in his life.

Now all he needed to do was plan a wedding and convince his future bride to marry him.

Chapter Twenty-Nine

'Brandon, I do not wish to look upon cottages today. Although I feel better since waking yesterday, I find myself feeling a bit weary this afternoon.'

Fiona leaned her head back against Brandon's shoulder and settled into his strength. The movement of the stallion beneath her and the warmth of Brandon's hold made her sleepy as they rode in the early-afternoon sun. The day and the weather were perfect. And she wasn't feeling weary at all—that had been a lie. She was feeling sorry for herself...which was ridiculous.

If only they were on a ride together like they'd used to have, exploring the glen and the lochs below. But this was no day's adventure like those that had marked their early love. Today she was picking out a cottage to live in with William. A cottage that would be far away from the castle, far away from Brandon's chamber, and far away from him.

She sighed. Of course she was grateful for such an option—truly she was—but the sting of losing him to another was still there. That barb would take a while to heal. Truth be told, her shoulder wound would heal much faster than her heart. But she'd promised herself she'd not let anything keep her from providing William with every happiness, even if it was the scraps of her pride that threatened it.

It didn't help matters that Brandon smelled especially divine today, freshly bathed with a hint of musk and spice. He'd even donned a rather fetching steel-grey overcoat with his tunic, and he wore charcoal trews—ones she'd never seen before. She was envious of Susanna Cameron, for she would be the one to admire him.

'When are your nuptials planned?' she asked, trying to practise and accept the idea of letting him go.

He chuckled. 'Soon.'

She rolled her eyes at his vagueness. She was truly trying to be civil, and he was being so very difficult. 'Was your bride pleased with the terms you agreed upon?'

'She requested a few changes be made, but in the end we were both pleased with the outcome.'

Another completely useless answer. Fiona shifted on the mount, agitation budding within her. Perhaps he didn't wish to speak with her about it—which was his right. She began a new line of conversation as she studied the first row of cottages in the village.

'These are quite nice.'

And they were. The areas outside had been swept and tidied, and small gardens promised new growth and potential blooms outside each one. Then it struck her.

'Where is everyone? It's so quiet, and no one is out of doors on this beautiful day. Seems strange, doesn't it?'

She furrowed her brow when he said nothing in response.

They continued on and crested a small hill that looked down into the centre of the village proper. Brandon brought the stallion to a halt and Fiona gasped at the sound of cheers and the sight of what appeared to be the entire clan in a large crowd around a small scaffold. The wooden structure was decorated in lace, tartan, and sprigs of colourful flowers.

She gasped again at the sight of it, and then her stomach curdled.

It resembled the scene of a wedding, except it was outside rather than in a chapel.

Had he brought her to his wedding to Susanna?

Sickness threatened, and she grasped at his hands that held the reins. She couldn't be a part of it. 'Brandon, please tell me you have not brought me here to witness your wedding to Susanna Cameron.'

'I have not,' he whispered in her ear, with a note of mischief in his voice.

'Then, by all that's holy, what is going on? This looks like a wedding.'

He gently lifted her chin between his thumb and fingers until she faced him. 'It is, Fi. I hope it to be *our* wedding.'

She searched his eyes for the truth and there it was, dancing about in the warm brown depths. 'What? You are not jesting with me? We are to be married today? Now?'

'Aye.'

He smiled, trailing his callused thumb softly, sensuously over her bottom lip, and she felt herself tremble against him.

'If you will have me. Will you marry me, my Fi?'

Shock numbed her body briefly before her mind attempted to work out its confusion.

'But what of Susanna?' she asked. 'Your agreement? You were engaged, if I remember correctly.'

'We agreed not to marry one another. New terms we were both eager to accept.' He grinned. 'She offered the help of her men to rescue you and William in exchange for me releasing her from our engagement and bearing any wrath her father might thrust upon us.'

'And...?'

'And helping her later, if needed.'

She twisted her lips. 'What of the elders? They can't support your decision. They abhor me.'

'I have stepped down from being Laird.'

A muscle flexed in his jaw and her throat tightened.

'What? Why? I never asked you to do as such. I never wanted you to give it up.'

'I know, Fi. It is what I want for myself. For us. For our son.'

'You gave that up for us?' Tears welled in her eyes. This wasn't what she wanted—not really. His sacrifice was too much. 'And if I refuse to marry you?'

'Then I will still choose not to be Laird.' His Adam's apple bobbed in his throat and he held her gaze.

'You are serious, aren't you?'

'Aye,' he answered, the breeze ruffling his hair.

She looked back at the crowd. 'And they are here knowing all of this? That you intend to marry me, not Susanna Cameron?'

He tucked a lock of hair behind her ear. 'Aye. They know. They are all here to celebrate us. And you.'

Tears threatened as she looked out into the crowd that had grown quiet, watching them from below.

'Why? They hated me but a week ago, and I have done nothing to deserve or earn their acceptance.'

'Oh, no? You risked your life to rescue our son. Took a dagger to the shoulder and still carried on to protect him.'

'But I put him in danger by fleeing in the first place. That was my doing.'

'Aye, but you fought your own clan and Audric to save him. So did your brother and Oric. They respect what you did, and they now understand that you are not to blame for what happened a year ago. They also know the truth about Oric and your mother…and of what happened to you in your attempt to save and protect our child.'

'They do?'

'Aye. Watch.' Brandon waved, and the men and women of the clan cheered. He put his hand down. 'Now you try.' He nudged her.

Was this a trick? A ploy to humiliate her?

But she had to learn to trust somehow, some way. She'd start now. She nibbled her lip, closed her eyes, and lifted her hand in a hesitant wave.

The roar of the crowd was just as loud, and she opened her eyes one at a time to see that it was for her. The people who had jeered and cursed her weeks ago upon her arrival now stood cheering for her and for Brandon. Her heart filled with hope and a tear fell down her cheek. Of all the things she had hoped for this day, it hadn't been this. This was beyond her imaginings.

Brandon pulled a ring from his coat pocket. A simple silver band with an emerald set in it. The very one she had stolen from his mother's jewels to give to William one day.

She gasped. 'The emerald!'

'Aye. It will remind us of the moment we almost lost one another, and how lucky we are that we didn't.' He held it before her. 'I also believe my mother would have wanted you to have it. It is as bright, fiery and dazzling as you. I love you, my Fi.'

She reached for it and held the ring in her trembling fingers, wondering if she was in a dream.

'So, Fi... Shall you be my bride?' Brandon asked huskily, resting his palm on her cheek, reminding her that he was real and so was this moment.

'Aye, Brandon Campbell, I will.'

As he pulled her close and kissed her the crowd erupted in a glorious cheer as big and as full of joy as Fiona felt in her heart.

'Are you ready?' Brandon asked after he'd ended their kiss.

'Marry now? Here? In front of everyone?' Nerves bubbled under her skin, duelling with her excitement and her desire to be his bride.

'Aye.' His eyes held an eagerness and happiness that rivalled her own.

'I am as ready as I shall ever be.'

He smiled and turned his mount to begin a slow, soft canter down the lush green hillside that was now flanked with people. They smiled and cheered as they passed, and colourful flower petals flew in the air against the bright blue sky.

Fiona laughed aloud. 'Those who once pelted me with curses now sprinkle me with flowers.'

'A great deal has changed since that day you arrived. I know I have changed. And all because of you and your love, Fiona. I am grateful for it...for you.'

Brandon's lips skimmed her ear and she shivered.

'As have I changed. We fought and found our way back to each other, did we not? No easy feat, but we did it.'

She clasped some bright pink petals as they blew towards them, rubbing them in her hands, releasing a soft floral scent. Looking farther away, she spied Oric and her brother Devlin, standing side by side with Rowan, Beatrice, Daniel and Miss Emma, who held wee William.

She sucked in a breath. 'Could you ever have imagined this moment? Look...' She gestured, pointing to their families, arranged side by side around the small wooden platform where they were to wed.

'Nay, it is a miracle, to be sure.'

'Aye.' Fiona smiled as she waved to their families and to all the clansmen and women around them. 'One of many, I'd say.'

Epilogue

Dusk whispered beyond the sunset that glowed in soft hues of pink, purple and orange along the Three Sisters of Glencoe, their grey mountain peaks reaching eagerly for the sky.

Brandon liked to think they smiled down at them, pleased to see him and Fiona walking hand in hand towards the loch, united by the vows of marriage. Finally they were officially husband and wife, and standing once again on the grassy bank where he'd found her weeks ago and thought her a thief.

He almost laughed aloud. What an adventure had begun that morn. And what gains he had made since that moment: a wife, a son, and a future. He'd repaired his tattered relationship with his brother, stepped down as Laird, and Fiona had found her true father in Oric— a man who loved and respected her. She'd also learned the truth about her mother, and now understood that she had not been abandoned by her as she'd long believed. It had all been a miracle.

Flowers and festivities had abounded this afternoon at their wedding, and the men and women who had once jeered at Fiona upon her arrival had showered her with praise, flower petals and love, recognising her as the brave and resourceful woman and warrior she was and always had been.

And now she was his wife.

'You take my breath away, Fiona MacDonald,' he murmured, full of pride and love for this woman who had not dared give up on protecting the life of their son or their love for one another.

'So do you take mine, husband,' Fiona chided, grasping his hand and pressing it to her cheek until he cupped her face. 'But I fear you must call me Fiona Campbell now, for I am yours.' A bright smile filled her face.

'And I'm proud to have you wear my plaid,' he said. Unlike that first morn, when he'd tossed it at her to cover herself, thinking she was unworthy of its stripes. What a bloody fool he had been.

They stopped at the water's edge of Loch Leven, listening to the cool lapping rhythm of the waves against the small smooth rocks residing on the shoreline repeating again and again.

Aye, she was finally his, as he'd always hoped she would be. Heat and desire flooded Brandon's body. *And love*. Love pooled deep in his belly. *This* was the Fiona of old and new. The woman he would follow into the glow of the sun and into the crush of battle, no matter where either might lead.

He caressed her face and slowly leaned down to kiss her. Her lips parted and the smooth warmth of her breath eased into him like honey along his veins. He kissed her again and again, until he could scarce draw breath in his need to consume her body and soul and make her his wife in every sense of the word.

A smile rested on her swollen pink lips. 'Shall we take a swim, husband? I feel over-warm.'

He chuckled. 'Aye, wife. A sound idea. The heat has flushed me as well.'

Fiona began a slow, seductive walk to the water, letting her dress loosen and slide down her body as she moved. Frozen, he watched the sun glow along the flesh of her form. And as she entered the water one step at a time she became the siren he had once imagined her to be, before that early morn of weeks past.

She disappeared into the loch and then stood up, with water cascading off her shoulders and breasts. Lord above, she was beautiful...and *his*.

He strode to the loch, flinging off his boots, removing his trews and jacket, and finally yanking his tunic from his body. The water cooled his heated blood.

Reaching for him, she slid her arms around his neck, wrapping her legs around his waist.

He moaned against her hair. 'Perhaps 'tis time to truly claim you and make you my wife in every way.' Pleasure coiled through him as he murmured the words along her neck.

Sliding down his slick body, she answered, 'Aye, husband. You are bound to me for the rest of your days.'

'Aye. Till the sun catches the moon, lass...till the sun catches the moon.'

She slammed her mouth against his and he groaned. He needed no further invitation. She would be his and his alone, as he would be hers. For ever.

* * * * *